CHIUN HEARD THE APPROACHING PACK LONG BEFORE THEY REACHED THE ROOM.

"They come!" Chiun said sharply.

The pair of imbeciles scrambled for cover. Chiun heard the rush of flesh and positioned himself in the middle of the room when the door burst inward, dead bolt shattered, pieces of the locking mechanism hurled across the room to scar wallpaper.

A gray wolf lunged into the room, immediately followed by another and another. To Chiun's left, the Gypsy woman screamed again and took off running for the nearest bedroom, with a snarling canine in pursuit. The white man yelped, his windpipe closing on him, hastily retreating to the balcony, where he would soon be trapped.

A manlike shadow loomed behind the wolf pack, filling up the doorway, but Chiun had no time to examine the intruder. A stocky canine rushed at him, leaping furiously toward his face.

Created by Murphy & Sapir

THE Destroyer™

WOLF'S BANE

A GOLD EAGLE BOOK FROM

W🌐RLDWIDE®

TORONTO • NEW YORK • LONDON
AMSTERDAM • PARIS • SYDNEY • HAMBURG
STOCKHOLM • ATHENS • TOKYO • MILAN
MADRID • WARSAW • BUDAPEST • AUCKLAND

First edition July 2003

ISBN 0-373-63247-9

WOLF'S BANE

To the Glorious House of Sinanju

1

What's in a name?

Shakespeare had posed the question, and now four hundred years later, Samuel Francisco had the answer. If you gotta ask, he told himself, you obviously haven't got a freakin' clue.

Take his name, for example. "Samuel Francisco" sounded as if his parents couldn't quite decide if he would be a Jewish prophet or a waiter in a Tex-Mex restaurant. He couldn't even trim the "Samuel" back to "Sam," because it came out sounding like a certain northern California city full of fruitcakes. It was perfect, salesmen on the lot going limp-wristed when they thought he couldn't see them, mincing little girlie steps as if they were trying out for fairy of the month instead of selling used cars to a bunch of idiots who couldn't tell a differential from a dipstick if their lives depended on it.

Nope, he caught himself. The proper term was not "used"; it was "previously owned."

That was another crock of shit, but one that he could understand from years of leeching off the public, one way or another. Dress up a dog turd with a little glitter and some parsley on the side, there would be some damn fool out there who absolutely knew for sure that he had found the bargain of the century.

The worst thing about Francisco's name, though, was the fact it wasn't even really his. Some pencil pusher back in Washington had picked it for him, maybe snoozing through a slow day, fat and happy with his civil-service paycheck, maybe paging through the telephone directory and playing mix-and-match until something caught his eye. Samuel Francisco had been two years in the federal program when he flipped on the television one night, started channel surfing and wound up in the middle of *Alien Nation* on TBN. Jimmy Cahn played a cop with an attitude, teamed up with a big-headed freak from Uranus or somewhere. Five minutes into the program, it hit him.

Sam Francisco didn't get his handle from the California fruitcake capital, after all. Some stupid bastard back in D.C. had been watching television, maybe getting high while he was at it, and decided he should name his next dumb pigeon for a bubble-headed alien. Someday Francisco hoped that he could meet the genius responsible and break his goddamn funny bone.

Not that his real name had been so terrific, mind you, but at least it had belonged to him, no crazy strings attached. He had been Aloysius Leroy Cartier for thirty-seven years, the name his sainted mama gave him, and he used to have some trouble over that name, too, before he learned to fight and everybody had begun to call him Bubba. He was getting on just fine, or thought he was, until the day some Feds showed up and hauled his Cajun ass to jail.

The rest was history. They had an airtight case, and Bubba Cartier was looking at a double deuce, all things considered, if he didn't make a deal. His training from the cradle up was that you should never talk to cops except to pay them off or tell them to go screw themselves, but Bubba had been taught another lesson, too, and that was looking out for number one. He could have gone away behind the federal charges, maybe have some oddball felonies appended by the state so they could ship him to Angola for a while. But his high and mighty bosses had been treating him like shit a month or two before the bust went down, and Bubba didn't feel like doing time to get them off the hook. He started thinking of the shit that happened even in the better jails these days—the race wars, contract killings, AIDS—and he decided, to hell with it.

After he agreed to testify, shit started happening like it was preordained or something, maybe laid out in those horoscopes from *TV Guide* his wife was always reading to him at the breakfast table, like he gave a damn. Bubba was short on faith in higher powers, even after being raised a Catholic—sort of—in the bayou country of Louisiana, but he figured maybe Uncle Sam could take care of his own.

He should have known better.

The marshals on the federal witness program had their rules to follow, little bureaucratic games to play. Bubba understood that kind of shit, but still it pissed him off when perfect strangers started playing with his life. The name, for instance. Some geek's little joke at Bubba Cartier's expense. And then there was the job they got him, covering a used-car dealership. He knew damn well that somebody had checked his file and seen the time he did for running chop shops, thinking, Hey! This asshole likes to work with cars, let's fix him up. Like that, the little things that wound up being Sam Francisco's life.

He didn't even want to think about the home away from home they had selected for him, all the way to hell and gone in Michigan. He could imagine Means or Sheppard, one of those guys, staring at a big wall-mounted map of the United States and wondering where they could send him so the bloodhounds wouldn't track him down. That ruled out Dixie and the border states, for starters. He could almost hear them talking: "Here we got ourselves a Southern boy, we better stick his ass up north somewhere. Nobody gonna look for him in Michigan, you think?" So be it.

Even so, he could have been worse off. They

could have sent him to Seattle, where it rained nine months a year, or up to Maine, where inbred fishermen ran lobster traps and answered ay-uh every time you asked them something. When Bubba thought about it that way, he believed that things were not the very worst that they could have been.

But Cadillac was bad enough.

They had to name it for a car, of course, it being Michigan. Not that he particularly gave a damn. The main thing was that he was living farther north than certain parts of Canada, where it started snowing in November, sometimes in October, and you froze your ass off through the end of March, more likely into April. Living in the bayou country all those years had thinned his blood, and it got damn cold up there, almost two hundred miles above Chicago. There were days the town closed up because the snow plows couldn't run, much less school buses, garbage trucks and squad cars.

There were also days when Bubba wished that he had gone ahead and done his time.

Too late to think about it now, and yet he couldn't help it. He was well and truly stuck, dependent on the marshals in the Witsec program—short for Witness Security—who had made his life over from scratch. No matter how he really felt, he couldn't piss them off too much, because he knew one thing as sure as hell.

The bloodhounds never really lost your scent. And if they found him, after all this time…

Rita was always bitching at him, over one thing or another. She was paranoid about the coloreds, and while Bubba couldn't fault her logic, he was all the time reminding her that colored money spent the same as any other kind, and they were big on buying cars. She blamed him for the fact that she could never see her friends again—small loss, as far as Bubba was concerned—and for the drop in income they had suffered when he left the outfit, started working eight to six and paying taxes. Rita blamed him when the kids got into trouble at their school. And sometimes, when the PMS kicked in, she even blamed him for the weather.

And so what if she was right. They wouldn't be in Cadillac if he had been a little smarter, quicker on the uptake, watching for the Feds. Once he was busted, Bubba could have kept his mouth shut, let the jail doors slam behind him, trusting that the outfit would have taken care of Rita and the kids. The truth was, though, that he had been shit scared of doing twenty years, had half convinced himself he couldn't do it, and they psyched him out. The deal was done, he had delivered on his end, and Sam Francisco of the Cadillac Franciscos was the end result.

But Christ, he couldn't get a decent plate of jambalaya anywhere within a hundred miles. He was reduced to eating store-bought gumbo out of cans.

Some days—most days, in fact, he wished that he had cut a bargain with the Feds to let him disappear alone, leave Rita and the rug rats out of it. His new life would have been a whole lot easier if Bubba weren't saddled with that baggage from the past. He could have saved a fortune, too, on aspirin for the headaches Rita gave him with her nagging, day and night.

What had attracted him to Rita in the first place? Thinking back, he knew it was her body, back when she was dancing at the Velvet Club, outside Metairie. Looking at her now, three kids and all those bonbons down the road, no one would guess that she had once been an A1 looker.

As for the brats...

Too late, he told himself. You're in it now, and no mistake. A man does what he has to do.

Yeah, right.

On Friday night, not knowing it would be his last, Bubba Francisco parked his trash cans at the curb, for pickup in the morning, and sat up to watch the best of Letterman. That wasn't much, in his opinion, but the fella with the big chin didn't do much for him, either, and the flick on HBO was some damn thing with Whoopi Goldberg.

Wonders never ceased.

Before he turned in for the night, he poured himself another double shot of Beam and went around to check the house, each door and window in its turn. He was supposed to be secure, up there in Cadillac, but you could never really tell.

The bloodhounds could be anywhere.

OUTSIDE, THE LEADER of the pack sat waiting for the windows to go dark. That done, he waited half an hour more, in case the man was pleasuring his woman, then he tacked on fifteen minutes more for them to doze. No time was ever truly wasted if you used it properly, in this case sniffing out the night breeze, studying the deeper shadows with his yellow eyes and looking for a trap. If there were hunters here, he had to give them credit for the way they had concealed themselves. He had to give them special credit for the control they exercised. His own craving was so strong it was almost too much to stand.

When he was sure as sure could be that he wasn't about to walk into an ambush, he went back to fetch the others. They were waiting for him in the van, unsettled by the city sounds and smells perhaps, but calm enough that he wasn't required to warn them about making noise. Six pairs of eyes intently focused on him as he opened up the sliding door.

''Come brothers, sister.''

They piled out and formed a ring around him, claws tap-tapping on the asphalt. When he started walking, after he had locked the van, two of them automatically took point, the others hanging back. The sleek bitch held her place beside him, on his left. They watched for traffic, crossing streets, and kept to shadows where they could. The residential neighborhood had streetlights at the intersections, but the houses in between were dark and still.

Surrounded as he was by things of man, the leader of the pack could smell the woods nearby. The neighborhood was no more than a half mile from Lake Cadillac and William Mitchell State Park, with Lake Mitchell and the Manistee National Forest a mile farther east. He wished they had the time to do some hunting for the hell of it, but business took priority. Within an hour, tops, they would be home-ward bound. By this time Sunday, he could turn the pack out on familiar ground. They could rejoin the rest of the pack and run amok if they were so in-clined.

But first they had a job to do.

He didn't know the target's name and didn't care. The men who hired him had supplied a photograph, which he had briefly studied, then devoured. It was his theory that ingesting snapshots of his prey gave him an edge. Before the men he hunted ever met him in the flesh, he had consumed a portion of their souls and thereby weakened them in preparation for the kill.

Or maybe he was full of shit.

Some thought so, back at home, though none of them would say it to his face. Even the ones who knew him best might doubt he had the ''power,'' but they never crossed him. Never more than once, that is. The leader of the pack possessed a fearsome reputation, which was well deserved. Even the bad boys knew it wasn't smart to piss him off.

The target had a five-foot wooden fence around his backyard, as if it would keep anybody out. The leader of the pack went over in a flash, the others following and forming up beside him in the darkness, waiting while he watched and smelled the house.

There would be no alarm, because the target thought that he was safe. You change a name, mock up some history. Time flies. What else was there to do? He was supposed to have protectors running interference for him in the big, bad world, but they were not in evidence this night. Except for bitch and whelps, the bastard would be on his own.

The leader of the pack advanced until he stood before the back door of the house. He crouched and sniffed around the doorknob, smelling whoever had touched it last. A tasty child-smell, meat so tender it would slip right off the bone, no problem. He could almost taste it now.

He straightened, threw back his shaggy head and called upon the power. It responded instantly, fire racing through his veins. He clenched his fists and felt his muscles swelling, straining at the denim fabric of his shirt. Long nails like talons bit into his palms. One of his brothers snarled, but he was used to that. They meant no harm.

He felt the power throbbing in him as he reached out for the doorknob, took it in his hand and twisted it with all his might. The lock resisted for a moment, then gave out a sharp metallic snap. The door swung open and he stepped inside.

He hesitated for a moment, just across the threshold, listening and sniffing at the house, to learn if any of its occupants had heard the noise. When no alarm was sounded, he stepped forward and the others joined him in the kitchen, heavy with the smell of good meat spoiled by fire. He understood that men preferred to char the sweet flesh they consumed, but he was still revolted by the practice.

He would take the real thing, raw and bloody, every time.

He led the pack beyond the kitchen, to a darkened hallway, picking up the odor of tobacco smoke and something else—perfume, cologne, some kind of makeup?—that would lead him to the target's bitch. He paused outside the room where two boys slumbered, opening the door without a sound and nodding to the darkness, smiling as a couple of his brothers broke formation, peeling off to do their work. The next room was a girl's. Another silent signal, and a supple shadow left the pack to go in search of something edible.

That left two brothers and the bitch to follow as the leader of the pack proceeded to a final doorway, also closed. He went down on all fours to sniff the carpet, baring yellow fangs. The sound that rumbled from his throat was out of place in human company.

He reached up for the doorknob, hesitating, head cocked so that one ear almost touched the door. Was that a voice he heard inside? The leader of the pack stood and squared his massive shoulders, grinning fiercely as he turned the knob and stepped into the master bedroom. Taloned fingers found the light switch, flicked it and a ceiling fixture blazed on, noonday bright.

In bed, the target and a woman with a double chin were sputtering toward consciousness. They saw the leader of the pack through bleary eyes, but it was still enough to startle them and make the woman scream.

"Surprise," he told them as he started toward the bed. "We just dropped in to have a bite."

ED BEASLEY HADN'T HEARD such screaming since…well, come to think of it, he'd never heard such screaming in his life. Oh, maybe on the late show, when they had a horror movie on, but he was more inclined to watch the Playboy channel.

The noise was coming from next door.

He glanced in the direction of the bedside clock and saw that it was nearly 1:30 a.m. Too late for parties in the neighborhood, and he had never known his neighbors, the Franciscos, as the entertaining kind. Kept mostly to themselves, they did, and there were no kids old enough to raise this kind of hell, unless...

He fought a brief and indecisive struggle with his sheet and blanket, dragging them behind him as he tumbled out of bed and made a beeline for the window. Pulling back the drapes, he peered across a redwood fence at the Francisco house. No lights were in evidence, and he waited for the screams to be repeated.

Nothing.

Beasley hesitated for another moment, wondering if he had been dreaming. Then he heard a crashing sound, as if some heavy piece of furniture had been upended, maybe hurled across a room and slammed into the nearest wall. He took a quick step backward from the window, trembling in his flannel PJs as he wondered what in hell he ought to do.

Call 911!

Beasley found the bedside lamp and switched it on reluctantly, half fearing someone in the outer darkness would discover him and burst in through the glass. He tapped out 911 and killed the lamp again, already feeling safer in the darkness. Three rings in his ear before another tape came on.

"You've reached the Cadillac Police Department emergency response line. All our operators are engaged at the moment. If your call is an emergency, please hold the line. If not—"

God*damn* it!

Beasley dropped the telephone, stood and lurched back to the window. Only deathly silence came from the house next door, so that he wondered if he had imagined the commotion to begin with.

Crash! Another heavy piece toppled somewhere in the darkened house.

He rushed back to the telephone and scooped it up. "You've reached the Cadillac Police Department's—"

Shit!

He slammed down the receiver, bolting for the bedroom door. He stepped on his cat and nearly lost it as the chunky tom spun out from under him, claws raking at one ankle.

"Move your ass, goddamn it!"

Beasley made it to his back door, fumbled with the dead-bolt lock in darkness, still afraid to show a light. He got it on the second try, but the damn door still wouldn't open, and he finally remembered the primary lock, a little button on the knob he had to press before the knob would turn.

Outside, the night was dark and still. The grass was cool beneath his feet, and Beasley cursed the haste that had permitted him to leave the house without his slippers.

Another crash from the Francisco house drew him toward the fence that marked the boundary between the two adjoining properties. He still had no idea of what he meant to do, unarmed and barefoot, barely dressed, but he would think of something when the time came. If he couldn't help his odd, standoffish neighbors, maybe he could catch a glimpse of the intruders and describe them to police. Sure, that was it. A simple witness didn't really have to get involved. Not like the wacky heroes who went charging into burning houses, dragging out unconscious strangers through the smoke and flames.

He reached the fence and stood on tiptoe in the soft earth of a flower bed. A rosebush snagged one leg of his pajamas, but he managed to ignore it, straining for a clear view of the house next door. From where he stood, he had the back door covered, with the steps that led down to a concrete walk around the east side of the structure. Everything was just like Beasley's house, the carbon-copy layout anyway, that readily identified tract housing from the early 1960s. Unlike Beasley, though, the neighbors wasted little time on sprucing up the yard. They cut the grass back twice a month and that was it. No pets that he could see, no flowers, no rock garden. Nothing.

He was staring at the back door when it suddenly

flew open and he had the clear view of the prowlers that he had been hoping for. Too clear, in fact, and Beasley instantly regretted wishing for a glimpse of the intruders.

Who was ever going to believe him now?

The dogs were bad enough, big shaggy mongrels, six or seven of them racing silently across the open yard, but Beasley had no time to wonder what a pack of mutts was doing there. His full attention focused on the man who followed them outside.

Scratch that.

He would admit, in subsequent interrogations by police, that he mistook the prowler for a human at first glance. The prowler had two arms and two legs and wore some kind of clothing, maybe denim, but the outward similarity to humankind stopped there.

Beasley had seen the creature's face and hands, all shaggy, sprouting long, coarse hair, like something from an old Lon Chaney movie. He couldn't be sure if the hair was brown or black, and didn't really give a damn. One glimpse had been enough to last a lifetime when the creature went down on its haunches, raised its head and howled at the moon.

2

His name was Remo, and he really didn't want to get involved, but somehow fate always found him.

All he had wanted was a bowl of rice, for crying out loud.

But before the bowl was half-empty he was called to duty. Defender of the downtrodden. Protector of the innocent. Smiter of evil. Was *smiter* a word? Whatever the hell, it was obvious he'd made a bad choice in restaurants.

It had turned out to be that kind of day, and it wasn't even noon.

He was en route to Folcroft Sanitarium in Rye, New York, when it occurred to him that he was hungry.

Remo started looking for a restaurant in Larchmont, shunning drive-ins with their greasy burgers, "extracrunchy" chicken parts and hot dogs drenched in chili that resembled something from the dysentery ward. He found the Happy Noodle, a decent-looking Chinese place on a side street near the heart of town.

A very pretty Chinese hostess took him to a seat. A male server brought hot tea in a ceramic pot and steamed rice. Remo was chewing away—it took a lot of chewing if you did it right—when trouble walked in off the street.

He counted seven of them, Chinese punks whose taste in clothing ran to leather coats or denim jackets with the sleeves cut off, tight slacks and high-gloss shoes with pointy toes. They all wore sunglasses, despite the dim light in the restaurant, and combed their hair straight back, like Dracula—Bela Lugosi or Christopher Lee. Most of them sported chunky rings that would do wicked damage in a brawl— assuming they made contact.

Remo watched the hostess move to greet the new arrivals, saw the nervous jitter in her walk as she approached them. The apparent leader met her with a smile, said something in Chinese, then shook his head at her response. The smile winked out, and he was pointing toward the back, in the direction of the kitchen, snapping orders that the slim young woman hastened to obey.

Remo assumed the older man who came to meet the punks had to be the Happy Noodle's manager, perhaps the owner. Remo didn't completely comprehend what was said, but he got the gist. Wherever they were found, established Chinese businessmen were often victimized by hoodlum gangs and forced to pay protection.

None of my business, Remo thought, and turned back to his meal. The loaded chopsticks were poised midway between his plate and mouth when he was forcibly distracted by the sound of knuckles striking flesh and a cry of pain. The hostess rushed to assist the fallen manager and yelled at the punks who loomed above him. There was nothing complimentary about her comments, and Remo saw the leader of the gang slap her hard across the face.

Remo, swearing under his breath, went to join the party.

On his right, one member of the gang saw Remo coming, nudged the punk next to him with an elbow, and it went along the line that way until the leader had him spotted, turning just his head to face the new arrival. He was smiling still, his eyes invisible behind the shades he wore, and Remo didn't care. It made no difference what the young man looked like with his glasses off. The eyes were helpful sometimes in a fight, but these punks weren't even a challenge. Rather, it would be a test of his patience and forbearance not to kill them when the first one made his move.

He came on slow and guileless, verging onto stupid, as the youngsters would expect a do-gooder white man to behave. They had grown up intimidating elders, picking out their targets based on fear or weakness. Thus far, the technique had served them well.

"Excuse me." He addressed the cringing hostess, seeming to ignore the young men ranged in front of him, likewise the restaurant's proprietor. "I'm finished, miss. If I could get my check now, please…?"

"Hey, man," the leader of the seven said to him, "does any one of us look like your damn waiter?"

Remo made a show of studying their faces and their clothing. "Gosh, no," he said at last. "My waiter didn't have a quart of oil in his hair, and there didn't seem to be a problem with his eyes. His clothes were nicer, as I recall. His shoes weren't greaser retro from the 1960s and he didn't use that cheap cologne. In fact, you ought to ask him for some pointers on style. I'm sure he—"

"Shut up!"

The young Chinese thug was livid, anger darkening his sallow cheeks. He stared at Remo from behind his shades, while the others muttered among themselves and fidgeted. A couple of them slipped hands inside their leather jackets.

"You got a big mouth for a round-eye," said the leader of the gang.

"You know, that's just what my wife says," Remo replied. "Somebody asks a question, I just fire back with the first thing that comes to mind. By which I mean God's honest truth, you understand. It gets me into trouble sometimes, I'm the first one to admit, but what the hey, that's life. Your hair, for instance. Now, I hope it didn't hurt your feelings when I said—''

''You wanna die, man?'' the leader asked him.

''Well, it's not as if I have a choice, now, is it? Certainly, like anybody else, I hope to live as long as possible, but let's not kid ourselves, okay? I mean—''

''I'm asking if you wanna die today.''

''Oh, well, that's different, isn't it? When you get down to the specifics of it—''

Remo heard the switchblade open with a snap before he saw it, glinting on his left. The farthest hoodlum from him was the first to draw a weapon, but the others quickly followed suit. He checked the hardware, counting off three knives, one cutthroat razor, one blackjack, one pair of knuckle dusters and a pair of plastic nunchakus. They might as well have armed themselves with some of the restaurant's signature noodles.

The leader twirled his nunchakus, making his companion on the right step back a pace to keep from getting swatted on the jaw. The members of his gang maintained respectful silence as he whipped the nunchakus through a short routine and caught the loose end underneath one arm.

''*Enter the Dragon,* right?'' Remo asked. ''Hey, I loved that movie, too. I must have seen it half a dozen times. I think I've even got the video at home. If I could make one observation, though... Your stance, I mean, well, it appears to me you're sort of leaning to the left, and—''

"You're a ninja, right? Some kind of expert, because you saw a movie?''

"A ninja? Oh, my goodness gracious, no! But, then again, it doesn't always take an expert to detect the weakness in an amateur's approach. Sometimes, I mean, the errors are just *quite* obvious.''

The hostess and the manager were staring at him now, clearly expecting Remo to be mobbed at any moment. He ignored them, focused on the nunchaku man, believing that the others wouldn't make a move until their leader gave the order.

"More tact,'' the Chinese hoodlum said, "is what you need. It's like you said, that mouth of yours. Besides—'' he nodded toward the scowling manager "—old Grandpa here could use an object lesson. He's too brave for his own good these days. That's not a healthy way to be, you know? He doesn't care enough about himself, his building, his employees. Maybe he still cares about his customers. You think?''

"I'm sure I wouldn't know,'' Remo said.

"Well, hey,'' the young man told him with a smile, "let's check it out.''

He had rehearsed the move; that much was obvious. Remo could almost see him posing with his 'chuks before a full-length mirror, maybe in the nude, and smiling at his trim reflection as he worked on different angles of attack. It didn't hurt to practice that way every now and then, but a person could overdo it, just like anything in life. Some mirror fighters focused so much on technique, the way they looked to others when they struck a pose, that they lost sight of basics. They forgot that fighting in real life had more to do with raw survival than with looking good. A handsome corpse was still stone dead, no matter how his hair was styled.

He gave another flourish of his nunchakus, letting out a "Yaoweeee" kind of sound he had to have borrowed from the late Bruce Lee. It warbled through two octaves, rising to a sharp soprano pitch before it ended with a startled-sounding "Oof!" The next move was apparently supposed to startle his victim, take him by surprise, but Remo Williams saw the windup coming from a mile away.

The self-styled tough guy whipped the nunchakus left to right from his perspective, counting on the backhand to connect with Remo's skull and take him down with one blow.

Remo hardly seemed to move, yet he ducked backward far enough to let the nunchakus whisper past his face with a quarter of an inch to spare. Before the young man had a chance to register his miss, process the information and react accordingly, Remo was gliding forward, still moving faster than the human eye could follow, one hand floating out in front of him to find his attacker's jaw.

Reach out and touch someone.

Remo pulled the punch, but the strike still carried force enough to shatter bone. One moment, Remo's enemy was snarling at him, showing gritted teeth; the next, his lower jaw had shifted two inches to the right. The change was accompanied by a sickly ripping sound, and a handful of his pearly whites exploded from between slack lips and pattered on the vinyl floor.

Remo was back in place and gaping at the young man as he fell. "Oh, no!" he said to no one in particular. "Did I do that?"

It took a moment for the other six punks to recover, and the next rush came from Remo's left. The grinner with the long bone-handled switchblade in his hand knew enough to hold the knife well back, against his right hip, while his left hand pawed the air in front of him. He was ducking, weaving as he came toward Remo, muttering some vulgar malediction in Chinese.

Remo half turned to face him, raising empty hands as if to placate his assailant. "Hey, wait a second here," he said, still clinging to his character. "I didn't mean—"

Remo brushed the empty hand aside as the other hand made the thrust that was designed to disembowel him. Remo wasn't in the mood to be disemboweled. He smacked the knife hand up, hard. The knife rocketed skyward, the hand broke and the blade man bonked himself in the head with his own forearm with such magnificent force he knocked himself out.

The impact left him stretched out on the floor, facedown, his right arm showing jagged angles that were never planned by Mother Nature. The unnatural speed of the movement of his arm had also shredded every tendon and ligament from the shoulder on down.

"My favorite Moe move," Remo explained.

The five remaining hoodlums had already seen what happened to their buddies when they tried to take the round-eyes one on one. Accordingly, the next rush was a two-man effort, more knives coming at him from the left and right.

Remo reversed his stance at the last moment, with a simple pivot on his toes, and saw the glimmer of the knife slide past his face as his right elbow rose to meet the youngster's rushing face. He was rewarded with a satisfying crunch of bone and cartilage, the cutter's nose and cheek imploding, impact robbing him of consciousness while sheer momentum kept him moving.

"Oops! Sorry!" Remo yelped as he gave the little punk an extra nudge and sent the limp form into his other adversary's path. "Coming through!" he warned.

The two young gangsters came together with a jolting impact, one a flaccid scarecrow. Remo heard a muffled grunt and saw the second attacker's blade slide home above the tumbling rag doll's hip. It shouldn't be a mortal wound, if Remo wrapped up his engagement in the next few minutes and the manager could summon an ambulance, but there was bright blood on the fourth man's knife as he and his comrade toppled to the floor.

"That has *got* to hurt," Remo commented.

The young man with the knuckle dusters seemed to have forgotten he was wearing them, or maybe he was simply frightened by the thought of closing to within arm's length of this most startling round-eyes. Whatever the excuse, he aimed a looping kick at Remo's face instead of striking with his fists. As with his leader, noise appeared to help the kicker with his move, a high-pitched yipping sound that may have been designed to psych out his adversary.

Remo registered the high kick as a rush of air before he turned to face it. Ducking back as the pointy shoe rushed toward his face, he caught the heel between his thumb and index finger, lifting as he pivoted, the kicker's other foot swept off the ground by leverage and centrifugal force. The knuck man's skull collided with the floor and he went limp, another flesh-and-floor-tile speed bump on the battlefield of life.

And that left two.

"You guys suck," Remo commented.

The young man with the blackjack should have

moved while Remo was demolishing his buddy, but he hesitated, checking out the odds and angles.

"Seriously. The Drunken Masters are better than you. The Crippled Masters are better than you. David Carradine is better than you and he's like eighty years old. You even make Jean-Claude Van Damme look talented."

"Shut up, Cauc!" His attitude told Remo that he longed to cut and run, but there was still his reputation to consider, and a witness who would tell the world if he showed yellow in a pinch. The razor man, meanwhile, was standing back and shooting glances toward the exit, measuring the distance, wondering if he could make it to the street.

"I hate to say this," Remo said regretfully, "but you know who you guys remind me of?" He winced and stage-whispered, "Steven Seagal."

That did it. A blend of rage and stubborn pride propelled the sap man forward, swinging wildly with his leather-shrouded weapon. Remo ducked beneath a reckless swing and poked a few stiff fingers up into the young man's solar plexus. He could easily have stopped the beating heart inside that rib cage, maybe ripped it out and placed it in the hoodlum's hand, but he was satisfied to drive the wind out of his adversary's lungs and spray the remnants of his breakfast on the nearest wall.

The sap man staggered, went down on one knee and lost his weapon as he clutched his burning abdomen. Still conscious, there was nothing he could do to help himself as Remo stepped in close and tapped him at the junction of his skull and spine, obliterating awareness. The slump became a sprawl, the punk collapsing on his side.

When Remo turned to face the razor man, his final standing target met him with a show of teeth that could have passed for either a smile or a grimace. He had grabbed the hostess and was holding her in front of him with one arm wrapped around her upper body while his free hand held the open razor to her throat.

''I'll cut her, man!'' he said.

''That wouldn't be the smartest thing you've ever done,'' said Remo.

''Oh, yeah? Why not?''

''Because your friends are still alive. They came at me, and I gave them a break. You cut the girl—'' he frowned and shook his head ''—no breaks for you.''

''She'll still be dead,'' the razor man retorted. ''Maybe she can be my prom date when I get to hell.''

''Did anybody mention killing you?'' asked Remo. ''Hey, not me. I couldn't bring myself to let you off that easy, kid. I'd have to break your legs in six or seven places each, the same thing with your arms. The spine's a little trickier, but I know how it's done. A simple twist, not too much pressure.

You're a basket case before you know it, paralyzed from the neck down, but still in constant pain. Can't scratch your nose or wipe your ass, but that's all right. You'll have a nurse to do it for you. Hell, the tricks the doctors know these days, you ought to live another sixty years, at least. I might drop in to visit you and celebrate our anniversary, make sure those pain receptors keep on functioning. Sound good to you?''

"You're fulla shit!"

"So call my bluff if you're feeling lucky, punk," said Remo. "Go ahead. Go for it. Make my day. One thing, though—make sure it's what you really want to do, because you'll wind up paying for it for a long damn time."

The hoodlum thought about it. To be fair, thinking was probably not something he did often. He certainly didn't do it well, and at this moment he made one of his least successful thinking attempts ever.

He decided to cut.

Remo saw the slight whitening of his knife hand and the smallest change in the indentation of the hostess's skin at the moment the pressure of the blade increased.

Remo moved. Fast. Faster than the kid would have thought possible, even though he'd seen the round-eyes do some pretty amazing stuff in the past minute or so.

But that was all nothing compared to what happened now. Remo moved in and took the razor out of the punk's hand—*before* the pressure was sufficient to slice into the flesh of the poor hostess.

Then Remo took the hostess away, as well.

She was surprised to find herself suddenly safe—for a heartbeat she had thought the guy was starting to cut her, and now where she was standing was several paces away from the action.

Such as it was.

The punk who until recently had been in possession of hostage and victim now was trying figure out where both had gone.

Well, there was his victim. What was she doing way over there?

Oh. There was a razor. The Caucasian with the quick moves had it. He was bending it.

That was a pretty damn good blade. Stainless steel. Strong. Bending it should be difficult. Twisting and squeezing it into a small metal ball should be impossible.

That's exactly what round-eyes was doing.

But his eyes weren't round anymore.

They were the shape of death.

Enlightenment came to the punk. He didn't know what the guy was, but he was way beyond normal. And he had made the punk a promise. Something about a lifetime of pain and paralysis.

The punk turned and tried to run out the door, but

the frantic movement of his feet wasn't matched by the rapid transition of the scenery from the interior of the restaurant to the exterior of Larchmont, New York. This had a lot to do, he decided, with the fact that his feet were not in contact with the ground.

The Caucasian had him by the collar and was holding him high without apparent strain.

"Just kill me," the punk begged.

Remo Williams smiled a smile that would haunt the nightmares of the punk for years and years.

"Sorry. A promise is a promise."

Remo quickly did what he had promised.

THE HOSTESS SAW IT ALL. Described it all to the police. She couldn't describe the perpetrator. She never got a good look at his face. Nobody did.

"You wouldn't be covering up for the guy?" the Larchmont detective demanded.

"Covering up for him?" she asked. "What is there to cover up for? He is a hero. If I knew who he was, I would go to the press and proclaim to the world that he is a courageous man who stood up for the unprotected ethnic citizens when the Larchmont police were conspicuously absent. *I know people in the media.*"

The detective lost his bluster. "Okay, miss, we're all on the same side here. No need to get Barbara Walters."

The hostess's dark eyes glinted with determination as she corrected him. "Connie Chung," she said distinctly.

The detective stammered for a minute. "Now, let's be reasonable—you can't go publicizing things like that," he whined. "People get in trouble. People get fired. It's not fair and it's just not true."

"Then why were our complaints ignored?"

"Complaints?"

"Six complaints called in to the Larchmont Police Department in three weeks. We recorded the calls. Would you like to hear our tapes?"

"That won't be necessary...."

"Aunt Connie would like to hear them, I bet."

Remo was already long-gone by then. When he noted the wail of approaching sirens, he left the restaurant, pausing briefly to choose a fortune cookie from a bowl beside the register.

He liked fortune cookies. Not that he ever ate them. It was the fortunes themselves, delivering their tidbits of erudition silently, unlike some other fonts of wisdom Remo could name. If you didn't like your fortune, you could just toss it out and forget it. A fortune cookie didn't follow you around nagging you for days. Or weeks. Or years.

Outside, he cracked the cookie open and removed the slip of folded paper from its ruptured heart. The fortune told him "You will meet a fascinating stranger when the moon is full." And underneath that prophecy, in smaller print: "Your luck number is seven."

Remo threw the cookie in the sidewalk trash can, but he put the crumpled fortune in his pocket as he walked on to his car.

3

Dr. Harold W. Smith reminded Remo of a lemon. His complexion called to mind a dimpled lemon rind. His expression typically suggested he'd bitten into something sour but was too dull to complain about it.

Before his long-running role as director of CURE, the supersecret crime-fighting and security organization, Dr. Smith had done a long tour of duty with the CIA, where he confounded Langley's staff psychiatrists.

They put him through a standard Rorschach test, but all that Smith could see was ink blots. Other testing was performed—crude by the standards of the twenty-first century but the state of the psychoanalytical art in the 1950s. The results were perplexing.

The CIA doctors were convinced that Smith was playing games or, worse, being deliberately misleading. Finally, they were convinced of the unbelievable truth.

In the words of one examiner, "The man has absolutely no imagination. None.'' The men in charge at Langley were delighted. Men with no imagination were exactly what the covert Cold War intelligence apparatus needed in those days. In the CIA, where he was sometimes called the Gray Ghost, his career had been highly successful.

He was often described as extremely competent, but his direct superior was known to add, ''*Competent* is the right word for Smith, but it's not a big enough word.''

The shrinks were wrong about Harold Smith, of course. They failed to understand that Smith was one who dealt in hard and fast reality. He could imagine Armageddon well enough, projecting what would happen if a raving lunatic in Moscow pushed the button, but he had no time for parlor games, no knack for spotting bats or butterflies in what were honestly and truly smears of ink. Case closed.

Aside from Harold Smith's steadfast fidelity to reality, he was possessed of an integrity that ran bone-deep and would put most public servants in the shade, where they belonged. Smith's honesty was such that he had never swiped a pencil, paper clip or piece of stationery from the office and never would.

Along with his honesty, Smith was distinguished by a patriotism that ran to the very fiber of his being. Even without tests to prove them, these traits were known to his superiors. And to their superiors. And eventually Smith was mentioned in the presence of the most superior official in the federal government.

It was back in the early 1960s, and the President of the United States was looking for a man just like Harold W. Smith—a loyal, pragmatic man, one utterly devoted to the precepts of liberty as described in the Constitution of the United States of America. His task would be to successfully control a great violation of that Constitution.

That violation had a name. CURE. Not an acronym. CURE was a cure for a sick world. CURE was an attempt to stabilize the magnificent constitutional democracy by violating its constitution. Organized crime didn't follow the rules. Espionage cells and other threats to the U.S. didn't follow the rules. CURE wouldn't follow them, either.

Smith had his doubts about the success of such an organization, but he would not, could not turn down an appointment by the President of the United States. He was retiring from the CIA and had already accepted an academic position, but instead he became head of CURE. He also became the director of the Folcroft Sanitarium in Rye, New York, where CURE was based.

In the early days, successes came slowly. When the young, idealistic President who had formed the organization was gunned down, murdered in front of thousands of spectators while riding in a motorcade next to his lovely young wife, Smith had been demoralized.

For all of twenty minutes.

Then he was back on the job.

Forty years later, he was still on the job.

In the intervening years he had ordered the commission of grave violations of most of the freedoms granted by the Constitution of the United States, but always with the goal of preserving it. And preserve it he had. CURE worked. No one—not even the Presidents under whom Smith served—knew the scope of activities it had been involved in and the disasters CURE had prevented.

Harold W. Smith was prepared to die by his own hand rather than share the secrets now locked inside his brain. If a threat ever materialized to undermine the federal government by exposing CURE, Smith would initiate a full-scale self-destruction of the organization, its computers, its records and even himself. He had the will and he had the pill.

Maybe, Remo thought, it was all that keeping-it-inside that made Smith sour. This afternoon, the director of CURE looked even more dyspeptic than was usual. He stared at Remo from behind his tidy desk, and while it wouldn't have been strictly accurate to call his look a scowl, it was the next best thing.

''The Happy what?'' Smith asked.

"The Happy Noodle," Remo told him. "Just down the road, in Larchmont."

"Ah." The lesson in geography didn't appear to calm Smith's nerves or roiling stomach. "How many were there?"

"Just seven," Remo said.

"Just seven."

"Well, now there's six and a half."

Dr. Smith steepled his fingers and braced them under his chin, as if the whirlwind of thought inside his head had grown too much for his ancient neck muscles to support.

"You couldn't let it pass?"

"Not really," Remo said. "The situation was escalating, getting out of hand. Besides, they're alive. No problem, Smitty."

"No problem? What about the publicity?" Smith said. "My God, I hate to think of it."

"No sweat," Remo said. "It's a restaurant, okay? It's not like they take names or check ID unless you walk in looking twelve years old and order booze. Which I don't and I didn't, and if they did card me I'd tell them I'm Remo Toohugandkiss or whatever the hell name I'm going by today."

"But you were seen," the director of CURE reminded him stiffly. "Keep in mind you're not exactly a stranger at Folcroft. Someone on the staff would know you if they saw you, and it isn't inconceivable that some of our staff were there or on the street. Larchmont's practically in our own back-yard.''

"I had my mean face on," Remo griped. "Nobody'll be able to pick me out of a lineup, I swear."

Smith spread his hands and turned his lemon face toward the ceiling, as if seeking guidance from the stained tiles. He shook his head at last, fingers coming to rest on the onyx surface of the desk and eyes focusing on the computer screen that came to life, hidden under the desktop.

"All right," he said, "let's all forget about this noodle business for the moment, shall we?"

Remo glanced behind him, wondering if Mark Howard, Smith's associate, had joined the party, but they were still alone.

Smith was focusing his attention on the glowing screen that was quite literally his window to the world.

"There's been some kind of cock-up in the federal witness program," Smith said. "We—"

"Some kind of what?"

The lemon face was raised. "Excuse me?" Smith appeared confused.

"Some kind of what?" Remo repeated.

"What?" Smith's frown showed irritation now.

"Nothing. Forget it."

"Right." Smith stared at Remo for a moment longer than was absolutely necessary, then his eyes dropped back to the hidden display. His fingers had never stopped moving, as if they had their own guiding will.

"The Witsec program has begun to leak," he explained. "Or, more precisely, it's begun to hemorrhage. We have three witnesses eliminated in the past two months, along with relocated members of their families. Nine victims altogether, plus a bystander who may have stumbled on the second hit in progress."

It was Remo's turn to frown. "This is something new? They go through witnesses like I go through shoes."

Smith looked at him sharply. "You don't go through shoes so much as waste them."

"They wear out fast," Remo said with a shrug.

The sour face Smith made was potent with doubt. "Perhaps you would like to see an accounting of CURE expenses arising from your shoe habit."

"Hey, what's wrong with having a shoe habit? Most of us have shoe habits. I hardly ever see you strolling around here in your socks."

"Your shoes are handmade in Italy."

"Forgive me for appreciating quality."

"And they are exorbitantly expensive," Smith persisted.

"So are yours, I'm sure," Remo protested.

Smith pursed his lips. "Remo, I have three pairs of shoes. Today I am wearing my newest pair. Black wingtips. I purchased them in 1989."

"They must be really stinky."

"A good pair of shoes lasts a long time, that's my point," Smith said in exasperation.

Remo made a resigned face. "Okay, Smitty, so when do you throw your shoes away?"

"When they're worn-out, of course."

"Me, too. Case closed. Now tell me why we should care about the Feds losing witnesses."

Smith knew Remo was right. Shoes was not the subject at hand—but he made a mental note to have Mark Howard generate the expense report he had mentioned.

"The federal witness program has had its glitches over the years, and a protected subject is inevitably lost from time to time," Smith admitted. "The typical scenario involves a homesick witness who can't resist a phone call or a visit home. He is spotted or traced, and then it's not long before he's neutralized. It is an effective reminder to other witnesses in hiding that the act of reaching out to touch someone is often tantamount to suicide."

"I guess it oughta," Remo said.

"Three witnesses in two months' time is different," Smith continued. "It defies the odds of mere coincidence. It should be impossible."

"Never underestimate the screw-up potential of a federal bureaucracy," Remo said. "Were the killings connected?"

"Indeed they were," Smith said. "Are you familiar with the Cajun Mafia?"

"They put hot sauce on everything," said Remo. "Cross them, and you wind up sleeping with the blackened fish."

Smith was used to Remo's quips and ignored them whenever possible. "In fact, they're ruthless. Deadly. Thugs and outlaws from the bayou country of Louisiana who have learned by watching other, larger syndicates, adapting the procedures to their own requirements. Since Marcello died, they've given the Sicilians lots of competition in New Orleans and throughout the state, with feelers out to Arkansas and Texas, drug connections of their own in Mexico, Colombia and Southeast Asia. They're involved in everything from vice to crooked politics and real estate. You name it, and the Cajuns have a slice of the potato pie."

"That's sweet-potato pie," said Remo.

"Whichever." Smith had already allowed Remo to distract him too many times and the conversation was only ten minutes old. "Until a few months ago, the leader of the so-called Cajun Mafia was Armand Fortier, known to his cohorts as the Big Crawdaddy. Please don't ask me why."

"Why?"

"Recently," Smith continued sternly, "after several failed attempts, he was convicted on a RICO charge including several homicides, extortion, drugs—the works. Unlike the previous attempts, which ended in acquittal or hung juries, this time there were witnesses prepared to talk, insiders who believed that Fortier was planning to eliminate them, just in case.''

"And was he?" Remo asked.

"Probably. What difference does it make? My point is that they testified, resulting in conviction, and all four were relocated, with their wives and minor children.''

"As opposed to major children?" Remo said.

Smith wished Chiun were there. The presence of the old Korean seemed to have the effect of humbling Remo or at least reducing the number of pointless comments. But Chiun was spending a lot of his time ''meditating'' these days. Smith had been assured the old Korean wasn't ready for retirement, but he wasn't sure what else the old Master's decreased involvement could signify.

The chief of CURE forged on. "As you may imagine, whether Fortier was after them before the trial or not, he wants them now. Or, rather, he wanted them, since three are dead. Mark will be here in just a moment with some shots from the crime scenes.''

There was a knock at that very moment and the door opened. Mark Howard entered with a manila envelope. "Remo," Howard said with a nod.

"Did he train you to do that, Junior?"

"Do what?"

Howard slid over the envelope and took the chair next to Remo. Smith opened the manila folder and removed a stack of photographs. He began to pass them across the desk, inverted, as if he were dealing outsized playing cards. The crime-scene photos were in living, bloody color, several of them close-ups. While they weren't the worst things he had ever seen, Remo decided they were bad enough. No slick, professional hits in evidence here. It was amateur night at the butcher shop.

"Okay, these are really nice and all, but do I care what the crime scene looked like?" Remo asked.

"The first one, on your left there," Smith directed his attention, "is what's left of Justin Marchant and his wife. They lived in Medford, Oregon, under the cover name of Wilson. Marchant was Fortier's accountant. One of them, at least. He juggled books to hide the income from a string of brothels, drug transactions, this and that. He testified. And now he's dead."

"Dead hardly covers it," said Remo. Peering at the photograph, he had some difficulty sorting out where Justin Marchant ended and his wife began. The bedroom—if it was a bedroom—was awash in blood.

"Next up," Smith said, "you have Adrian Pascoe and friend. The woman was identified as Louise Lascar, no connection to the case. Pascoe apparently hooked up with her after his relocation to Scranton, Pennsylvania, as William Decker. They were sharing quarters.''

The way Smith sounded when he spoke of "sharing quarters,'' Remo half expected him to add that Pascoe and his lady had been living in sin. It hardly mattered, though, since neither one of them was living any longer.

''Yech. Bet it was a closed casket. What was the link to Fortier?'' he asked.

''Pascoe was muscle, but ambitious muscle,'' Smith replied. ''Apparently, he started out on the New Orleans docks as an enforcer for the union. Cajun stock, of course. His father and a couple of his uncles have done time for poaching, liquor violations, felony assault, grand theft. His testimony helped sink Fortier on contract killings dating back to 1987.

''Third photo,'' Smith said. It showed what could have been a shattered mannequin, except for all the blood and scattered viscera. The setting seemed to be a lawn or grassy field.

''That's Wyatt Greaves,'' Smith said. ''He was a neighbor, more or less, no evidence of any personal connection to the witness. Greaves apparently liked late-night jogging. The police surmise that he heard something as he passed by Pascoe's house, or maybe he just met the killer coming out. In any case, it was bad timing.''

"Bad is right."

"The last three shots," Smith said, "show Aloysius Cartier, his wife and their three children. Cartier ran chop shops for the Cajun mob and worked his way up into middle management. The FBI caught him red-handed with some stolen property and squeezed until he sang. The family was relocated to Cadillac, Michigan, with the surname of Francisco. They were safe, from all appearances, until three days ago."

Now they were safe again, thought Remo, as only the dead were ever truly safe from harm. But Jesus, what a way to go. The man and woman tangled up in bloody sheets, another bedroom transformed into a mad surgeon's operating theater. The children...

"What's the weapon?" Remo asked. "Machete? Ax? A chain saw?"

"Teeth," said Dr. Smith.

Remo Williams said nothing for a long moment. Then he said, "I see."

He did see. He saw it as big as death.

Smith didn't typically involve CURE in something as mundane as organized-crime murders. Now Remo knew why Smith was involving them this time. "Goddamn it!" he growled.

"Autopsy reports on all nine victims are consistent," Smith continued relentlessly. "Medical examiners from three states have confirmed their findings with the FBI in Washington. It would appear the victims were attacked and killed by one or more wild animals. Aside from the dismemberment, there is persuasive evidence that parts of several bodies were, well, devoured.''

"As in eaten.''

"That appears to be the case.''

"In addition to the damage you can see, the female victim in Nebraska was discovered to have several canine hairs clutched in her hand,'' Mark Howard said.

"Canine as in dog,'' Remo stated, feeling hollow.

"There was a witness to the last attack,'' Smith added. "Or, rather, a witness to the getaway. A neighbor of the Cartiers, one Edward Beasley, heard some kind of a commotion at the time of the attack and ran outside in time to see the, um, the suspects fleeing from the scene.''

"Suspects,'' said Remo, "as in more than one?''

"It gets a little shaky here,'' Smith said. "The witness has described a pack of dogs, no breed confirmed. They were, he says, accompanied by a monster.''

"What kind of monster?''

"His words, not mine,'' Smith said. "A hairy monster, if you want to be precise.''

Mark clarified. "Specifically, he called it 'A hairy wolf man howling at the moon.'''

"To top it all off,'' Smith said, "saliva from a

number of the wounds has been identified as human.''

"That bitch!" Remo stated harshly.

"Judith White," Smith intoned morosely.

"Who else?" he demanded angrily. "I let her get away."

"She engineered an escape," Mark Howard said.

"Whatever."

Smith took a deep breath. "We don't think it's her, Remo."

"Huh? Of course it's her."

"There are a number of things about it that don't fit," Howard said. "Even if she is still alive, you did close down her stable."

"So what? You know how fast she works when she sets her mind to it. You drink her special blend, and next thing you're a human animal hungry for meat. This is right up her alley."

"It's not, though," Howard said. "Judith White wouldn't work for organized crime. Why would she?"

Remo gave him a bitter stare. "We're not talking about a woman with a lot of scruples, Junior. She needs cash to fund her little mad-scientist research labs. She wouldn't have qualms about doing hits for the mob if it pays for the Bunsen burners."

"She'd know the crime scenes would be full of odd clues to tip off law enforcement, for one," Smith said. "And she is not fond of publicity."

"Also, the hairs at the scene were canine," Mark Howard reminded Remo. "White has not been known to make much use of canine DNA in her gene-splicing experiments."

Remo was exasperated and angry. "Earth to stupid guy—that bitch put a little of everything in her special brew. A little tiger, a little leech, a little whatever. If there happened to be a stray dog raiding the garbage cans, she'd have wrung his neck and dumped him into the pot, too."

There was a moment of silence while they considered this. Then Remo sighed. "You're right. These killings aren't her style. That means it's one of her pups."

"Now I think we are on the same wavelength," Smith said, nodding. "We have to consider that's the source of this so-called monster."

Remo laughed hollowly. "What the hell else *would* we consider?"

THE OLD ASIAN WAS about to say something when Remo walked into the duplex. Maybe something derogatory. Maybe just a mild insult. Whatever it was, he swallowed it when he sensed Remo's smoldering self-recrimination.

Chiun, Master of Sinanju Emeritus, said simply, "My son?"

"Little Father." Remo paced the nearly empty living room.

A minute later he lowered himself to sit cross-legged on the mat, facing Chiun, and started again. "Little Father. I failed."

"How did you fail?" asked the little man in a singsong voice that held a deep compassion at rare times. Like now.

"Judith White. She's started killing again. Or one of her litters, anyway." He told Chiun all the details.

"She got away from me in the end," Remo said. "If I would have stopped her then, this wouldn't be happening."

"But Emperor Smith and the young Prince believe this is not her," Chiun mused.

"They think it's probably connected to her. A bad batch of her potion that she threw out or forgot about or just didn't care about. A bunch of rabid Rin Tin Tins that slipped through the net. The way they're behaving, Smith thinks they might have even been operating for several months, maybe years."

"So how could you have known of their existence, let alone been responsible for their removal?" Chiun asked in a very straightforward way.

Remo sighed. "I don't know."

"You could not," Chiun summed up. "They may have been created before we last encountered Dr. Judith White at her water factory."

"That lets me off the hook? That just means it was my first kill-Judy failure rather than my second.

Either way, I let her get away and now people are dying.''

"There is no way you could have known she did not die in the fire. There was no way you could have foreseen her slippery escape in Maine.''

"Aren't I supposed to be the freaking Master of Sinanju?''

"You are the Master of Sinanju. There is no 'freaking' and there is no 'supposed' about it. As the Master of Sinanju, you have skills beyond any possessed by other men. But this does not make you omniscient.''

Remo frowned. "Omniscient means knowing everything?''

Chiun sighed heavily. "Yes.''

"So you're trying to say I don't know everything?''

"Yes, as you've just demonstrated wondrously.''

"So how come I feel like I let those people die?''

Chiun didn't answer that. He could have harangued on the subject for a half hour if he wanted to. And he probably would. Later.

"Smitty and Junior aren't even convinced it's her or her kids,'' Remo said bitterly. "Get this. The FBI thinks maybe it's just some guy dressed up in a monster costume. You can buy them anywhere, mail order if you want to skip the stores. Full head and gloves, the feet, whatever. Smitty tried telling me the Feds might be right.''

"And the other canine creatures?"

"The theory is they're attack-trained dogs," Remo said. "That's easy. You can train a dog to do almost anything. They had a German shepherd in L.A. a few years back, somebody trained him to snatch purses on the street. In Argentina, when Perón was still around, the state police had special handlers training dogs to rape their female prisoners."

"Trained dogs and monster masks do not explain human saliva in the wounds," Chiun said.

"Smith says maybe the guy's just a biter," Remo said. "I guess stranger things have happened. Look at Dahmer."

"What of the witness who survives?" asked Chiun.

"His name's Jean Cuvier. Some kind of second-string lieutenant in the Cajun mob before the FBI grabbed Fortier. His specialty was fixing sporting events. He started yapping to the Feds and wound up with a contract on his head and asked the government to help him out. He squealed on the stand about Fortier's dabbling in extortion. He told the jury about Fortier acid-blinding a jockey who forgot he was supposed to lose a race. After the verdict, Cuvier was relocated to Nebraska. Omaha."

"He will be next," Chiun said, not making it a question.

"Maybe," said Remo. "I'm gonna go baby-sit him for a while and hope the wolf man comes back.

Then we'll know for sure if it's one of Dr. Judy White's little experiments or a guy in a wolf suit. But somebody is bound to try for Cuvier. Fortier's attorneys have a motion for a new trial pending in the Seventh Circuit, and it could go either way. If it goes back to trial and he's eliminated all the prosecution witnesses, Fortier walks."

"When the killers come for this Cuvier, they will be forced to reveal their true nature," Chiun mused. "This will put your mind at ease."

"Huh? How?"

"To know their origin is to understand them. Once you understand them, then you will know you are not responsible for their being or culpable in their crimes. It is as the Emperor says, Remo—they are not necessarily the offspring of the madwoman Judith White."

Remo wasn't buying it. "But another set of cannibal killers springs up just a few months after Dr. White slips through the net? Not likely."

"Maybe it is. Since we encountered the cannibal woman, Smith has doubtless inveigled his electronic information machines to look for the telltale signs of an attack matching the nature of Dr. White. The killers were there, but only now has it come to the attention of Emperor Smith."

"I think you're reaching for straws."

"I do not reach for straws. Ever. Also, consider that perhaps this creature is not a product of Dr.

White and is not a masquerader in a costume, but a true wolf man.''

"Huh?"

"Spoken like a true Master. It is unlikely, I agree, that an American would have such powers. All the more since his ancestors came from France. If he was Asian, now, perhaps…''

"You don't believe in werewolves, do you, Little Father?"

Chiun regarded Remo with a frown. "Such tales are not unique to Europe and America," he said at last. "Koreans have never sought communion with the lower beasts, but it is not unknown in China and Japan, where degradation of the species is routine."

"A Chinese wolf man?"

"In fact, the were-*fox* is more common," Chiun replied. "No doubt, the lowly Chinese once attempted to improve their ignoble mental state by interbreeding with a wiser animal. The end result, predictably, was not as they intended."

"You're not serious." Remo had conjured a mental image. "I can't picture it. I mean, I guess I can see a Chinese were-fox, but what I can't picture is the actual mating between the human and the fox."

"I chose not to even attempt to visualize such a thing," Chiun said rancorously.

"Especially since you gotta know the fox is not going to be a willing partner," Remo added before

Chiun could continue. "So the poor thing probably had to get tied up or something."

"Doubtless."

"So you're talking about Chinese bondage bestiality."

"No," Chiun replied firmly, "it is you who keeps talking about it."

"It's outlandish. I don't believe it."

"That is because you are incapable of using a computer and thus cannot know that such outlandish things are reality. Ask the Prince Regent to locate such material on the Internet. I seriously doubt he will fail to find photographic evidence of some poor fox enduring what I have described. I'm sure you will find it utterly fascinating and it may pique your interest in a new hobby. Now may I continue with my story?"

Chiun's tone told Remo that it was a rhetorical question and he had better not answer at all if he didn't want to get slapped upside the head.

"It is well-known that in some parts of China there are foxes who can take on human form at will," Chiun said sternly. "For some reason best known to themselves, they nearly always take the form of women, to entice some lowly peasant from his toil and trap him in a web of sensual delights before they rob him of his meager senses and his life."

"That sounds more like a succubus," said Remo,

"but we're talking werewolves here. Full moons and silver bullets. Pentagrams and Michael Landon. Did you ever see the movies?"

"There is, of course, a classic story of a werewolf from Korea," Chiun said. "The fairy tale told to Korean children says the man in the story is a common woodcutter. What the Korean legend fails to recall is that it was actually a Master of Sinanju."

"I hope it's not Master Pak," Remo warned.

Chiun looked at him askance and slightly confused. "Why do you hope it is not Master Pak?"

"Because Pak's the one who met the vampire, right?"

"Yes. Why does this matter?"

"Come on, Chiun, didn't you ever see the Universal black-and-whites where they started pairing up monsters without logical explanation? Even when I was a kid it strained my credulity."

"Are you speaking of motion pictures?"

"Yeah. Like in *Frankenstein Versus the Wolf Man.* They had the wolf man just happen to stumble across Frankenstein's castle. So, never mind that the wolf man could have been running around in any forest in all of Eastern Europe, it's pure coincidence he finds the one place where there's another monster."

"Do you have a point?" Chiun demanded.

"There was one that was even worse but I can't remember which—it had the Frankentsein monster *and* the wolf man *and* Dracula. The big three 1940s monsters all ending up together for no adequately explained—''

''Enough!'' Chiun barked.

''What? What?''

''You are babbling, imbecile!''

''I'm just trying to tell you that I'm gonna have a hard time believing that Master Pak ran into both a vampire and a werewolf.''

''It was you, not I, who mentioned Master Pak!''

''So was he the one who met a werewolf?''

''No, white blabbermouth, it was Master Hun-Tup.''

Remo considered that and nodded. ''The guy who rode around with Marco Polo.''

''As you would have learned long, long ago if you would only have exerted the will required to lock your grotesquely swollen lips together long enough to allow me to speak!''

''Long ago? We just started discussing it thirty seconds ago.''

''An eternity of interruptions.''

''Hey, fine,'' Remo said, tightly closing his mouth and pantomiming locking them with a key. ''Mm. Mmmmm?''

''I'll be satisfied only if you manage to keep them like that long enough for me to finish telling the history of Hun-Tup's encounter with a werewolf.''

Remo looked at nim expectantly and, Chiun noticed, not a little sarcastically.

"Master Hun-Tup was traveling when he came to Kanggye. The people, when they realized they had a Master of Sinanju in their midst, came to him in great numbers, offering to collect a great sum of gold from every citizen for miles around if he would rid them of their terrible menace—a wolf of enormous size, who attacked and devoured men, women and children. Hun-Tup turned down their offer, for the Masters of Sinanju worked only for kings and emperors. Not the common rabble. Still, he was intrigued, and he went into the forests near Kanggye and quickly found the spoor of this great wolf."

Remo fought back the urge to ask, "You have wolves in Korea?"

Chiun glared at the almost-interruption he had seen on Remo's face. "Master Hun-Tup followed the trail and found himself face-to-face with a ferocious wolf. Hun-Tup wounded him mortally with a single blow to the skull, but didn't kill the beast instantly. He was curious about the beast, and where it went to die, he hoped, would tell him something of its nature. And he was correct. He followed the fleeing beast's trail of bright blood, which led him to a lonely peasant's hovel. There, inside, he found an old hermit lying on the bed, naked except for bloody rags wrapped tight around his wounded skull. Hun-Tup attempted to speak to him, but the old man would not answer. Soon he died and was transformed into a wolf once more.''

Remo looked dubious.

''Speak now!'' Chiun said. He disliked having the history of Sinanju doubted, especially by Master Remo the Illiterate.

''But you said Koreans don't—''

''The hermit was Chinese,'' Chiun replied. ''If you applied yourself to study of geography, you would have known that Kanggye stands beside the Yalu River, but a few miles from the Chinese border.''

''Ah. Of course, it all makes sense now.''

''You are skeptical,'' said Chiun.

''Sounds like a fairy tale,'' Remo replied.

Chiun made a little sniffing sound, as of dismissal. ''I despair of bringing the great history of our village to the blighted desert of your mind.''

''Hey, I've got a hell of a lot of Sinanju history stored up here,'' Remo protested.

''Prove it. I will quiz you.''

''Love to but I gotta run,'' Remo said with a glance at his watch and getting quickly to his feet. ''I'm on the next flight out to Omaha, at six-fifteen,'' said Remo.

''I'll come, as well,'' Chiun said, rising.

''I thought you had a lot of meditating to do.''

''I will meditate in the hotel room while you go about serving your Emperor and performing your duties as the Reigning Master of Sinanju. And on the aircraft you can take my quiz.''

''That,'' Remo said, ''would be wonderful.'' Remo was lying. It would, in reality, suck.

''I knew you would think so,'' Chiun sang out brightly. Chiun was lying, as well. He knew Remo would hate it. That was part of what made it fun.

4

The flight to Omaha was perfectly routine. Routine required that Chiun, the Master of Sinanju Emeritus and veteran of more airplane flights than the entire flight crew, spend the majority of the time staring out at the wing. Watching for the signs that it was about to snap off. He lost interest in quizzing Remo somewhere over Kentucky.

The flight was over its quota on annoying and obnoxious travelers, including a bigmouthed businessman crammed in next to Remo. A bleached-blond single mother and her two unruly children swarmed into the row in front of them. A red-haired boy with catastrophic freckles stood on his seat and spotted Chiun, calling out to his mother, "Lookee at the Chinaman!"

Remo could feel Chiun steaming in the seat immediately to his left. The mother shushed her brat, and Remo was relaxing when the stranger to his right said, "So, your friend's Chinese?"

"Korean."

"Too bad. I was in China for a couple months

last year. Wide-open marketplace for auto dealer-
ships, you know. Fantastic. I don't know about Koreans, but the Chinese people are the nicest folks
you'd ever want to meet. Of course—''

"You've got a piece of lint there," Remo said
and reached out toward the salesman's lapel.

The slightest touch was all it took. The businessman who liked Chinese people went to sleep. He'd
regain consciousness about the time they landed in
Omaha.

"Sweet dreams," said Remo, making his face
into an evil sort of grin.

The red-haired child saw it all and watched wide-
eyed.

"I think he'll stay quiet now," Remo said with a
manic grin. "Will you?"

The boy nodded, mouth agape, and sat in his seat.
He didn't make another sound.

Chiun's face was blank but his breath came out,
"Heh heh heh."

"You're welcome," Remo said.

"Heh heh heh."

AT OMAHA'S EPPLEY AIRFIELD they picked up a
midsize Chevrolet sedan in the Avis lot. Remo puzzled over the Auto Club street map and drove them
north and west of Omaha on Interstate 680, catching
Highway 6 eastbound, for a run past malls and hos-
pitals to Eastland Park.

Jean Cuvier—alias "Rick Baker"—lived alone in a smallish house near the Elmwood Park country club. Small didn't mean cheap in that neighborhood, and Remo wondered briefly if the informer would miss it.

Not that it mattered. He was leaving, one way or another. The witness had run out of options. He could leave or he could die.

Remo found the house after only a couple of wrong turns and parked half a block away, to the west. He had already worked out the move with Chiun, who had decided at the last minute to come along.

Remo waited for a moment near the car, while Chiun vanished into the backyard of a house two doors from Baker's. He gave the Master of Sinanju a few seconds, then ambled down the block and up to Baker's door.

Inside the house the doorbell played a little tune that Remo couldn't quite recognize. He rang it again. The door opened and he was still trying to figure out the song so he rang it a third time.

"Oh," he told the man at the door. "The Rocky theme. Oh, brother."

Remo had been expecting some sort of a tough guy to answer. What he got was an animated version of the Pillsbury doughboy.

"I don't want nothin'," the man said.

"I guess that makes you one of a kind."

"Says what?"

"Everybody wants *something*," Remo answered.

"Not me. Now go away."

"Staying alive. I bet you want that, don't you?"

The eyes narrowed. "Does I know you?"

"I know you, Mr. Cuvier."

It took a second for the name to register, then the doughboy recoiled—and backed into Chiun, who'd come in through the rear without making a sound. The witness yelped and Remo caught his arms before he started sending windmill punches at the old Korean.

"See, now *that* will get you killed," Remo chided Cuvier. "I've already saved your life, and we've only known each other fifteen seconds."

Remo carried him into the living room and propped him upright on the sofa. Cuvier started swinging again as soon as Remo freed his hands, so he grabbed them again. Cuvier found his hands locked in twin steel vises. The guy wasn't even putting an effort into holding him prisoner.

"All right," Cuvier said at last, slumping. "Go on and do what you come for."

"That would be the saving-your-life thing I was talking about," Remo told him.

"You all want to explain that?"

"Three of your former associates have been killed recently." Remo gave him the names, watching the color drain from Cuvier's face as he spoke. "Someone traced their new identities and ran them down. It wasn't pretty. You're the last in line.''

"How were the killings done?" Cuvier demanded.

"The medical examiner suspects a pack of animals.''

"Loup-garou!" Cuvier nearly bolted from the couch, despite Remo's restraining grip.

"What's that again?" he asked.

"Never you mind.''

Remo looked at Chiun, who looked bored. "Loup-garou is werewolf," he explained.

"I'm getting out of here right now," Cuvier declared.

"That's exactly what we had in mind," Remo said.

5

The rabbit had been dead for half an hour, maybe forty minutes. It was crossing Highway 85, between Papillion and La Vista, when it met a Dodge Intrepid doing half-past sixty in the northbound lane and was dispatched to bunny heaven on the spot.

It was a clean kill, relatively speaking: fractured vertebrae and shattered skull, with visible extrusion of the brain, but no great damage to the carcass overall. In fact, the rabbit's body still retained a hint of warmth that pleased the leader of the pack, his nostrils flaring.

He was a carnivore by breeding and by inclination, craving meat and mostly passing on the veggies when his stomach growled for food. As it was growling now.

The little problem that isolated him from humanity also prevented him from strolling through a supermarket, loading up his basket with a pile of steaks, chops, ribs and such—but still, he had to eat. Back home, in the bayou country, he would go out prowling with the pack, or sometimes on his own, and not stop looking until he had satisfied his hunger. On the road, it was a different story. He could pack meat with him, ice it down, but it would only last so long and stretch so far. When he ran out, or the supply on hand went bad, the leader of the pack improvised.

Roadkill, for instance.

It was everywhere, though obviously more abundant in some areas than others. If you had the time to shop around, the nation's highways offered up a menu that would rival that of any gourmet restaurant. A savvy shopper had his pick of snake and turtle, squirrel and chipmunk, raccoon and opossum, rabbit, woodchuck, every now and then a deer to feed the whole damned pack. Some districts had their local specialties, like Texas armadillo, prairie dog on the Great Plains and wolverine in Michigan. He didn't care for cities, where the bill of fare was mostly cats and dogs, but meat was meat.

This night, the rabbit was an appetizer. There wasn't enough of it to go around, and he wasn't inclined to offer any of it to the pack. They leered and grumbled at him, little whiny noises from the bitch, but he ignored them. They would all be feeding soon enough.

And so would he.

In truth, he could have passed by the rabbit and waited for the main event, but they had time to kill, and there was no point wasting food. If life had taught him anything, it was that you could never count on getting lucky. When you saw a free meal lying on the center strip and failed to stop, you could just as well go hungry down the road.

He twisted off the rabbit's shattered skull and slit it down the belly with a ragged talon, disemboweling it before he peeled the skin. A glance in each direction told him that he had the highway to himself, no traffic at the moment, but solitude was like luck.

It didn't last.

The leader of the pack wasn't inclined to reminisce in any great detail, but there were times, like now, when he considered the peculiarities of life. A simple accident of birth had made him stand apart from others of his kind, shunned even by his father and his older siblings. When his mother stubbornly refused to give him up, the old man thrashed her and expelled them both, to live or die according to their wits. His mother had been smarter than the old man reckoned, though, devising ways to make ends meet. Survival was the first priority, pursuit of food and shelter, leaving little room for dignity. They had survived, all right, but it had worn his mother down by degrees, with physical exhaustion, personal humiliation, finally disease, until the beast-child found himself alone at ten years old.

He had never been to school in all that time, of course—it would have been impossible, unthinkable—and there was no thought of it now that he was on his own. His mother loved him, but she recognized that others would not share her sentiment, so she had concealed him from the world at large. So skilful was the deception, that at her death, no social workers had come sniffing after him to place him in a foster home. Nobody came at all, in fact, until the next month's rent was two days late, and Mr. Landlord used his master key to let himself inside the miserable two-room flat. Later, when he was babbling to the lawmen, they smelled whiskey on his breath and would have locked him up to sleep it off, if not for the ragged bite marks on his arms.

There was no living in the big town after that. His mother had been Cajun through and through. Her roots were in the bayou country, and she used to take him there sometimes, on the rare occasions when she had some free time on her hands. Not to visit her people, mind you—they would certainly have viewed her monster offspring as a curse from God—but to show him the ways of nature, teaching him by bits and pieces how the greater system worked. It wasn't long before he had the basics figured out.

Kill or be killed.

Once he was on his own, he went back to the bayou country. It was touch and go, the man-child trying to compete with predators who had their act down cold. He lived on carrion at first, and precious little of it, but he learned. And it was almost good enough.

Almost.

A careless accident had nearly ended it, when he was coming up on twelve years old. He should have seen the moccasin, its thick body draped across a drooping mangrove branch, but he was concentrating on the fish that darted just beneath the surface of the brackish water. When the snake struck him, going for the face, there was no warning but a blur of motion and the stinging impact as its fangs sank home.

Between his panic and the poison coursing through his system, he had nearly died. He would have died were it not for the old Cajun hermit who had found him and decided it was worth a try to save the boy-thing's life. He had recovered, slowly, and the old man let him hang around, taught him the fine points of survival in the swamp…and other things.

It was the hermit who had taught him he was special, blessed with certain powers that made other people cringe from him in fear. It was the old man who had shown him what it meant to be a loup-garou.

By teaching him to accept and even embrace his true nature, he had been prepared for the next great change that came over him.

Years later, when the hermit was too old to scrape

a living out of the harsh and merciless bayou, his young protégé was more than skilled enough to provide for them both. But the hermit was worried for the young beast he had adopted. The beast was mature, full-grown and vibrant with energy and vitality that should not be confined to their isolated corner of the swamp.

Then fortune, for the first time, smiled on the hermit. The strange woman appeared out of nowhere and offered the hermit cash money. In exchange, he gave her a piece of paper allowing her to set up her house trailer on their lonely bayou for three months.

She wasn't on vacation, and her mobile home was different from any RV the hermit or his ward had ever seen before. It was a living machine, always humming with energy. There were generators and air-conditioners and other roof-mounted machinery. The smells that came from inside were not to be believed.

The woman was fascinated with the hermit's young beast. She spoke to him without pity and exhibited no fear of him or his bizarre appearance.

She was a scientist, she said, and she recognized the young man's condition as nothing more than a standard case of hypertrichosis. Well, maybe a little more extreme than the cases she had heard of. "All victims of the condition are covered with dense hair all over their bodies," she explained matter-of-factly.

Aside from his mother and the hermit, this scientist woman was the only person he had ever known who treated him as something other than a freak.

When he told her he liked being what he was, the scientist smiled and asked, "Why?"

He told her about his love of the hunt.

The scientist began to show a glint in her eyes. Suddenly, the young man knew. It seemed impossible, but he knew. The woman scientist also enjoyed the hunt, strange as it seemed.

"What if you could be more of what you are?" she asked him then.

He was confused.

"What if you could be faster, stronger? The ultimate hunter? The leader of your own pack?"

He wasn't even sure what she was talking about.

But of course he answered, "Yes."

WAY NORTH, from the direction of La Vista, the leader of the pack saw headlights coming, shining like a distant pair of luminescent eyes. He finished with the rabbit, tossed the clean-picked bones aside and walked back to the van. His brothers and the bitch all crowded in to lick his bloody fingers, and he left them to it. It would whet their appetite for what was coming.

The final target lived near Elmwood Park in Omaha, a few blocks from the College of St. Mary.

Cruising in his Dodge Ram cargo van, the leader of the pack watched street signs, checking them from time to time against the map he had draped across the shotgun seat. His eyes were keen enough to chart a course without the dome light, following the trail that he had marked out with a yellow felt pen on the map when he was laying out the hit. The others huddled close behind him, bright eyes peering through the van's bug-speckled windshield as he drove.

This was the last one. When this night's work was completed, he could go back home, rejoin the rest of his pack and recuperate for a while from the stress of being on the road. The balance of his money would be paid as usual, delivered by a pair of jumpy shooters who would drop the satchel at a designated point and speed away to minimize their risk of meeting the recipient. So far, the system had worked well enough. If he was lucky, there might even be some roadkill waiting for him on the highway near the drop.

He found the street he wanted, signaled for the turn and held the van a mile or two below the posted speed limit. No cops in sight, but it could be a problem if he met one. There was bound to be a hassle, and he couldn't guarantee that his reaction would be swift enough to drop the officer before he reached his weapon, much less handle two of them if they were traveling in pairs. That would mean shooting, and while he wasn't concerned about the bullets on his own behalf, the noise alone would cancel any hope of taking his appointed quarry by surprise.

This one was Cajun, like the last three, and he might know things. A trick or two for dealing with a loup-garou, perhaps. The leader of the pack had no desire to take that chance, if he could help it. It was better all around if he could catch his prey asleep, or at the very least distracted, tied up with the mundane chores of life when death dropped in to pay a call.

The house was dark, as he had hoped it would be. Likewise with the neighbors, at this hour of the night. Nebraskans came from farm stock, as he understood it, early to bed and early to rise. His target was a working man, as well, some kind of minigolf amusement park where children gathered, chasing little balls on artificial grass. The leader of the pack had hoped he wouldn't have to take his prey at work, where there were witnesses. It would be so much cleaner this way, better for all concerned.

He drove past the house and found a vacant house four doors down. There was a realtor's sign out front, and the carport was empty. He killed his headlights as he nosed the Dodge in off the street. His brothers and sister, handpicked by him from the pack for this arduous journey, were obedient. They would wait for him, as always, while he checked the house. It made them restless, but they understood the rules and didn't challenge him.

He left the van and closed the driver's door behind him softly, pressing gently till the latch engaged. It was a challenge, keeping to the shadows with a light directly opposite, but he was good at tracking, stalking prey. A little dog was yapping at him from a yard across the street, but it was no real threat. He worried more about the mongrel's owner waking, glancing out and spotting him, but he was almost at his destination now. A few more yards…

He slipped into the target's backyard through a side gate. The grass was several inches long, in need of mowing. It was obvious the man he came to kill was not a conscientious gardener. He left weeds in the flower beds and didn't trim the shrubs that grew close in against his house. Not that it mattered now. A few more minutes, and his worries would be over for all time.

He kept an eye out for security devices, spotting none. He was surprised from time to time that those he hunted made no greater effort to protect themselves. Not that a burglar alarm would have prevented him from doing what he came to do, but still, his quarry could have made the hunt more challenging.

He found the back door, reached out with his thick, dark fingers. He tried the knob, gently, and was startled when it turned. Unlocked? He crouched and sniffed around the door, suspecting something in the nature of a trap, and drew back without noting any kind of threat.

Should he go in without the others? They would never let him hear the end of it if he deprived them of a feast, but he could always scout the territory first, make sure the way was clear before he fetched them from the van. The kill itself was less important to the pack than feeding, after all.

He took the chance.

There was no word for protocol in his vocabulary, but he understood that he was stepping out of line. It was a small thing, but he told himself the others wouldn't mind. They would forgive him when they saw the kill and tasted blood. And if they didn't, well, it would be too damn bad.

But there was something wrong.

He knew it when he crossed the threshold, entering a little claustrophobic place that some would call the mud room, but was more a skimpy corridor than any kind of room at all. The house was quiet, as he had expected, but it was not sleeping quiet. Rather, it felt dead, abandoned, vacant.

No, he thought. The kitchen still bore cooking smells—another man who ruined his meat with fire—and there was glassware in the cupboards, silverware and other items in the drawers that flanked the rather dingy sink. He moved beyond the kitchen, traveling silently in darkness, and turned left down a corridor that took him to the living room. The place was fully furnished down to magazines splayed on the coffee table, and smelled strongly of cigar smoke.

He didn't possess his quarry's scent. The men who hired him didn't work that way, but they had left him photographs instead. It mattered not that they were out of date. The leader of the pack would know his prey on sight, and that was all he needed. Still…

He knew the feel of houses that have been abandoned. Something left them when the people departed, beyond the noise and everyday aromas that life generated: sweat, urine, feces, sex, the rest. When houses stood unoccupied, the smells began to fade, a little at a time, but there was more to it than that. An empty house felt empty, and it made no difference how much furniture was left behind to clutter up the lifeless rooms.

Could he have missed his final target? It defied all logic, but his senses told him that the man was gone. It seemed impossible, but life had taught him early on that anything could happen, and the worst shit came upon you when you least expected it.

Damn! The last one on his list before he went back home, and now the hunt would have to be prolonged. Worse, he had exhausted all the helpful information his employers could provide. Once he left

Omaha behind, he wouldn't have the faintest glimmer of a clue where he should look.

He was a werewolf, damn it, not a fortune-teller.

Maybe visiting? he asked himself, and clutched the slender reed of hope in shaggy, taloned hands. There was no rule that said his quarry could not have a friend, unknown to those who paid to have him killed. The others had their women, one with children who were tender and delicious in the end. Who said the final target couldn't have a—

No.

He knew that it was wrong. The house didn't feel gone-to-visit empty, waiting for the occupant's return. The ceiling, floor and walls boxed in dead air. Not long dead, granted—maybe no more than a day or two, but it may just as well have been a year. In his world, gone meant gone, and he couldn't pursue the stranger on his own without a scent.

Keep looking.

He pretended there was still a chance that he might be mistaken, moving back along the silent corridor in the direction he had come from. Past the doorway to the kitchen, past a bathroom on his left. Its door stood open, showing him a sink and toilet. There was no need for a light to prove the indoor privy was unoccupied.

There were two bedrooms at the south end of the house. He tried the smaller of them first, eliminating possibilities, and found the room unfurnished, used for storage, several stacks of boxes standing shoulder-high. One of them had been neatly labeled with a black marker, the name R. Baker printed on the side directly facing him.

He didn't know the quarry's name, but guessed it wasn't Baker. Something French, he would have wagered, for the moneymen had set him hunting Cajuns this time, targets who had scattered from the bayou country, moving north, then east or west, and covering their tracks.

But not quite well enough.

One room remained, and his last hope of an easy kill evaporated as he turned the doorknob, stepped across the threshold into darkness. Nothing, even though the bed was rumpled and a night light burned inside a small adjacent bathroom, barely large enough to hold the mandatory sink and toilet.

Gone. His frustration and his unsated hunger brought on the rage. First he felt the burning in his stomach, then the too-familiar clenched-fist feeling in his chest—yet he kept his balance, lashing out in blind, instinctive fury at the nearest objects he could reach. Trashing his quarry's lair, in case the yellow bastard ever tried to move back in.

When he was finished, he would mark his territory, urinating on the walls and doorjambs, defecating in the middle of the living room. But first…

He couldn't see the moon, but he could feel it, tugging at the tide within his body as he ran amok, gouged flimsy plaster walls with jagged fingernails, grabbed bits and pieces of his quarry's wasted life, destroyed each object in its turn and flinging it aside.

And somewhere in the middle of it, he began to howl.

"GODDAMN DOMESTIC BEEFS!"

Patrolman Roger Miller was responding to the code-two call—with flashing lights, no siren—but he didn't like it one damn bit. Domestics were the worst, especially at night or in the early-morning hours, when the parties had had all day to let their ancient bullshit grudges marinate in alcohol. You never knew what you were walking into, whether one or both of the belligerents would turn on you and vent their rage against the uniform. A little change of pace from beating on their spouse or lover, maybe reaching for a pistol or a butcher knife to make the point.

I oughta call for backup, Miller thought, but didn't. He would take a gander at the situation first. If the racket was enough to wake the neighbors, he should have a fair idea of whether help was needed by the time he rang the doorbell.

Anyway, it broke up the monotony of what had been a long, dull night. He had the eight-to-four this week and next, before he cycled back to days, and while the graveyard shift meant nonstop action in some precincts, Miller's beat was strictly middle-class. No drive-by shootings, only one convenience store to watch, no bars or teenage hangouts where the booze and blow made tempers short, drove pimply punks and Milquetoast working men to raucous feats of derring-do. Most nights he had it easy to the point that he was bored out of his freaking mind.

But not this night.

He had been counting on the usual: some moving violations, maybe a white-collar DUI, perhaps a residential burglary discovered once the perps were long gone with their swag. There was a curfew on the books these days, as well, and that meant rousting kids on Friday night or Saturday, but weeknights were a snooze.

The young policeman—twenty-six come next July—knew that he should have thanked his lucky stars for the assignment. Others from his graduating class at the academy had gone directly to the ghetto, hassling with the brothers every night, chasing graffiti taggers, dodging bricks and bottles—sometimes filled with gasoline—as they were watching out for car thieves, crackheads, any kind of human garbage you could name. The white-trash precincts were no better, stupid rednecks with their stringy hair, motheaten beards and blue jeans frayed in back from dragging on the pavement when they walked, their John Deere caps on backward. Up close, they smelled like beer and cigarettes, teeth stained orange and brown from packing snuff.

Patrolman Miller used his spotlight, mounted on the driver's door, to check house numbers as he rolled along the quiet residential street. On either side, the reflections of his own blue-and-white emergency flashers bounced back at him with a strobe-light effect, distorting shadows so that they appeared to take on life and dance in weird, surrealistic shapes.

He found the number he was looking for and pulled into the driveway, switching off the flashers as he killed the engine. Miller took a moment to inform the radio dispatcher that he had arrived. Still no request for backup, as he sat there with his window down and listened to the night.

There was no racket emanating from the house in question, damn it. Miller wondered if he had been called out on a wild-goose chase, some idiot's idea of an amusing prank. Dispatch would have a record of the caller's number and a tape recording of the call, but you could always phone in from a public booth, disguise your voice and give a bogus name. It was like sending taxis or a dozen pizzas to a neighbor who had pissed you off somehow. Embarrassment was all that counted, never mind the waste of time for a patrolman who could otherwise be elsewhere, maybe interrupting crimes in progress.

Right, thought Miller. Like they caught me in the middle of a freakin' crime wave.

Darkened windows all around and silence on the

block. Miller was just about to write it off and check back with dispatch, when someone turned the porch light on next door. A yellow bulb, to keep the bugs away. He glanced in that direction, saw a stocky woman in a quilted bathrobe waving at him.

"Jesus H."

He stepped out of his cruiser, gave the silent house in front of him another glance, then moved across the intervening strip of grass between two driveways, toward the woman on the porch next door.

"It stopped just when I saw your lights," she said.

"What did?"

"The noise I called about. It sounded like somebody screaming, only different. For just a minute there, it could have been some kind of animal."

"The people here keep dogs?" he asked.

"Not people," said the woman. "Just one man, by himself. No dogs at all. I would have seen or heard them, don't you think? I mean, he's lived there for eleven months."

"And you are...?"

"Lucy Kravitz," said the woman. "My husband Joe's away on business, or he would have—"

"What's your neighbor's name?" asked Miller, interrupting her.

"Well, I'm not sure."

"How's that, ma'am?"

"We haven't actually met, you understand, but still—"

"I see."

She doesn't know his name, thought Miller, but she's positive he lives alone and doesn't have a dog. Another freakin' busybody. Christ!

"And when I heard these sounds, the shouting and the crashing noise—"

"A crashing noise?"

"Like someone was destroying all the furniture!" she said.

"Okay," he said reluctantly. "Why don't you go on back inside. I'll check it out."

"Well, if you think—"

The sudden crashing sound made Miller jump. He covered it by pointing to the Kravitz woman's open door and telling her again to get inside. Backtracking toward the darkened house next door, he was beside his cruiser when the growling started, loud enough to reach his ears from somewhere in the house, but muffled somewhat by the intervening walls. Sure didn't sound much like a freakin' dog.

Patrolman Miller thought about the backup one more time, but he was already embarrassed by his first reaction to the noises from the house. Old biddy next door had to be thinking he was yellow, and he would confirm her judgment if he called for help. It was a rule, of course, to call for backup, but the rules were bent or broken every day.

He drew his pistol, making sure he had the safety off, and eased around the south side of the house. The noise was coming from a room in back somewhere, and Miller didn't feel like leaning on the doorbell when he could retain the prime advantage of surprise.

It was pitch-black behind the house, a bank of clouds obscuring the moon, but they began to break up moments later, letting Miller find his way. The noises from the house were growing closer, louder. Christ, forget the dog. It sounded like a freakin' leopard in the house, or something.

Maybe I should go back for the 12-gauge, Miller thought, and then the back door blasted off its hinges with a crash, propelled halfway across the scruffy yard. A walking nightmare followed it outside, half crouching, shoulders hunched. Patrolman Miller took it for a burly man until the moonlight fell across its face.

By that time it had spotted Miller and was rushing toward him, snarling as it came, with outstretched talons.

And there wasn't even time to scream.

6

The federal penitentiary outside Atlanta, Georgia, was among the toughest in the nation. There was nothing to suggest the "easy ride" or "country club" approach to housing prisoners so often noted in the press and by potential office-holders in election years, when fear of crime translated to votes. Atlanta's federal pen received no white-collar swindlers, kinky televangelists or presidential campaign managers who got caught with their fingers in the public cookie jar. At one time, it housed Al Capone, before he was transferred to Alcatraz—the Rock—but Alcatraz was now a kind of morbid theme park, while Atlanta's federal prison endured.

Atlanta's clientele included drug dealers, bank robbers, kidnappers, self-styled gangstas. A majority of those confined were black, but there was also room for redneck "soldiers" in a race war of their own imagining, a handful of Sicilian mafiosi, certain careless Teamsters, Cubans and Colombians, a spy or two.

And Armand Fortier.

The Cajun godfather was in a bad mood when his lawyer came to visit him on Saturday. It always pissed him off to see the shyster who was charging him three hundred bucks an hour while he sat in prison on a bullshit RICO charge that should have been thrown out at the preliminary hearing. Fortier had canned his trial attorney—literally, at a plant outside Metairie, where they turned decrepit horses into dog food. But the new guy hadn't shown results, either, in their pursuit of an appeal. He had a new-trial motion bogged down somewhere in the system, plus a handful of concocted "evidence" so thin you could have read the Sunday funnies through it, but the key was getting rid of those who had betrayed Armand the first time out. The traitors who had sold him down—no, up—the river to Atlanta in the first place. Scumbag ingrates.

Fortier had put his best man on it—if you thought of Leon Grosvenor as a man—and he had thought that things were working out all right.

Until today.

"What you mean, he missed them?" Fortier demanded, leaning forward with his broad, big-knuckled hands spread on the table that was bolted to the floor inside the room reserved for inmate visits with attorneys. Theoretically, the room was soundproof and the screws were barred from eavesdropping, but Armand kept his voice down all the same, despite a sudden urge to scream.

The lawyer swallowed hard, as if he had a fish bone or a little piece of oyster shell lodged in his throat. "Um, well, I mean there was a problem. The fellow seems to have, um, well, moved on."

"What the hell you mean, moved on?" the Cajun snarled. "Cost me two hundred grand to find out where they at, them dickwads, and you tellin' me it's wasted."

"Well," the lawyer said, frowning, "three out of four—"

"Ain't good enough!" said Fortier.

"But if the man has disappeared—"

"Feds hid him one time, they can hide him twice. What you use for brains there, little man?"

An angry flush suffused the lawyer's cheeks, but he didn't possess the courage to reply in kind. Instead, he tried to humor Fortier, play to his mood. "We found him once before, we can—"

"We found him?" Fortier was staring at him with the rapt attention of an entomologist who has unearthed a new and unexpected insect species. "I hear you said we found him? Make it sound like you been out there lookin', instead of sittin' on your ass and billing me for shit, half the time I don't know what."

The lawyer found a thimbleful of nerve. "If you're in any way dissatisfied—"

"I'm in a damn zoo with crazy blacks and a

bunch a guys that think they Hitler. Now you want me to be satisfied?"

"I meant—"

"Screw what you meant," the Cajun said. "I tell you something true, I guarantee. You don't mean shit, hear what I'm sayin'? You take my money, say you going to do certain things for me, I expect them things to be done. You come round here with sad old stories, asking for more money, I start thinking maybe you be screwin' me."

"No, sir, I can assure you that—"

"Thing is, when I get screwed, I wanna know it's comin', see? That way I can enjoy it, like. Your way, it's just a big pain in the ass."

"He can't go far," the lawyer said.

"You know that for a fact? He call you up and say, 'I don't be going far'?"

"Well, no, but—"

"What you do is listen now, and do just what I say."

"Yes, sir."

"Reach out for Leon and remind his hairy ass he still owes me a pelt. He let me down on this, it be wolf season where he at, I guarantee. Then next thing, you call up that boy what took two hundred grand to do a job that still ain't done. Feds got old Jean, I wanna know the zip code by this time tomorrow."

"Suppose the Feds don't have him?" asked the lawyer. "What shall I do then?"

"You bring your high-rent ass back here and tell me that. What you use for brains, boy? Seem like chicken gumbo."

A GUARD ESCORTED Fortier back to his cell in Ad-Seg, which he understood was fedspeak for administrative segregation. Once upon a time, they used to call it solitary, and it was reserved for punishment of prisoners who broke the rules. These days, Ad-Seg still housed its share of troublemakers, but it also held inmates who were isolated for their own protection: snitches, racial activists, high-profile cons whose very notoriety had made them targets for the rank and file of mainline prisoners who hoped to build a rep by shanking someone famous. They were strictly one-man cells in Ad-Seg, and the chosen few were fed right where they lived, without exposure to potential dangers in the mess hall. When they exercised, it was in groups of three or four, a private corner of the joint where they were safe from shivs and prying eyes. The Cajun's closest neighbors on the cell block were a former agent of the CIA who sold out brother agents to the Russians in the last days of the cold war and a transient pedophile who sometimes killed and ate his victims as he roamed from state to state. They both seemed nice enough, but Fortier wasn't concerned with making friends.

He wanted out, and soon. The wheels were greased, but he could never make it work while any of the witnesses who sent him to Atlanta in the first place were alive.

Three down and one to go.

He meant to see it done, or know the reason why. And if the plan fell through, there would be one extremely sorry loup-garou to answer for it.

"No more Mr. Nice Guy," Fortier informed his empty cell. "I guarantee."

REMO COULD SMELL the stagnant swamps ahead of him before the interstate conveyed them out of darkest Mississippi and into bayou country. Everything from that point on would have a kind of continental flavor once removed, which made Louisiana stand out from the other Deep South states. It was the only state in Dixie where the Roman Catholic Church claimed a majority of Christians, counties were called parishes and everything from food to architecture had a strong French accent. The swamps were "bayous" here, and many residents still put their faith in voodoo—from the French *voudun*—regardless of their race or ethnic origin. If there was any place in the United States today where legends of medieval lycanthropes still clung tenaciously to life, Louisiana fit the bill.

"You grew up here?" Remo asked their reluctant navigator in the front passenger seat.

"Louisiana born and bred, that's right," the Cajun said.

"You like it?"

Cuvier considered that one for a moment, frowning as if Remo's question puzzled him, presenting issues he had never taken time to ponder.

"Like it?" Shoulders thick with muscle lifted in a shrug. "Is where I'm from. Like it or don't like it, what difference? Tell you one thing true—I like it more than Omaha."

He stretched the last word out as if its syllables were unfamiliar to him, something from a foreign language—which, Remo decided, was a fair enough description in the circumstances.

"You may not be safe here," Remo told him, "even if we find the man who's tracking you."

"I told you three, four times already, ain't no man," said Cuvier. "Armand done hire himself a loup-garou. You find him, he find you, don't matter which. That's all the trouble you going to need."

"Tell me something," Remo said. "In all the time you worked with Fortier, did he have lots of werewolves on the payroll?"

"Go on with jokin'," said the Cajun. "That's all right. You meet old loup-garou, then you'll be laughing out the wrong side of your face."

"I wasn't joking."

Cuvier gave him a quick sideways glance and they rode in silence for a few more minutes, Remo concentrating on the road, Chiun pretending to be asleep in back, before the Cajun spoke again.

"There's not just one loup-garou around here, if you wanna know. Not many, but a few. A few is all it'll take. Pass on the secret and the power."

"But you never met one?"

"Not me, no," said Cuvier. "My grandpa seen them, back a time, before I was born. See one, it last you for a lifetime, if you live that long."

"I'm only interested in recent werewolves. You don't know *this* werewolf," Remo pressed him. "Where he lives or what his name is, anything to help us track him down."

"Done told you not to worry about that thing. He'll find us when he feel like it, I guarantee. He find us, and that's all she wrote."

Remo veered to a different tack. "What would you pay your average wolf man for a job like this?"

"A contract? All depend on what he ask for, what he needs. I reckon some take money, just like common folks. You can't be sure, though. Loup-garou might ask you something else."

"Such as?"

"No tellin'. He be lookin' for someone to carry on the line, might ask you for a soul."

"How's that?"

"Your firstborn baby girl, for example. Raise

them up a litter that way, keep the pick and lose the rest.''

Remo was trying to get real-world answers, and this guy was hanging out in the twilight zone.

''The white man in his arrogance assumes that he knows everything,'' Chiun said from the back seat. ''He visits distant lands, interrogates the people who have lived there for a thousand generations, then dismisses half of what they say as fantasy, the rest as lies.''

''Is there a point?''

A bony index finger, moving with the speed of thought, tapped Remo sharply on the head. ''Your point is sadly obvious,'' the Master of Sinanju said. ''Do not take wisdom for granted. A man with wisdom accepts that there are things he does not know. Koreans understand this basic truth. Even Chinese and Japanese can grasp it, with some effort. White men, on the other hand, display their ignorance by claiming knowledge of all things.''

''Okay, I get your drift,'' said Remo, switching to Korean for privacy. ''But I wasn't raised on spooks and demons. We know what this werewolf is and what it's not. This wolf man is brought to you by Judith White, not Hammer Horror.''

''I assume nothing. Perhaps this creature is not what we think it is, but what the Cajun criminal thinks it is.''

''Huh? You trying to tell me that you believe in

werewolves? The supernatural kind? Silver bullets and all that?''

Chiun answered with a haughty silence.

Remo sighed. ''Okay, Little Father, look—this has the signature of Judith White's little projects. Judith White ran away just a few months ago. Seems to me Judith White's the most likely culprit.''

''Perhaps,'' Chiun replied without conviction.

Cuvier was looking concerned at the unintelligible conversation going on around him. Remo didn't want him freaking out on them. Not while he was still good bait. He switched back to English.

''So,'' he said, glancing over at the Cajun, ''how does someone go about becoming loup-garou?''

''Some born that way, what I been told,'' said Cuvier. ''Them others go on out lookin' for it. Wanna grab the power for themselves.''

''Is there some kind of formula?''

''Ain't made no study on it,'' said the Cajun. ''Heard some stories, long time back. One say you gotta have a wolf skin, other say you don't. One talks about some kind of ointment made of herbs. Another one tells how you gotta say the right words at a certain time of night.''

''That's helpful,'' Remo muttered.

''Ain't no help to get,'' the Cajun said. ''Go on up against old loup-garou, best say you prayers before you start.''

''I'll make a note.''

"One thing I'm happy 'bout," Cuvier said.

"Oh, yeah? What's that?"

"Time we be gettin' into New Orleans," said the Cajun, "we'll be right in time for Mardi Gras. We have a little party before the end."

HUMILIATION and frustration kept Leon from sleeping on the long drive home. The leader of the pack didn't need the others grumbling at him, but they did it anyway—except the bitch, who simply glared at him from time to time, then slowly turned away without a sound, a gesture of supreme contempt.

The pack was pissed because Leon had made a kill without them, and there was no time to share. The cop had stumbled into it as he was leaving, more than likely summoned by a neighbor who had wakened to the noise of Leon freaking out and tearing up the absent target's house. It had been close, that one. Not from the aspect of a risk, since he didn't think an ordinary bullet would have fazed him, but because there could have been another cop, one who escaped if he was lucky, sounding the alarm.

Leon's chief weapon, other than the pack, his teeth and talons, was the fact that 99.9 percent of all Americans would swear upon a stack of Bibles that there were no loups-garous. That kind of ignorance protected him and made him stronger than he was already. Granted, one scared cop wouldn't be able to convince the world at large—hell, they would more than likely slap him in a straitjacket—but if enough people reported a phenomenon, somebody from the government was bound to check it out eventually, and that spelled no end of trouble for a werewolf on the prowl.

So all of them were angry for different reasons as he drove around the clock to get back home. His brothers and the silent bitch had their noses out of joint because they hadn't had a chance to chow down on the cop—as if he had—and they were making due with cold ground beef from several all-night markets strung along the highway.

Leon, for his part, was mad and worried all at once, because it was the first time he had blown a paying job, and he had no idea what his next move should be.

The shopping was a problem, same with gassing up the van, but he had worked it out with help from the old man who raised him long ago. He had to hide his face and hands when he was out in public, meaning off the bayou, anywhere on the road. You couldn't travel far in the United States, even by night, and remain invisible. Even if he could satisfy the pack with roadkill, there would still be stops for fuel, other essential shopping expeditions, maybe even rare occasions when he had to ask directions from the locals.

The old man's solution was to purchase a hat and

raincoat from the Goodwill people, with a pair of roomy leather gloves, and big rolls of gauze. Dressed up, with gauze wrapped all around his head beneath the snap-brim hat, sunglasses on, the leader of the pack resembled someone who had suffered facial burns, or maybe was recovering from some kind of extensive plastic surgery. The old man took one look at him back then and beamed. "Just like Claude Raines," he said.

Whoever that was.

Leon didn't care for movies—had no television at his present den, in fact—because they always ended wrong. He had to have seen two dozen movies about loups-garous when he was growing up, and every stinking one of them had all the facts backward. They inevitably showed the loup-garou as a half-pathetic human—always agonizing over how he had been "cursed"—and half-demented monster who was forced to change against his will and run amok, so crazy-stupid that he would attack his mama if she didn't wear a sandwich sign.

Bullshit.

The movies had it all wrong, which was no surprise to Leon. They were advertised as "science fiction," after all. He knew nothing about the science part, but there was plenty of fiction in the werewolf movies he had seen. The moon, for one thing, how it was supposed to make a loup-garou transform against his will. That was a load of crap. The moon was nice for hunting when you needed light, but it couldn't compel the change. Leon had heard that some loups-garous transformed by will, regardless of the season or the hour. Others, like himself, had grown so comfortable with their primal state that they had basically forgotten how to slide back into human shape—come to think of it, had he ever known how?

Leon was different, and he was better than all the other loups-garous. The woman had seen to that. She had taken what was nothing but your average bayou werewolf and made him into something spectacular.

When he was growing up, when the old man was teaching him how special he was, he'd been full of pride. But then *she* came. She remade him into the baddest loup-garou that ever was. And all it took was a glass of water to do it.

He was ecstatic with the new him, and his appreciation for the strange woman—what was her name?—was boundless. She was his savior. She was his angel. He had fallen in love with her.

Then she betrayed him.

LEON HAD NO USE for motels and less for restaurants; all risk aside, they were a waste of money spent on luxuries he didn't crave and meat that was spoiled by fire. Whatever groceries and other things he couldn't pick up in the swamp, he had delivered by a black youth who was smart enough to do his job and ask no questions. When he needed new clothes, every second year or so, he put on his disguise and made a quick run into St. Charles after dark, to the Goodwill store, to pick up blue jeans, overalls and denim shirts.

Around St. Charles, they figured Leon had some kind of skin disease, mostly likely leprosy, that made him hide his face and hands that way, go shopping only once or twice a year, and always on the razor's edge of closing time. He didn't know it, but the gray-haired folks who ran the Goodwill store kept kitchen tongs behind the counter, underneath the register, against those days when Leon paid a call. They never touched his money with their hands while it was lying on the counter, but waited until he was gone before they grabbed the tongs.

It would have made him laugh to see the "normals" going through their paces, acting like the power of a loup-garou was something you could catch like mumps or measles, rubbing shoulders in a crowd. Hell, if it worked that way, Leon wouldn't have been the only loup-garou he knew, and he would have more friends to talk to than the members of his pack.

You didn't catch it like a disease. You were born with it, and then, if you were lucky, you drank the strange woman's special water to make you complete.

Not that he knew of others like himself. He was

alone, except for the pack, and they weren't *really* like him. His brothers and the bitch weren't exactly acting very friendly at the moment. It would take some time, he knew from past experience, for them to lay the grudge aside and stop their sulking. Being home again, with the entire pack, the whole family, would make things feel right.

But the pack had learned to covet human flesh and blood; it was a delicacy they enjoyed far more than the venison, raccoon or rabbit he collected on his night runs over Highway 90. None of them were capable of checking out what the old man had called the long view, sometimes the big picture, which meant looking down the road to what might happen days or even weeks ahead.

Leon himself had trouble with the long view, but at least he understood the process, realized that simply living in and for the moment, like a full-fledged wolf, could lead you into mortal danger.

Not that laying plans was any guarantee of long life and success, by any means. He had sat down and planned his latest road trip, even buying road maps from the retard who worked graveyard at the Texaco in Luling, but it all came down to shit if one of his intended meals skipped out ahead of time. The Cajun who was paying him had given Leon names, addresses, everything he needed to complete the job, but he had seemingly ignored the possibility that one or more of Leon's targets might evacuate before the loup-garou arrived, and he couldn't wait around to see if number four was coming back.

Not after he had trashed the house and killed that cop in the backyard.

The Cajun would be furious; that was a given. Leon thought about that for a moment, and decided it was logical for him to worry. Not because he feared the man, per se, but rather for the knowledge his employers had. Someone behind the Cajun knew enough to seek a loup-garou, which meant he not only believed, but he had also done his homework and would have a few tricks up his sleeve.

Like silver, for example.

Leon felt his hackles rising as he thought about it, and the bitch picked up on something, possibly a subtle variation in his body odor, peering at him curiously from the shotgun seat. She knew the fear smell of a human, but it had no place among the members of the pack. She studied Leon as he drove a good five miles, and finally decided not to push it.

Never let them fool you, Leon thought. The bitch was smart.

He had to be smart, too. He had to think carefully about his employer, the big man behind the Cajun who gave orders and expected prompt results. The name of the employer was Fortier, and everyone knew Fortier was a man to reckon with. He could be generous or vengeful, depending on the circumstances and his mood. These days, since he was locked up in a cage for violating human laws, his mood was seldom jovial. It would be less so when he heard that target number four had slipped through Leon's paws.

The leader of the pack knew he had to come up with a plan quickly if he intended to retain his lucrative employment. And yet, no matter how he tried to concentrate, no plan announced itself. His mind was filled with jumbled images of blood and violence, but nothing that would qualify as strategy.

It'll be better once we're home, he told himself, and hoped that it was true.

7

Remo took one look at the New Orleans streets, decked out for Mardi Gras, and recognized a good news–bad news situation off the top. The Crescent City was in jubilant chaos, swinging with the massive party residents and tourists spent a whole year looking forward to, and no district of New Orleans was more rowdy than the teeming French Quarter. Remo watched the costumes and figures lurching past him, everything from painted dwarves to looming giants, all apparently intoxicated and intent on staying that way for the next several days.

A vacationing trio of sophomore coeds from Northern Illinois University ran up under Remo's balcony and yanked their shirts up to their chins. Remo found himself admiring their bare breasts, each pair more pleasing than the next.

"Sorry, girls," he said. "No beads."

"You don't need beads, shweetie!" one of them slurred. "We'll show you whatever you want! For free! How 'bout we come on up?"

"Cops!" Remo called. "Here they come!"

The coeds couldn't focus well enough to see that it was a lie and jogged off into the seething crowds.

Smith and the insidious tentacles of CURE had reached out from Folcroft Sanitarium and somehow managed to get hotel reservations on Tchoupitoulas Street. Such rooms were normally sold out a year in advance of Mardi Gras, many of them to a clientele that showed up every year like clockwork. Remo and Chiun had one large room with a bed and a sleeper sofa, together with a tiny balcony that overlooked the crowded street and faced a rank of quaint saloons across the way.

The crush of inebriated flesh would complicate the task of finding Cuvier's old cohorts from the Cajun mob and squeezing them for leads on the elusive hit man. Staring at the freak show on parade below, Remo decided that a real-life werewolf would have no difficulty strolling down the boulevard and plucking victims from the crowd. No look was too grotesque for Mardi Gras, no behavior too bizarre. There would be witnesses, of course, but most of them would laugh it off, assuming that the act was some kind of burlesque, a Grand Guignol performance staged for their amusement.

Chiun had the television on. His ages-old infatuation with American soap operas, which had dimmed when they became too heavy on the gratuitous sex and violence, had recently reemerged with a twist. These days the old Korean was drawn to Spanish serials.

It got worse. Remo had recently begun to suspect that the ancient Korean was leaving the Spanish-language stations on a bit too long after the soap operas ended. Remo was wondering if maybe Chiun had become interested in…

No. Couldn't be. It was too horrible to contemplate.

But the guy on the screen right now was bad enough, and he spoke English, more or less. It was some kind of infomercial with a white-haired Southern statesman-type gesticulating for the camera, grinning like a used-car salesman. Was he selling fried chicken? No, Remo realized, it was politics.

"Now, my esteemed opponent likes to quote the Good Book in his speeches, tellin' you all the Lord Himself would vote Republican if He was registered in the great State of Louisiana. My dear old mama always taught me it was rude to argue with another man's religion, and I ain't about to go against her teaching now. But I will take a moment to remind you all of what the Book of Proverbs tells us, chapter twenty-six, verse five. It says, 'Answer not a fool according to his folly, lest thou also be like unto him.' By which I mean to tell you all—"

"Who's the windbag?" Remo asked.

"That's Elmo Breen," said Cuvier. "Big man here in the parish and all across the state. He's friendly with Armand 'Big Crawdaddy' Fortier, I guarantee. The two of them are like that.'' He raised a hand, the first two fingers intertwined.

''This seersucker's running for office?''

''Governor,'' Cuvier said sincerely. ''I expect he's going to make it, too, less Marvin pull a bunny out his hat.''

''Who's Marvin?''

''You all ain't heard of the Reverend Marvin Rockwell?'' Cuvier appeared to have some difficulty grasping the idea.

''We're not from around here,'' Remo explained.

That was no excuse, Cuvier's expression told him. Out loud the Cajun said, ''Reverend Rock, I call him. He got a show on TV where you can save your soul without ever having to get up off your sofa. Fact is, Reverend Rock got him a network out of Shreveport there. They call it JBN, I think it is. The Jesus Broadcast Network, or something like.''

''And he's running for governor, too?'' asked Remo.

''Bet your life he runnin'. Runnin' hard, I guarantee. Old Rock got most of the Jesus people prayin' for him, sendin' in their money to help redeem the State of Louisiana. Throwing away their money is what they're doing.''

''You're not a believer?''

''I believe in me,'' the Cajun said. ''What else I got?''

"I thought all of you were Catholic down here," Remo said with a shrug.

Chiun ran through the channels once more, found little besides political announcements and Mardi Gras coverage, and glared hatefully at the television.

"Praise God for your video recorder, eh, Little Father?"

Chiun pinned Remo with a baleful glance. "I will offer no thanks to meddlesome carpenters or to bumbling sons."

"Hey, what's your problem with me all of a sudden?"

"You have displeased Emperor Harold Smith in some way, that he sends us to such barbarous surroundings."

"You may recall that you volunteered to come along," said Remo. "And the trip was my idea, not Smitty's."

"Even worse," Chiun huffed. "No consideration for others. No regard for your frail Father."

"Say," the Cajun interrupted, "is you all related some way?" It was the first time Cuvier had spoken directly to the old Korean. He had shown an extreme reticence toward Chiun since the old Korean gave him a mild traumatic shock by sneaking up on him in his own house.

Chiun made a disgusted sound. "Related?"

"Yes," Remo said.

"No," Chiun insisted.

"We're from the same bloodline," Remo explained.

"We are related as the pigeon is related to the eagle," Chiun clarified.

"Just asking," Cuvier replied, then turned to Remo. "How you figure to go lookin' for the loup-garou?" he asked.

"I thought I'd start with some of your old cronies," Remo said. "They may have an idea who Fortier is using for the contract."

"Best you try another way before you talk to anybody in the family," Cuvier suggested.

"What did you have in mind?"

"You best go see the Gypsies right away, before you get yourself in some kind of mess you can't get out of. They set you straight about the loup-garou."

"Gypsies." It was perfect. Now, if he could only get directions to the good witch of the west, Remo decided he would have it made.

"You be surprised what Gypsies know," said Cuvier. "Might teach you something if you listen close and keep your mouth shut."

"I suppose you know where I can find some, just like that?"

It was the Cajun's turn to smile. "Fact is, I do," he said. "I do indeed."

"Y'ALL THINK it went all right?" Elmo Breen asked of no one in particular.

"You looked great," said Elmo's lackey, Maynard Grymsdyke. "Phones are ringing off the hook already, with the new spot. Answering old Rockhead from the Bible made the difference, like I said. You're winning hearts and minds."

The candidate stopped short and turned to face the shorter, balding Grymsdyke. "Son," he said, "how old are you?"

"How old?" The lackey paused and thought about it, as if searching for the proper and politically correct response.

"Your age, for Christ's sake!" Elmo snapped at him. "It ain't a loaded question."

"Forty-two," Grymsdyke replied, still frowning.

"Forty-two," the white-maned politician echoed, almost wistfully. "So, you was still in diapers when we got our asses kicked by little point-headed folks in Vietnam. That right?"

Grymsdyke delayed responding for another moment. This time he was counting. "Not quite, sir. I was eight years old when Mr. Nixon—"

"Never mind!" Breen snapped. "My point is that you make me nervous sometimes, Maynard."

"Sir?"

"That crap you're shoveling about winning hearts and minds. Our people used to say that all the time in Nam. Went on and on about how the majority of dinks just loved us. Couldn't wait to help us kick the Commies out, they said. 'We're winning hearts and minds.' Thing is, we lost that war, in case you disremember.''

"I recall that, sir. In fact—"

"In fact," Breen interrupted him, "I never put much stock in phone calls stirred up by a TV ad. Been my experience in thirty-nine years as a public servant that folks who'll take the time to call and praise you are the ones who would of voted for you anyhow. Same things for polls, most of 'em. Some guy asks a couple dozen people what they think about abortion or campaign finance reform and tries to say he knows what everybody's thinking. That's a pile of bullshit, and you know it well as I do.''

"Sir, if you could try to keep your voice down…"

They were moving briskly toward the ninth-floor elevator in the east wing of the Crescent City Hilton, and they had the spacious hallway to themselves, but Grymsdyke nurtured his paranoia like a gift from God. He wasn't happy, Breen had long ago decided, if there did not seem to be at least the risk of spies and eavesdroppers. The threat of being overheard and somehow shafted with the very things he said made Grymsdyke feel important, useful, even vital to the cause. Without that feeling of supreme importance, Elmo Breen had long ago decided, Maynard Grymsdyke would have shriveled up and blown away.

There wasn't much left of him, as it was. Grymsdyke stood five foot two or three, almost completely bald, and weighed perhaps 120, counting shiny wingtips and the two mobile phones that he carried wherever he went. As if it weren't enough to have one with Call Waiting, in case some great thinker was trying to reach him and pour out the secrets of life. He wore one of the phones on his belt, while the other was snug in his left armpit, cradled in some kind of harness that looked like a holster. Breen used to call his flack and campaign manager "Two-Gun," until he saw how Maynard flinched each time and realized that he had hurt the stubby gofer's feelings. It had shamed him for a moment, as if he had been caught teasing a disabled child.

Looks were deceiving when it came to Maynard Grymsdyke, though. Inside that shiny head reposed the knowledge of a Princeton Ph.D. in political science, which meant that he knew everything the books could tell him about nailing down elections. What he didn't know so well, as yet, was people. After all those years in classrooms, seminars and such, he still put too much faith in raw statistics for Breen's taste.

Elmo himself had barely lasted two years in a third-rate junior college, never quite acquired the units necessary for a grand Associate of Arts degree in history, but he knew people inside out. He knew what turned them on and off, the knee-jerk issues that would make a bloc of voters love or hate you once you took a public stand. He knew the rules, of course: blacks "always" voted Democrat; white born-agains were "always" staunch Republicans— this list went on and on. One thing Breen knew that Grymsdyke had not fathomed yet.

A lot of it was bullshit.

There were ways around the rules, he understood, if you appealed to people, touched them where they lived. For most, that meant the pocketbook, religion, family, sex—the basics. A successful politician made a point of finding out what his constituency wanted out of life, and he would promise to fulfill those needs by any means at his disposal. Clearly, most of what he promised was impossible—a left-wing Democratic president could never overhaul the welfare system, for example, if conservative Republicans controlled Congress—but you didn't really have to do that much in public office. It was more important that you seem to try. And if you failed, well, there was always some reactionary, radical or plain old crooked bastard you could point a finger at, make him the scapegoat for your failure. Lay it off on someone else.

Going up against a TV preacher, now, that was a special problem. Ticklish. Any other candidate, Breen could have started slinging mud right off the bat, hoping that some of it would stick, but with a preacher man you needed special mud—a bimbo in the woodpile, for example, or a Cayman Islands bank account where all that "seed faith" money went to hide—but so far Grymsdyke's people hadn't found a thing on the Reverend Mr. Rockwell.

It was time to pull an ace out of his sleeve, and that meant Breen would need some extraspecial help. Before the Feds put Armand Fortier away for life and then some, Elmo would have made a phone call, talked it over with his friend and struck some kind of bargain. Cash or favors in return for pictures of Reverend Rock cavorting with a prostitute, perhaps—or better yet, a little boy. Presumably, Armand's successor had the same kind of connections, held the same strings in his hand, but Elmo didn't really know him as he had known Fortier for years on end.

Still, this was war, and he couldn't afford to let some grinning Holy Roller beat him to the statehouse. Quoting scripture on TV was one thing, but he would feel better, closer to the finish line, if he nailed down the Devil's vote, as well.

"Maynard," he said at last, his mind made up, "get me a private meeting with Merle Bettencourt."

"I DON'T BELIEVE he has the everlasting nerve to throw back scripture in my face. Do you believe it, Jerry?"

Jeremiah Smeal displayed the same sour face he wore around the clock. "Sin's what it is," he said, his high-pitched voice unsuited to a man who measured six foot one and topped the scales around 350 pounds. "A shameless mockery."

"Still, it could hurt us," Reverend Marvin Rockwell said in answer to his aide.

"The faithful—"

"Screw the faithful!" Rockwell cut him off. "This ain't some kind of weekend show or camp revival meeting, Jerry. This one is for all the marbles, son. If I'm elected governor of this great state, think of the grand work I can do for Christ our Lord!"

"Yes, sir."

And all the perks, thought Rockwell, keeping that one to himself. What he came out with in its place was: "We must not allow him to preempt us, Jerry. I'm God's candidate, and everybody knows it! Spirit-filled at nine years old, I was, speaking in tongues before my whole damn class in Bastrop. I've healed the sick and lame from Dallas all the way to Pascagoula. I heal people on TV, for Christ's sake! What more do they want?"

Smeal shrugged. "'Even the Devil can cite scripture for his purpose,'" he replied.

"That's perfect!" Rockwell said. "What verse is that?"

"It's Shakespeare, sir. *Merchant of Venice.*"

"Shit! I can't go literary on these yokels. Give me something I can use!"

The fat man, suddenly disconsolate, was trying to

stare holes in his black loafers. Rockwell could almost hear the cog wheels grinding in his head, trying to conjure a rebuttal for their adversary's latest TV spot.

"There's Jeremiah 7:4," he said at last.

"'Trust ye not in lying words,'" the televangelist recited, knowing it by heart. "Could work. Keep thinking, though."

"Yes, sir."

The trouble went beyond quotations from the Bible, Rockwell understood. That peckerhead in Houston, Pastor Benny Bobbit, hadn't helped the cause when *Sixty Minutes* caught him skimming money from his ministry to keep an eighteen-year-old strumpet in the mood for steamy fun and games. It had been bad enough that Bobbit was a preacher in the first place, but he also paid for thirty minutes twice a week on Rockwell's Jesus Broadcast Network. Reverend Rockwell had been a guest on Benny's show, for God's sake. They had stood together in the spotlight, grinning, shaking hands. Now Rockwell had to cut the bastard loose and pray that not too many of the faithful started drawing close comparisons.

"Get thee behind me, Satan!"

"Sir?"

Rockwell didn't realize that he had spoken until Jerry Smeal's shrill voice intruded on his gloomy thoughts. Now he was talking to himself, goddamn it, and in front of witnesses.

"Just praying, Jerry. Never mind."

"Yes, sir."

It was a tough job, trying to escape the stereotype of a money-grubbing TV preacher, all the more so when he fit the mold so perfectly. Rockwell had hopes that politics would save him, launch him from the Christian junior varsity into the Lord's own Super Bowl contingent. Then and only then would he be recognized by millions for the man he truly was.

Or, rather, for the man he wanted them to think he was.

The yellow press had made a run or two at him already, looking into his credentials, sniffing after the diploma mill that had declared Rockwell a doctor of theology in 1986. That piece of paper cost him fifteen hundred dollars, but at least he never had to crack a textbook other than the Bible, and the Ph.D. had granted him a measure of respect among survivors of the TV holy wars. A year's apprenticeship on Christian Airwaves International, and he had launched off on his own, building the Jesus Broadcast Network from a single run-down station in Metairie to a web of thirty-seven stations scattered through the hard-core Bible Belt. Come Easter, he would crack the Southern California market, and with all the nuts out west, he hoped the money would be flowing soon, to justify his effort. In the meantime, though...

The first time Rockwell had thought of running for the statehouse, it had been hilarious. A joke. Then Jerry Smeal had talked to him about it for a while, pointing out some of the advantages—state matching funds, to start with—and had told him there was actually a chance that he could win. Of course, he had to edge by Elmo Breen to win the primary, and that was no small challenge in itself. Elmo had been around forever, held most every office in the state except for governor at one time or another, and his easygoing style appealed to voters in Louisiana, where the choice between a raving Klansman and a proved thief had been too close to call, a few years back. That was the kind of atmosphere where Rockwell could let his hair down, use his gift for hellfire oratory to the utmost, and perhaps—just maybe—make a slim majority of the benighted yokels buy his vote-for-Jesus rap.

The free publicity was working to his benefit already. Three new stations were asking if they couldn't please become a part of Reverend Rockwell's great network for salvation, and you had to love a country where that kind of thing was possible.

The polls told Rockwell that he was trailing Elmo by a hefty nineteen points, and Pastor Bobbit's trial was coming up in three or four weeks' time, a golden opportunity for Breen to point a finger and remind the no-neck voters of exactly what they could expect from TV preachers. Never mind that he was right. It damn well wasn't fair!

I need an angle, Reverend Rockwell decided, and this time he caught himself before he spoke the words aloud. Instead, he spoke a name.

"Merle Bettencourt."

"Sir?" Jerry Smeal was visibly confused.

"Still praying, Jerry," Rockwell informed his aide. "Never you mind."

THE GYPSY CAMP WAS situated three miles south of town, outside Westwego, with the stagnant bayou close enough that Remo smelled it even with his windows rolled up tight and the air-conditioning on high. There was a dead snake in the middle of the highway, seedy strip malls off to either side, and Remo wondered where it had been going when its time ran out.

He hadn't asked how Cuvier knew where the Gypsies would be found. They were supposed to drift around the countryside, and since the Cajun had been up in Omaha for something like a year, presumably without connections to his former stomping grounds, it puzzled Remo. Still, he let it go. He had enough things on his mind, werewolves included, without trying to discover if his witness was a closet psychic.

In the old days, he had been led to believe, the

roving Gypsies packed their lives in horse-drawn
wagons, gaily painted, drifting aimlessly from town
to town as they told fortunes, read the tarot cards,
picked pockets, rustled livestock—anything, in fact,
that would keep money flowing in without the grim
necessity of taking honest work. There had been
Gypsies in New Jersey, back in Remo's former life.
He had arrested one of them for swindling senior
citizens, some kind of scam involving eggs and evil
spirits. No one in the suspect's family had seemed
especially resentful of the bust. It was like weather,
something you could never really change.

These Gypsies had progressed from horse and
wagon to an ancient school bus painted green, with
different-colored swirls resembling psychedelic
cloud formations on the sides and rear. He was reminded of the sixties and a song about a magic bus,
some kind of acid groove, but quickly pushed the
reminiscence out of mind. Behind the bus, an old
VW van sat on the shoulder of the road, more primer
gray than any other hue, and there were three mopeds lined up behind the van.

Beyond the bus, an open field lay in between the
highway and the swamp. The Gypsies had a campfire going, and a mismatched pair of portable bar-
becue grills was producing aromatic smoke that almost canceled out the rank smell of the swamp.

Almost.

The kids saw Remo first as he pulled up behind

the mopeds, killed his engine, stepping from the
Blazer. There were six or seven of them, Remo was
sure, plus three apparent teenagers, and better than
a dozen adults, ranging from late twenties to a crone
of seventy or eighty. By the time he cleared the van
and started to approach them, they were all aware
of Remo, and he could have sworn that other eyes
were following his progress, from the van, the bus
or both.

Must be damn crowded when they're on the road,
he thought, and then dismissed the thought as being
of no consequence.

As Remo neared the fire, a forty-something Gypsy
with a fierce mustache stepped out to intercept him.
He was dressed in a bright red shirt with bishop
sleeves, long collar points and shiny buttons, black
pants resembling jodhpurs and riding boots that
gleamed like patent leather, fitted out with silver
buckles on the sides. His neck and hands were bright
with gold, including rings on six of his eight fingers.
As the gap between them lessened, Remo noticed
that the Gypsy's left eye was possessed of a nervous
tic that made it blink and twitch, as if the orb were
trying to escape its socket.

"You have business with my family?" the Gypsy
front man asked, with twenty feet between them.

Remo nodded toward the teenagers and tots. "All
yours?"

Broad shoulders rolled inside the crimson shirt.

"Some mine, all Romany," the Gypsy said. "I think you didn't come here for no genealogy."

"You must be psychic," Remo offered, but the joke fell flat. "The fact is, I was told... I mean to say I'm hoping you can help with some information."

The Gypsy smiled and stroked the side of his nose with a nicotine-stained index finger. "You are looking for New Orleans, yes? You must go back the way you came."

Strike one on fortune-telling, Remo thought. He said, "It's not directions, Mr....?"

"Ladislaw," the Gypsy said. No telling if it was his first name or his last.

"Well, Mr. Ladislaw—"

"King Ladislaw," the walleyed man corrected him.

Remo let that one pass. "I'm looking for a different kind of information. I'm not sure—"

"About your future, yes?" The Gypsy's smile increased in wattage, pearly whites on bold display. "You come to the right place, all right. The Romany have powers. But, of course, it is no easy thing. We must—"

"It's not about my future," Remo told him, interrupting the sales pitch. "I need to ask about...well, um, a loup-garou."

The Gypsy lost his smile as if someone had wiped it from his dark face with a washcloth. Remo watched his left eye jiggle for a moment, dancing to a different beat, before both pupils locked like gun sights on his face.

"Who sent you here?" King Ladislaw demanded. "You said someone told you to come here."

"Slip of the tongue?" Remo suggested.

"Now you lie."

"Okay, you're right. It was a Cajun friend of mine," he told the Gypsy, stretching the relationship. "I'm not at liberty to give his name, but I can tell you that he wishes you no harm. I'm not with the police or—"

"Why should Romany have fear of the police?" asked Ladislaw, his bad eye veering sharply north-northwest.

"No reason I can think of," Remo said. "Let's just forget it, shall we? My friend was obviously wrong."

He turned to leave, but barely took a step before King Ladislaw called out to him, "You stop!" Remo turned back to face the Gypsy, waiting.

"You say this friend of yours is a Cajun?"

Remo nodded, kept his mouth shut, waiting.

Ladislaw reached up to tap his own forehead, above the jerky eye. "Is he a special man, this friend?"

"I doubt it," Remo answered frankly. "If he had the power and knowledge, I suppose he wouldn't send me here, to you."

The Gypsy's left eyelid came down, as if to better study Remo without interference from the rebel orb. "You are a wise man, I believe."

"I know an old Korean who would disagree."

"Excuse me?"

"Forget it. Can you help me?"

Ladislaw had found his smile again. "My eldest daughter has considerable knowledge of such matters. She is, how you say?" The Gypsy raised a hand and tapped his head again.

"Brunette?" Remo suggested.

"Sensitive!" King Ladislaw seemed pleased that he was able to recall the word. "Of course, it still requires great effort, sometimes pain. For something dangerous, like loup-garou, two hundred dollars."

It was Remo's turn to smile. "I'm after information, not the pelt," he said. "I'll give you fifty down, and match it afterward if I'm completely satisfied."

The Gypsy king seemed infinitely pained, but he was clearly in his element, adept at dickering. "For such a risk," he said, "one-fifty is the best that I can do."

Remo considered it, deciding what the hell. It was CURE's money, anyway, and fifty bucks was nothing to the organization that had eluded government auditors for decades on end.

"Half down," he said.

"A deal!" King Ladislaw relieved him of the

cash and led him to the former school bus, where the back door—once reserved for exit in emergencies—now stood ajar.

"Step in, my friend," the Gypsy said, "and learn what you must know. I only hope you do not see too much."

8

The windows in the rear part of the bus were painted over, but some fading daylight spilled in through the open doorway, and the space inside was lit with candles. Remo counted twelve candles while he was waiting for his eyesight to adjust, examining the portion of the bus that had been artfully converted to a kind of sitting room. The rug beneath his feet was clean and looked handwoven. Furniture consisted of some large embroidered pillows in the place of chairs, with a low table just in front of him, standing ankle high. Remo was put in mind of certain geisha houses he had visited…until he saw the girl.

She occupied a cushion on the far side of the table, sitting with her back against a folding screen that blocked his vision of the bus interior beyond that point. In fact, he didn't care what lay beyond the barrier, so captivated was he with the girl. She wore an off-the-shoulder peasant blouse with puff sleeves and a ruffled skirt that hid her legs completely. Tawny cleavage showed above the scoop neck of her blouse, but Remo's eyes were drawn inexorably to her heart-shaped face, framed by jet-black hair that spilled across her naked shoulders. Her complexion was a light café au lait, and while she didn't have her father's eyes, it seemed that perfect teeth ran in the family.

"Your father said—"

"Sit, please."

Her voice was soft but firm. He did as he was told, and quickly scanned the tabletop, noting the crystal ball that stood to one side, near a deck of tarot cards.

"I am Aurelia Boldiszar. And you are...?"

"Remo," he replied.

"Not such a common name. What is it that you wish to know?" she asked.

Remo was tempted to suggest that she tell him, but Master Chiun had frequently reminded him—in diplomatic terms, of course—that no one liked a smart-ass.

Remo said, "A Cajun friend of mine told me that Gypsies—"

"Romany," she said, correcting him.

"Okay, that Romany could give me information of a certain nature, and your father told me you're the one to see."

"My father." There was something in her smile, but Remo couldn't make it out and told himself it was a waste of time to try. "This 'information of a certain nature,'" she went on. "Can you be more specific?"

"It concerns a loup-garou."

If she was startled by his statement, she concealed it like a pro. There was no show of fear, not even hesitation, as she ordered, "Let me see your hands."

"Say what?"

"Your hands. Palms up, please."

"I don't need—"

"I need to see your hands," she told him, with enough steel in her voice that Remo offered up his open palms.

Aurelia studied each in turn, some twenty seconds each, and then sat back, appearing to relax. "You are not loup-garou," she said.

"I could have told you that."

"A loup-garou would lie," she told him. "Some, despite their power, strive for greater knowledge, greater skill. They do not shrink from subterfuge."

"Uh-huh." He made a vain attempt to hide the skepticism in his tone, but her expression told him he had failed.

"You don't believe in loups-garous," she said, "and yet you come in search of information on their habits—and, I think, their weaknesses. Why do you waste your time and money, Mr. Remo?"

"Just plain Remo."

"You avoid my question, Just Plain Remo."

"What I search for is a loup-garou, but it is one that is made by science. Not magic."

She considered that. There was wisdom residing in the depths of her eyes. "Does it matter?"

He was wondering how much to tell her. If she was possessed of psychic powers, there would be no point in trying to conceal the truth. Conversely, if she was a charlatan, he had already wasted time and money on a wild-goose chase.

"Well, yeah. I mean, I assume a mutant created by science is not going to behave like a guy who goes all feral when the moon's full."

"And you seek the loup-garou why?"

"I'm a security consultant," he said, treading softly on the borderline of truth. "My present client, one whom I have promised to protect, is being hunted by bad men."

"In other words, he has a contract on his head." Her smile was almost taunting. "I'm not an idiot, all right, Just Plain Remo? Just run it down."

He smiled in spite of himself. "Okay. Some of my client's late associates have died—been killed— in the past few months, apparently attacked by a large animal. The man I'm working for insists they were the victims of a loup-garou, a werewolf. He insists the thing is coming after him and that there's no way to avoid it. He suggested I talk to Gyp—I mean, to Romany, and get more information. I decided that it wouldn't hurt to humor him."

She sat there looking at him before she gave him a nudge. ''There's more to it than that. You think this is a laboratory-created monster.''

''Yes.''

''So you do not disbelieve in the loup-garou. That's strange enough for a policeman. Or—'' Aurelia Boldiszar smiled slightly ''—whatever you are.''

Abruptly she was all business, turning her gaze intently into his hand. ''This I see. You are indeed protecting someone, but he is not your employer. You would not take money from this man, but someone else prevails upon you to defend his life. You demonstrate humility in describing yourself as a security consultant—you are certainly a great deal more than that.''

''Well…''

''You did not seek me out to humor anyone,'' she declared flatly. ''For that, you could have left your client where he is and simply gone to dinner. Kill some time, then tell him that you saw the Gypsies. He would never know the difference. You are here because you seek out certain information for yourself.''

''Meaning?''

''You want to believe the loup-garou is what you think it is—a science experiment gone bad—but you're not sure. You have seen something else, long ago, not in America, I think, and it makes you wonder. Something...'' She considered it for several moments, finally shook her head. ''No. Much about you is shrouded in darkness. Your past is a swirl of images that seem real and can't possibly be real. Your present is like the presence of something giant and huge out of the old myths. Except I don't picture the giants of legend wearing goofy grins like they just saw their first dirty magazine. Your future—''

Aurelia Boldiszar shuddered.

Remo Williams stopped the goofy grinning. ''What about my future?''

''It is difficult—'' What was difficult she did not say. Even the speaking seemed to be an effort.

''Tell me,'' he commanded sharply.

She looked up. Her dark eyes glimmered with moisture. ''It is indecipherable,'' she said, her words fracturing, and for the first time she was something other than in control.

''You're lying,'' Remo snapped.

She shook her beautiful head very slightly. ''No. I speak the truth, Just Plain Remo. I see something that I think is your future. I see you. I see the swirling darkness and chaos of your life. I see your fathers and your daughters and your sons, battling one another....''

Remo blinked. ''You got the part about the fathers right,'' he said. ''But as for the daughters and sons, there's just one of each.''

She just looked at him.

"Tell me the truth," he said quietly.

"Somehow, you would know if I was lying to you," she said. "I believe that what I say is true, and believe it because I have seen it. You must decide if what I *see* is true."

She was right. Remo could hear her conviction in the beat of her heart and the rhythm of her breath. He could see it in the pattern of her pupils' dilation.

"I have one son," Remo Williams declared flatly. "I have one daughter. That's all."

They both knew he was trying to convince himself. He felt his face warm up and willed his circulation to get control of itself.

"You're distressed."

"Distressed?" Remo demanded. "Lady, three minutes ago my biggest concern was a swamp-dwelling wolf man and how to talk you out of your Romany uniform. Now you tell me I've got more kids than I know about and soon they'll be fighting among themselves."

"I did not say soon," she protested. "I did not say when."

"Whatever. Just threw me for a loop."

"That means you believe in what I say?"

Remo looked at the Romany princess and exhaled a long, long time and it sounded like the word "crap" stretched out inhumanely.

The problem was, he didn't want to believe in this kind of mumbo jumbo. The other problem was, this was the kind of mumbo jumbo that came true for him with annoying frequency.

"Back to the subject in hand, so to speak," he announced, trying to get his own mind back on track. "The Loopy Garou of the Backwoods Bayou."

"Whether he is the product of dark art or dark science, he's not to be taken lightly," the dark-eyed woman chided him. "This is advice that comes not from a vision. It comes from something I have seen with my own eyes."

"You've seen a werewolf?" Remo asked.

"I've seen enough," Aurelia Boldiszar said. "Beyond that, I can tell you that there is a loup-garou near by. Within a day's walk of New Orleans, perhaps. Whether he is the one you seek—or who seeks you—I cannot say. If so, it won't be long before he takes your scent. Your client is at risk, and so are you."

"I should be stocking up on silver bullets, then?"

"You're pleased to joke," she said. "So be it. But remember this, Remo. Like you, the loup-garou is not as other men. He can be beaten, even killed, but it requires more dedication to the task than you may be accustomed to."

"How do you know what I'm accustomed to?" asked Remo, curiosity encroaching on uneasiness. Would Harold Smith consider a seer's seeing as a breach in CURE security?

"Loups-garous and Romany have never been good friends," she said. "I may be able to assist you in your search."

"Well…"

"At the moment," she continued, "I do not know where this loup-garou is hiding, if or when he will approach you, but I may be able to discover more if I apply myself."

"How much?"

"My treat," she said, and flashed another dazzling smile. "I am interested in the manner of man you are. Tracing palms and looking into the crystal and reading the tarot, these are imprecise methods of divination. To understand the person and his soul and his fate, one must live within the arm's length of his or her aura."

"Yeah, well, maybe I'm one of those people you don't *want* to know," Remo said, and he realized he was offering her a way out. But he was fervently hoping she wouldn't take it.

"My choice, my risk," Aurelia said.

He saw no downside to it and responded with a shrug. "Why not? I'm at Desire House, in the Quarter. That's on Tchoupitoulas Street. Don't ask me how to spell it."

She was smiling now. "Desire House?"

"From what I've seen, it's nowhere near as friendly as it sounds."

"You'll hear from me," Aurelia said. "Good night."

Outside, King Ladislaw was waiting to accept the other half of the one-fifty. Remo handed it over.

"You are satisfied?" the Gypsy asked.

"Ask me again tomorrow," Remo answered. "If I'm still alive."

LEON WAS DRESSING out a raccoon, ready to discard the guts for anyone who might desire them, when the bitch heard trouble coming. Privately, he could admit that every other member of the pack had keener senses than his own. It galled him, but there was no arguing with simple facts of life. Whenever it began to get him down, Leon consoled himself with a reminder that he had the only working set of thumbs in camp, and thus was still the only one among them who could drive the van.

He had no license, registration or insurance, granted, but such details were a bore. Leon dismissed them out of hand. He liked to think of the Dodge Ram as his inheritance, although its former owner was no kin of his. They hadn't even known each other, really. Their acquaintance lasted all of six or seven seconds, while his shaggy hands enclosed the driver's head and twisted sharply to the left, with force enough to snap his neck and end his life.

Good eating, he had been. Not scrawny, like so

many of the bayou dwellers Leon saw when he was out on hunting expeditions. Mr. Dodge Ram had been positively plump and redolent with health, a feast unto himself. A gift of Providence, which Leon had accepted in addition to the van.

Now he laid the 'coon aside, rose from his crouch, pricked up his ears. The others had begun to melt into the undergrowth before he rose, anticipating his command and acting on it while the thought was taking shape in Leon's head. It never crossed his mind that maybe they were leading him, and not the other way around.

He was the loup-garou. He ruled the pack and he always would.

At least as long as he was cozy with the bitch.

He started moving toward the water, following his nose and instinct, picking up the first sounds from the skiff before he cleared the chest-high reeds. Deep night and trailing Spanish moss concealed him as he watched the lone intruder moving closer, paddling his cheap flat-bottomed boat and watching out for landmarks on the bank.

He didn't recognize the boatman yet, moonlight behind him making him a silhouette against the restless water, but the man was close enough now that he caught a smell he recognized. It was the smell of fear.

Off to his left, Leon heard one of his brothers approaching the water's edge. A "normal" man would probably have missed it, but the leader of the pack knew swamp sounds, and he knew at least approximately where the others were right now. The bitch was roughly fifteen yards to Leon's right, downstream, which put her closest to the new arrival. If the man kept veering toward the shoreline with his skiff, she could spring out and join him by the time he reached her hiding place.

The small man in the skiff stopped paddling then, as if he had picked up on Leon's thought somehow. It made no sense, of course. More likely he was tired, or maybe lost. Good luck if that turned out to be the case. A man could sit for hours in the bayou country, searching for familiar landmarks, and come up with nothing. He could sit forever, until the ants and larger scavengers arrived to pick his bones.

But this one wouldn't go to waste. Leon had already forgotten the raccoon. It was a simple appetizer. This was food.

Just when he knew the bitch was winding up to make her leap—a bit too far, in Leon's estimation, but he couldn't tell her that—the small man in the skiff produced a match and struck it on the gunwale of his old flat bottom, holding up the tiny light beside his face. A wave of feral disappointment surged through Leon as he recognized the thin, dark face.

He knew this man. They had a deal of sorts. It would be wrong to share him with the pack...at least until he found out what the slender Gypsy had to say.

Leon wasn't much good at whistling, with his teeth and all, but he produced a low-pitched warning sound that told the others to stand back. No sooner had the order passed—a whimper from the brother on his left, a quick snarl from the bitch—than Leon stepped from cover, moving toward the water's edge. This man had seen him and was theoretically prepared. There was no point in hiding when a frightened man came all this way to bring him news.

"What is it you want?"

His throat felt dry, the words emerging as a raspy whisper. With the pack, he mostly spoke their language—yips and growls and whines that drew their meaning from the circumstances of a given situation. It was a fact that Leon often muttered to himself, sometimes in French, sometimes in English, but he tried to keep it down so as to not offend the pack. It was a very different game to speak deliberately with "normal" men, so that your words conveyed coherent meaning.

In the skiff, his uninvited visitor recoiled, then caught himself and tried to make it look as if he simply had a nervous twitch. The overall effect was laughable, but Leon missed the humor in it, scanning back upstream in case the Gypsy had turned traitor on him, leading other "normal" men to find the pack. So far, there was no sight or sound of followers.

"I have news," the Gypsy said.

"I am listen," Leon said, suspecting that his choice of words wasn't exactly right but guessing it made no difference.

"Stranger come by the place today." The Gypsy didn't have to say which place, and time had little meaning in the bayou, once you drew a line between the daylight hours and the hungry night. "Asked some funny questions about you."

The wolf man felt his hackles rising, curled his upper lip to show a flash of crooked yellow teeth. His shaggy hands flexed in the darkness, talons scratching at his palms.

"He call my name?" asked Leon.

"Didn't have to," said the Gypsy. "He said he was looking for a loup-garou. I hear that, and think of you."

Leon tipped back his head and scanned the crazy quilt of stars above him. They were timeless, changing with the seasons and rotation of the earth, but always coming back again, as inescapable as weather, permanent as death.

It took a moment for the bayou night to mellow him, but he was getting there. When Leon spoke again, his voice was calm, no snapping at the messenger, no matter how he longed to roar and tear the Gypsy limb from limb.

"So, what did you all tell him?" Leon asked.

His uninvited guest first looked dismayed, then terrified. It was a good choice in the present circumstances.

"Now you joke with me," the Gypsy said, lips spasming into the semblance of a smile. "Man didn't talk to me at all. What do I know?"

"You know how to find me," Leon answered. "Know about where I live."

"I never talked to him," the frightened man repeated stubbornly. "Man comes, he talks to Ladislaw, then goes in to spend some time with Aurelia. Paid Ladislaw handsome for whatever Aurelia had to tell him and then he goes away. Use your second sight and see if I be lying."

Leon wasn't big on second sight, but he stared at the quaking Gypsy for a moment more before he spoke. "Got what he come for," said the leader of the pack. "Got his palm read."

"I can't say that," the trembling Gypsy said, "but that Aurelia sees things. She has powers."

So do I, thought Leon. "That's it?" he asked.

The Gypsy nodded, jerky little motions with his head. His hands clung desperately to the oars. If he was lying, Leon thought, the little man deserved some kind of an award.

"All right," the wolf man said at last. "You told me something, now I'm telling you. Don't go on right back to where you been. Find some other place to spend the night.''

The Gypsy mulled that over for a moment, then finally nodded. The full weight of his betrayal made his shoulders slump and forced his head down, eyes avoiding Leon's sharp chin almost resting on his chest.

''Go on now,'' the leader of the pack commanded. ''I got things to do.''

He didn't wait to see the Gypsy turn his skiff and paddle back the way he came. Retreating toward his dark camp, Leon heard the others padding in around him, stony silence from the bitch, a couple of the others whining questions.

''We're going to take a little ride,'' he told them, smiling in the darkness. ''Maybe get a bite to eat.''

AURELIA BOLDISZAR HAD not told Remo everything she saw and felt when she was in his presence.

Then again, she never told outsiders everything. It was a lesson she had learned, partly from the instruction of her mother, but more by trial and error. She was twenty-five years old, and that was plenty old enough to understand that even members of her family, the Romany, did not desire to know the whole truth of their futures or to realize how much she knew about their secret pasts.

In truth, the other Romany rarely consulted her these days. They were polite enough, and treated her

like family—her father was their leader, after all—
but she still caught them glancing at her furtively,
as if afraid that she was "reading" them against
their will. They feared she would learn secrets they
had closely guarded over years or decades, sometimes even from their wedded mates.

And they were right.

Aurelia didn't understand the power, but she had
it. That was all that counted in the end. It didn't
operate continuously, or she would have lost her
sanity when she was just a teenager. Instead it came
and went, influenced to some indefinable degree by
her attempts to focus, calling on the energy or whatever it was to let her see behind the public masks
that men and women wore in daily life.

This Remo, now, he was a different matter altogether. From her first glimpse of him, there had been
confusion—not because he was inscrutable, but
rather because she saw so much. Aurelia couldn't
always say when those about her would face death,
or how; in fact, that dark, oppressive knowledge
thankfully eluded her most of the time. With Remo,
though, there had been the inescapable sensation
that he had already known death. Maybe that first,
irrational impression was what had muddled everything else she saw when she was with him.

She knew he was an orphan—or had been one,
rather, until he had found a father figure relatively

late in life, and then, much later, found his biological father.

Aurelia felt that Remo was basically a good man, though his path had taken him to many places he would not have chosen for himself and forced him into contact with a brooding cast of villains. Most of them were dead now, she was certain, and she had no doubt that a majority of those had died by Remo's hand.

Consumed with her thoughts of her enigmatic visitor and his equally strange task, Aurelia missed the early-warning signals that might have saved her people.

Then again, it was entirely possible that the impending danger—like so many others—would have failed to warn her, even if she had been concentrating, actively pursuing any strange vibrations in the night.

When she heard the first scream, it took her utterly by surprise.

There was a vicious snarling, and a young girl cried out again. Aurelia thought it had to be Janka, but the knowledge didn't help her. Even as she struggled from her sleeping bag and pressed her face against the nearest window of the bus, the cry was cut off with a brutal, inescapable finality. Aurelia felt the life force torn from little Janka as if it had been her own. She didn't have to see the child to know it was too late to help her.

More of her people shouting now, some of them men. There was confusion, fear and anger mingled in their voices. Where the snarling, baying canine sounds originated, she couldn't be sure—until it struck her like a swift blow to the solar plexus.

Loup-garou!

The cursed man-thing had been smarter than she reckoned. It had found her out and tracked her down within a few short hours of her conversation with Remo. Something in the werewolf's cunning nature drove it to make a preemptive strike, to prevent her from assisting Remo with his hunt.

A flash of insight, crystal-clear, told her the best way to protect the others was to flee. The wolf man wanted her, and while she knew he wouldn't hesitate to massacre the Romany in search of her, there was at least an outside chance that he would follow if she ran.

There was no time to plan where she would go, grab any items from her minimal belongings. Gypsy life meant traveling, and traveling efficiently meant readiness to leave at a moment's notice. Thought translated into action almost instantly, and she exploded from the bus into the milling chaos of the camp, beelining for the mopeds parked behind the old VW van.

Before she traveled half a dozen strides, Aurelia almost stumbled on a corpse. The dead man lay facedown, but she could tell it was Sebestyen from his shirt—what there was left of it. He had been mauled, pale ribs exposed on one side, where the flesh and muscle had been torn, and blood was everywhere.

Aurelia glanced back toward the bus, in time to see a canine form leap through the open doorway she had vacated. Around the corner of the vehicle, a hulking man-shape suddenly appeared, moving with massive shoulders hunched, arms flexing, fingers opening and closing, seeking prey. She didn't see the creature's face and had no wish to, sprinting past the van.

One of the mopeds was missing, but that knowledge barely registered before she was astride the first in line, stamping on the kick starter. The two-wheeler was old but lovingly maintained, its engine sputtering to life upon demand. Aurelia hung on for dear life and whipped it through a tight U-turn, part of her terrified that she would fall, another part assuring her that she would not.

Behind her, an inhuman voice roared out stark fury. She was on the blacktop now, and had the moped's throttle open. It had not been built for speed, like some two-wheelers. Could it outrun a loup-garou…or more than one?

It struck her that she had been wrong, somehow, about the local wolf man being on his own. There had been two of them, at least, and from the sounds she heard as she was running for her life, Aurelia guessed that there were still more in the camp.

How many? She had no idea, and no sensation spoke to her as she drove north, the night wind in her face. The Gypsy camp was better than a mile behind her when it came to her that she was driving without lights. When she had remedied that situation, she felt safer from collision with oncoming motorists. Police would be another matter if they stopped her, since she didn't own a driver's license, but at least there was a chance she could persuade them to go back and check the camp.

By which time, she assured herself, it would already be too late.

She knew where she had to go.

Desire House.

Remo didn't know it yet, but he was waiting for her. And there was a chance, although it seemed increasingly remote, that she might even save his life.

9

At half-past midnight Remo was asleep and dreaming of Lon Chaney, Jr. The dream was in black and white. Just like when he dreamed about the Three Stooges.

He recognized the street scene as an image from another time and place. He couldn't have identified the town, wasn't convinced it had a name, but knew that he had seen it many times before. The cobbled streets and architecture told him that he was somewhere in Eastern Europe, in that blissful time before the War to End All Wars. Behind him, if he glanced across his shoulder, Remo knew that he would find the full moon just emerging from a mass of brooding clouds.

Lon was somewhere in front of him, most likely hiding in the pitch-black alley to his left, a half block farther on. Remo hadn't yet laid eyes on him. But he could feel what was supposed to happen next. Lon had ducked offstage to don his wolf-man costume, but he was returning shortly, with a vengeance. You could bet on it.

There came a strange sound from the alley. Not growling, or the scuffling sound of semihuman footsteps Remo had expected. Rather it was the thud of feet on a carpeted floor, far away and coming closer on the run. It was a panicked run.

Remo sat up in the same instant as Chiun. They were both on mats on the floor of the hotel suite they were sharing with Cuvier. The mob target was snoring on the bed.

"Well, are you going to answer it?" Chiun demanded. A second later there was a frantic rapping on the door.

Cuvier was a light sleeper, too. He snorted and snuffled back to consciousness and feebly grunted a warning. "It be the loup-garou!"

"Don't think they knock," Remo said. He was already opening the door, and the delicate aroma coming from the hall identified the visitor before he saw her.

Aurelia Boldiszar looked shell-shocked.

"I didn't know where else to go," she said by way of greeting. "There's a chance it may already be too late."

Remo stood aside, then poked his head into the corridor and listened. It was empty and there were no suspicious sounds.

"What may be too late?" he asked, closing the door and flipping on the light.

Aurelia uttered a small "Oh!" and put her hand

to her mouth, as if to stifle a cry of alarm. She stared directly into the vivid emerald eyes that resembled those of an intense child. But the head they were inside of was covered in yellowed, water-wrinkled parchment.

"I'm sorry," she apologized. "It's just that I've seen—"

"I understand, child," said the ancient Master.

Remo caught the unexpected compassion in Chiun's voice and realized he hadn't exactly been quick on the uptake. Chiun had sensed that what had brought Aurelia there in the middle of the night wasn't just a sense of urgency. It wasn't even just an emergency.

"I've made a terrible mistake," she said. "There is not one loup-garou, but several. I've seen them."

"Excuse me?"

"They came to the camp," Aurelia said, and her eyes seemed to grow hollow. "They were killing us. Killing and killing. I don't know how many. The loups-garous were after me. The best thing I could do was get away."

And lead them here, thought Remo. But instead of saying it, he asked, "When did this happen?"

"Half an hour, maybe forty minutes. It took time for me to locate the hotel."

"And now you're telling me you actually saw these things?"

"Two of them," she replied. "One was trans-

formed completely, while the other…I can't do it
justice. It was manlike, walking upright in the shadows, but its face…''

Aurelia's voice trailed off. She met his eyes, then
turned her gaze away, as if embarrassed. Why? Because she had run out on her companions, even with
the best of motives?

Remo and Chiun knew she was telling the truth.
They could read it in her breath and the pulse of her
blood under the skin of her throat. Cuvier knew she
was telling the truth because he had faith.

Faith in the existence of the loup-garou.

Remo thought of going back out to the camp to
see it for himself, but quickly scrubbed the notion.
If Aurelia had been followed—even if she hadn't—
it was far more likely that the loup-garou would try
for Cuvier at their hotel than wait around the Gypsy
campsite for a little one-on-one with Remo.

They could hole up in the hotel, thought Remo,
or he could approach the problem from another angle. He could do, in fact, what he probably should
have done as soon as they were settled in New Orleans.

''You'll be safe here,'' he told Aurelia, wondering if it was true. Chiun could handle any man alive,
but if their adversary wasn't human…

''Why?'' Aurelia pinned his eyes with hers.
''Where are you going?''

Remo hoped his smile was reassuring, but it

didn't feel that way from where he stood. Still, he plastered on a smile. "Let's say I've got a hankering to see Mardi Gras."

MERLE BETTENCOURT WAS happiest when telling other people what to do. He loved the sense of power and authority that came with giving orders, telling his subordinates to jump and noting that they didn't even ask how high. The power of life and death especially excited him. It was better than sex.

At the moment, though, Merle Bettencourt was mired down in the bog of party politics. Venal politicians were a key part of the system, human cogs that kept the great machine moving forward, but that didn't mean he had to like them. Every time he was compelled to work with some asshole who styled himself a "statesman," it made Bettencourt feel he ought to take a long, hot bath. Given a choice, he would prefer the company of killers, pimps and pushers—they were at least honest about their motives and desires.

But here he was in an election year, and the primaries were unusually early, due to anticipated irregularities. Armand had to find it inside himself to finesse the oily bastards who were bent on suckling from the fat teats of the body politic. It seemed to Bettencourt that this year's candidates were worse than usual, and that was saying something in a state where politics and criminal behavior had been more or less synonymous since the days of Huey Long. The Kingfish was a pioneer of sorts; he set the tone for all that followed, teaching future generations of disciples how to realize their dreams, be all that they could be, and during his tenure graft had been refined to an elusive art form.

Still…

Gut instinct made him want to go with Elmo Breen. Breen was a lifelong veteran of gutter politics and had the morals of an alley cat, disguised by oily charm. He had started out with the Sicilians, in Marcello's pocket, but the changing times had prompted Breen to look for sponsorship among the native-born. For the past ten years or so he had been snuggling up to leaders of the Cajun outfit, kissing major ass at any given opportunity. He was a pro who asked no questions and provided value for the money he received, dodged nasty questions with the flexibility of a sidewinder and never let his patrons down.

Unless, of course, he saw the chance to cut himself a better deal.

It was an iron-clad rule of Armand Fortier's, with which Merle Bettencourt agreed, that you could never really know what the stupid voters might decide to do once they were shut up in the polling booth and confronted with a list of names. That being true, it only made good sense to have friends on both sides in any given contest, just in case. No matter how the dice came up, that way, the outfit couldn't lose.

Which brought him back to Reverend Rockwell. The TV preacher was a hopeless ego-tripper, like so many of his colleagues, with a penchant for insisting that his words were Jesus Christ's. Whether the Rock believed his own spew or not, Merle Bettencourt had no idea, nor did he give a damn. Old Rockhead was amusing in his way, but he could also be a liability in public office if his fire-and-brimstone calls for cleaning up the state were taken seriously. As it was, however, Bettencourt had learned enough about the pastor that he felt he could relax.

Rockwell was living, breathing proof of Romans chapter three, verse twenty-three, where it declared that *all* have sinned and come short of the glory of God. Not that the pastor was a womanizer, pedophile or any suchlike kinky specimen; in fact, there was no solid evidence that he engaged in sex of any kind, or ever had. He didn't drink or play around with drugs, as far as Bettencourt could tell, nor did he squander cash on games of chance. There were suspicions—at the FCC, the IRS and elsewhere—that he might be skimming more than his reported salary from JBN, and there was no real doubt that he had flouted campaign finance laws, but that was small potatoes when you got down to it, hardly worth the cost of an investigation, much less months or years in court to prosecute and maybe see him wriggle off the hook.

No, Bettencourt had finally decided, Reverend Rockwell's great sin was pride, a driving need to lord it over others with his stern self-righteousness and tell the whole damn world how it should live. His TV network was a vehicle for self-promotion, plain and simple, with the holy smoke screen dazzling Rockwell's simpleminded followers. The pastor spoke to them in tongues, which sounded more like bullshit baby talk to Bettencourt. He dubbed the ones who sent him money on a monthly basis "soul survivors." Stupid puns were something of a trademark with the Rock, in fact. He had been known to call the money sent in by his TV flock "hellfire insurance," and sufferers from terminal disease—who somehow lacked the faith required for Reverend Rockwell to heal them of their ailments—were harangued to "cram for finals" by enrolling in a cut-rate Bible correspondence course. At one point, early in his televangelism days, he had sold tiny bits of rock and concrete swept up from construction sites and advertised as chippings from the Rock of Ages.

Bettencourt admired that kind of gall, and it had been no great surprise when Rockwell's campaign put out discreet but urgent feelers to the Cajun Mafia. The pastor knew of Elmo Breen's connection to the mob, and while it suited him to blast his opposition as a crook and friend of crooks, Rockwell also knew that big-time money was required to win the statehouse. Even with the Jesus Broadcast Network pumping covert thousands into his campaign, he needed more, as much to fox the watchful Feds as to defray his costs. Of course, the Rock couldn't be seen with Bettencourt or any of his Cajuns, but that didn't stop his bagmen from soliciting, collecting and transporting better than a million dollars from the mob to Rockwell's primary campaign.

That kind of money came with certain obligations stamped into the greenbacks like a hidden watermark. In public, Rockwell continued to denounce corruption and the men behind it, promising a swift return to ''ancient family values'' if he was elected governor, but in the meantime he had reached an understanding with his covert benefactors. If he won—and there was still no guarantee, despite the extra million in his war chest—Rockwell would keep his campaign promises by going through the motions of a shake-up, mostly concentrated in Baton Rouge. There would be raids, investigations, show trials and convictions, but he promised to avoid disturbing his supporters any more than might be absolutely necessary. If the Cajun mob saw fit to offer scapegoats—say, perhaps, their leading competition in the drug trade and illegal gambling, loan shark and extortion rackets—Reverend Rockwell's investigators would accept the sacrificial goats and let it

go at that. Come next election year, they could ne-
gotiate new terms.

But now, with the primary just a few weeks off,
both candidates had started calling Bettencourt at
crazy hours, whining that the money wouldn't
stretch to cover all their needs, asking if maybe there
was something Bettencourt could do about the no-
good rotten bastard who obstructed the path to the
governor's mansion. Bettencourt would have been
tickled pink to smoke them both, but those tech-
niques had mostly gone out with the Kingfish. For
the moment, all that Merle could do was lend a sym-
pathetic ear and keep on filling briefcases with cash.

Whoever won the race would be presented with
a bill, detailed and itemized. If he contested it or
tried to bluff his way out of the game, Merle Bettencourt had tapes—both audio and hidden-camera
video—that would be guaranteed to change the
rebel's mind in nothing flat.

So much for politics. It took a measure of finesse,
but Bettencourt was getting there, remembering to
watch his temper and keep stroking the gargantuan
ego that every politician carried like a monkey on
his back. Some months earlier, in private, he had
started browsing through the dictionary and thesau-
rus, peppering his speech with new words, cutting
back on the profanity when there were ladies—as
opposed to whores and bitches—in the room. Merle

had begun to think that maybe he could fill old Armand's Gucci loafers, after all.

But there was still one problem to be dealt with, and he couldn't let it slide now that the wheels were turning, even if he didn't really give a shit about Armand's new trial. The Cajun godfather still had his loyalists in the family, enough of them to stir up holy hell if Bettencourt appeared to give the liberation effort less than everything he had.

Which meant, in turn, that he couldn't afford to let the final witness get away, no matter where he went to hide. And he couldn't afford to let a freak like Leon Grosvenor take him for a ride.

He needed something in the nature of an update from the wolf man, and he needed it right now. The trouble was that Leon didn't have a telephone or mailing address, living on the bayou like some kind of half-assed sideshow freak, away from other men. Which meant that Merle would have to reach out to him personally, even though he hated the idea.

A damn loup-garou.

What next?

REMO HADN'T EXACTLY memorized a lot of Dr. Smith's file on the Cajun Mafia. From what he gathered, they were little different from the traditional crime families that had controlled New Orleans since the latter decades of the nineteenth century. The new breed favored jambalaya over ravioli, and they leaned toward dogfights rather than the ponies, but they still touched all the bases of illicit enterprise. Their specialties were drugs, extortion, prostitution, gambling and a quirky sideline in the smuggling of endangered species for discriminating pet owners. The latter operation had apparently begun with Armand Fortier himself, who doted on exotic birds but now confined himself to watching sparrows in Atlanta when he was allowed outside to exercise.

Remo did have a slip of paper with some names and addresses. Not far from the hotel, on Jackson Avenue, was an operation that masqueraded as a pawnshop, but there was more to Ham's Hock Shop than met the eye. The registered proprietor, a Cajun named Étienne DuBois, was nicknamed "Ham" after his run-in with a wild boar on the bayou back in 1969. Étienne's first shot had failed to drop the monster, and it took him down, goring him repeatedly before he got it in a headlock, drew his twelve-inch bowie knife and cut its throat. Weakened by loss of blood, too badly wounded for the hike back to his skiff, DuBois was stranded for six days, subsisting on raw pork and boar's blood until he was strong enough to travel. He had been "Ham" ever since, to friends and enemies alike, and didn't seem to mind.

His injuries from the abortive hunting trip included some outlandish scarring, which he stub-

bornly refused to have corrected, and a hobbling
walk that put Étienne on disability. The fact that he
had never held an honest job before the hog attack
didn't prevent the state from compensating him for
"loss of wages due to work-related injuries." His
patron, Gaetan Fortier, had pulled the necessary
strings in Baton Rouge, and when old Gaetan went
to his reward, Étienne went right on working for the
son, Armand, to show his everlasting gratitude.

Not that Ham's Hock Shop was a terribly demanding gig. He dealt with drunks and losers,
mostly, where the terms weren't synonymous. Some
junkies, the occasional sneak thief if he had mer-
chandise that Étienne could move with no risk to
himself. He was a tightwad, and the shop made
money on its own, but it existed equally to serve the
Fortier crime family as an outpost in New Orleans,
where intelligence could be collected from the
streets and funneled to the proper ears. Sometimes,
in boozy conversations with selected friends,
Étienne compared himself to famous secret agents
of the cinema. He had been known to introduce himself as "Bond, Ham Bond," his Cajun accent making Bond sound just enough like "bone" for it to
draw obligatory smiles and anemic laughter.

Remo's maxim was that information, by its very
nature, flowed both ways. Those who received could
also share, if they were so inclined. He just had to

incline them. Inclining people was one of the things he did best.

He plunged into the jostling crowd on Tchoupitoulas Street and made his slow way eastward, weaving through the crush of partiers toward Jackson Avenue.

Unlike the carnival in Rio, there were laws forbidding outright nudity at Mardi Gras, but the occasional police he spotted on his trek appeared to be more mellow than your average Southern cop. At Tchoupitoulas and Louisiana Avenue, he saw two spit-and-polish lawmen joshing with a trio of young women dressed in G-strings, fishnet stockings, pasties and stiletto heels. The women also wore headgear resembling fish bowls with antennae, while the cops were wearing leering smiles. Everywhere were women, and men, in painted-on clothing. You had to look closer to realize they were completely naked.

It took him a few brisk minutes of weaving among the revelers to reach the pawnshop. Ham's Hock Shop was open, more from force of habit than with any hope of drawing business from the crowd outside. Some of the revelers paused long enough to press their faces to the windows, ogling saxophones, trombones, guitars, a nice display of ersatz switchblade knives, but no one went inside. Remo was the exception, a cow bell clanking overhead as it was jostled by the swinging door.

"Help you?"

Étienne DuBois was a man of average height who ran to fat. He clutched a sturdy wooden walking stick in his left hand. The leg on that side seemed to have an extra joint, more like an insect's, that encouraged it to wobble every time he took a step. On the right side of his face a long scar like an inch-wide lightning bolt zigzagged between the Cajun's jaw line and his eyebrow.

"I'm looking for a loup-garou," Remo said, cutting through the small talk.

Étienne DuBois allowed himself a crooked grin, the pale scar crinkling like rubber.

"You got a better chance a findin' one out there," the Cajun said, and pointed with his free hand toward the street. "Most anything you want will be out there tonight."

"I wouldn't be surprised," Remo said, moving closer to the Cajun, "but I'm looking for the real thing, not a fake."

DuBois's smile did a flip and wound up as a frown. "You're drunk or a crazy one, my friend," he said. "Somebody needs to check you out or something, you go looking for a real-life loup-garou."

"You don't believe in werewolves?"

"Not since I'm old enough to know better," the Cajun said.

"That's funny."

"Funny how?"

"Well, see, the thing is, I was told your boss man had a loup-garou he uses for his special jobs."

The frown was gone now, too. Its passing left the Cajun's face deadpan. "This place you standing in belongs to me," he said. "I got no boss man."

"Well, damn, I must've got it wrong, then. You don't work for Armand Fortier? Or maybe Bettencourt, now that the big guy's in Atlanta?"

"Don't guess I recognize those names."

"Uh-huh. It couldn't be that you sustained brain damage, could it, when that hog was chewing on your head?"

"You best get out a here right now," the Cajun said.

"We haven't finished talking."

"Oh, yeah, we finished," said DuBois. "You just don't know it yet."

He swung the heavy walking stick with force enough to split a watermelon—or a skull—but Remo saw it coming five minutes before it would have hit him. Remo brought up his right arm casually and allowed it to take the impact. The cane snapped and the broken-off piece spun aimlessly across the shop.

"Strike one," he said. "What say we keep talking as I suggested? 'Cause if that's the best you've got…"

DuBois was staring at him, features doubly puckered by the scar and a peculiar frown, still clutching half a cane. The broken end was lighter than the outer layer of wood by several shades, reminding Remo of a tree branch snapped off in a storm.

The scar-faced Cajun did not try to swing his shortened cane a second time. Instead, he jabbed the broken end toward Remo's face, as if to gouge an eye or plug the stranger's mocking mouth.

Remo grasped the wrist behind the cane and twisted, feeling wrist bones snap and dislocate. DuBois gave out a squealing cry of pain that fit his nickname and released the walking stick before he sprawled, headfirst, into a drum set standing in the middle of the floor.

"Strike two," Remo said when the Cajun had retrieved enough of his disjointed wits to understand the spoken word. "You're out on three, so make it good."

DuBois leaned on a cymbal when he tried to rise, but it spun out from under him and dumped him on his backside. Favoring his shattered wrist and crippled leg, he eventually tottered to his feet.

"Who sent you?" he demanded.

Remo answered with a question of his own. "It doesn't really matter, does it? You can talk to me, or you can have the worst night of your life. The last night."

Étienne DuBois was staring at him, gripping his right arm in his left hand while leaning back against a long plate-glass display case filled with cameras, watches, compact radios. The Cajun shot a quick glance toward the windows and the teeming street beyond, but it was hopeless. No one in the Quarter would have rushed to help him on an ordinary day, and Mardi Gras was in full swing, legitimizing aberrant behavior for the next two days.

"These things you ask about," the Cajun said at last, "they get me dead."

"You're dead already, Ham. My way, at least you get a running start."

"Hey, where you learn that kung-fu shit?"

"My father taught me," Remo said. "And if he heard you calling it 'kung fu' even I wouldn't be able to save you. Quit stalling, now. You want to talk or dance?"

"That loup-garou you ask about, I think you don't believe me if I told you."

"Try me out," said Remo. "You may be surprised."

10

It was a fluke that Fortier's gorillas ever caught a glimpse of Remo, but a fluke was all it took sometimes. He was emerging from Ham's Hock Shop when he met another caller coming in. The man was five foot two or three, built like a fireplug, with the bullet head to match. He wore a suit so shiny it was almost iridescent, but without a tie. His oily black hair was combed back from his sallow face in a lopsided pompadour. His sideburns would have set the King to spinning in his grave from envy.

Remo brushed on past the sawed-off thug, confirming with a feather touch that he was packing heat. Intent on getting out of there and merging with the crowd, he didn't spare the shop a backward glance until he heard the cow bell clank again and a gruff voice shouted, "Grab that guy!"

He had his adversaries pegged and counted in two seconds flat. Besides the fireplug, now emerging from the shop with murder in his eyes, three others were hanging back, clustered beneath a balcony where a young woman turned her shapely backside to the crowd and proved she was a natural redhead. The three goons heard their comrade shouting, followed his accusing index finger to the spot where Remo stood, and moved as one to cut him off.

The vast, amorphous organism of the crowd engulfed him, sucked him in, reminding Remo of *The Blob,* with Steve McQueen. This was a different kind of monster, though: more complex, yet more simpleminded, oozing through the Quarter without seeming purpose, fueled by alcohol, randomly shedding cells on every side, absorbing new ones to replace those lost. A man could get lost in a crowd like that and evade his enemies.

Remo didn't want to get lost.

Of course, he'd prefer not getting any revelers shot. Especially all those friendly college coeds.

Remo had no idea where he was going, other than away from Ham's Hock Shop and Jackson Avenue. He wouldn't lead the shooters back to his hotel. Remo slipped and slid through the crowd heading westward, leading his pursuers through the crowd, giving them the occasional glimpse to keep up their enthusiasm. His adversaries pushed and bullied their way through the crush of gaudy costumed bodies.

Fireplug had glimpsed the shop in ruins, maybe spotted Étienne DuBois behind the counter sleeping off the nerve pinch Remo gave him when he had run out of useful information.

Remo assumed the goons were Cajun Mafia, soldiers of Armand Fortier and his lieutenant, Bettencourt. They wouldn't relish going home without an explanation for the ruckus at Ham's Hock Shop, and the best thing they could hope for was to bag the culprit, take him with them when they went back to report.

On tiptoes he could make out a surge of motion through the crush, heads bobbing, bodies rippling as the spearhead of pursuit drove past them. It reminded Remo of snake-hunting in tall grass, the way you had to watch for subtle movement in the grass, because your prey remained invisible.

A mounted cop came out of nowhere, surging through the crush, proceeding in the general direction of the goons who hunted Remo. Had he seen them from his higher vantage point and known that something was amiss? Would he chastise them for their rude behavior, shoving through the crowd?

Then the cop veered off course, proceeding toward the distant outskirts of the mob. On that side of the street, a woman who resembled Shelley Winters in a Dolly Parton wig was dancing naked on a balcony, the sight of so much cellulite in motion making Remo vaguely ill. The mounted cop seemed bent on stopping her, an effort that evoked mixed cheers and booing from the audience.

"That's gotta be a felony," Remo muttered, and began moving through the press of bodies again, searching for a place where he could confront the goons without endangering the revelers.

From Ham DuBois he had gleaned a first name, bits and pieces of a story that could still be crap, despite the fact that his informant seemingly believed it. Remo needed more, and he was hoping that the four punks on his tail could add a few more bytes of information.

Remo began negotiating his way through the crush, moving inexorably toward the north side of the street. The human current had already passed Desire House, drawing Remo and his tail toward the terminus of Tchoupitoulas Street at Jefferson Avenue, with Audubon Park just beyond. South of Tchoupitoulas, the Mississippi River snaked its way along the outskirts of the Crescent City, dividing New Orleans proper from the suburbs of Westwego, Harvey, Gretna and Marrero. Narrow side streets had their own block parties going on, no respite from the crowd, and even alleyways were populated with partiers whose costumes mingled 1950s horror movies and sci-fi with all the trappings of a modern-day Gay Pride parade.

Ten minutes after leaving Ham's Hock Shop, he found what he was looking for. It wasn't perfect, but he would find nothing better at this end of Tchoupitoulas Street.

A cemetery.

How appropriate.

He wormed his way in that direction, left the surging crowd behind him as he broke into a trot.

JEAN CUVIER HAD NEVER made it with a Gypsy, and the more he thought about Aurelia Boldiszar, the more that lapse in judgment struck him as a critical mistake. She had the kind of look he had always liked in women: slim but not emaciated; elegant, even though her clothes were far from stylish; intelligent but quiet, keeping to herself a bit instead of showing off how smart she was.

The women in the past, let's face it, had been mostly bimbos. They were good at what they did, but without the bedroom and the shopping mall they had no purpose in life. With a Gypsy, now—this Gypsy, anyway—he had the feeling that he would be traveling uncharted territory. It excited him to think about it…but, predictably, there was a problem.

When Aurelia looked at him, which wasn't often, it was as if her eyes glazed over and kept on moving, anxious to find something else to focus on. Okay, the Cajun knew he wouldn't pass for Mel Gibson or that younger guy, Matt What's-his-name, but he had never been described as hideous. Some women went for him, some didn't. But none of them had ever told him that they couldn't stand to look at him.

The more he thought about it now, the more it troubled him. A part of his brain told him that his manly honor was at stake, he had to make the Gypsy really see him, but another part was getting worried. Cuvier was wondering if what he saw there, when her eyes glazed over, was in fact revulsion toward him as a man, or maybe something else.

He thought about the stories he had heard about the Gypsies when he was growing up. He had believed them as a child, and still believed enough of them to recommend that Remo seek out the Gypsies for information on the loup-garou. Some of the stuff he'd heard was crazy, while some other parts made sense. Jean Cuvier had never really stopped to dwell on whether Gypsies could predict the future. Tell someone when they were going to die, for instance. Maybe tell them how.

But what if this Aurelia babe could see his fate? Suppose that what she saw, just glancing at him from across the room, was so damn horrible it turned her stomach and she had to look away or lose her dinner right there on the coffee table.

What if she was seeing him dissected and devoured by old loup-garou?

The warmth that he had felt between his legs, watching Aurelia move around the room or simply sit there, paging through a magazine, was gone now. In its place there was tightness, as if his scrotal sack were shriveling to peanut size, attempting to retreat inside his body. Cuvier felt nauseous, dizzy, trying to imagine what the Gypsy's powers had revealed to her about the graphic details of his death.

He crawled back into the bed, tried to sleep but couldn't. He pictured monsters rushing at him from the shadows, tearing into him with fangs and talons, eating him alive. That was the worst part, fearing that the damn thing wouldn't kill him outright, that he would be conscious when it started gobbling his flesh and gnawing on his bones.

After a couple hours of that, he knew that he would have to face the Gypsy, find out what she knew. She might not want to tell him right off, but he had some money squirreled away. If that failed, or the price tag was beyond his reach... Well, he would simply make her tell him. Who was there to stop him? The old Chinaman?

He took it easy getting out of bed, no noise to warn the Gypsy or disturb the old man on the sleeping mat on the floor. Aurelia had the folding cot, had taken it when Remo left. Jean hadn't understood much of their whispered conversation, but he meant to hear the details now and find out what was coming to him, one way or another.

She seemed to be asleep as Cuvier crept to the cot on tiptoe. He stifled a curse as he collided with a corner of the coffee table and a bolt of pain shot from his shin up to his knee, and so on to his skull. He stood there, frozen like a statue, waiting for the pain to subside, afraid to breathe in case the sound had roused Aurelia from her sleep.

But she was still unconscious, with the sheet pulled up across her shoulder, bare skin showing in the dim light from the curtained window.

He knelt beside the bed and woke Aurelia with a hand pressed tight across her mouth. She was prepared to struggle, but the sheet got in the way, and he was leaning down to whisper in her ear by then.

"Relax," he said. "It's only me. We need to have a talk."

She glared at him, dark eyes above his hand, but then she nodded. He drew his hand away reluctantly, still feeling her soft lips against his palm.

"What do you want?"

"I seen you lookin' at me there, a while ago," said Cuvier. "Gypsies can see things, sometime, like what's coming, yes?"

"Sometimes," she said.

"So, what I wanna know is this—what's comin' after me."

"You know the answer," she informed him, "or you wouldn't ask the question."

He felt bright anger flare inside of him. "I don't need riddles from you, I guarantee," he told her, leaning close enough for her to smell the garlic on his breath. Aurelia tried to shrink from him, but there was nowhere for her to go. Her breasts made lumps beneath the sheet and set a faint alarm bell clanging in his head.

"You want to know if you're in trouble," the Gypsy said. "Well, you are. You made this trouble for yourself, and now you can't escape it."

Curiously, it aroused him, listening to her pronounce his death sentence. He couldn't help it. Even as he willed himself to concentrate on business, yet another part of him was thinking what did he have to lose?

"I wanna know what's left," he told her, climbing awkwardly onto the yielding mattress. "You're going to tell me how much time I got."

His left hand settled on her breast, began to knead the pliant flesh through layers of fabric. "How much time?" he said again.

"Not much," she answered, bringing up a knee between his meaty thighs.

The impact stunned him, overwhelmed him with a blast of pain eclipsing anything he could remember from a lifetime of hard knocks. He barely noticed as her right arm freed itself and whipped a rock-hard fist into his face.

The next thing Cuvier remembered, he was lying on the floor beside the bed. Aurelia was kneeling on the mattress, miles above him, cursing him in languages he didn't even recognize. The lights were on, and would have hurt his eyes if there had been a spare nerve left to carry more pain signals to his

brain. Too late for that, though, with the piercing
agony that clutched his groin.

The little Asian stood over him, regarding Cuvier
with an expression that may have been curiosity,
amusement or disgust.

"Sleepwalking is very dangerous," Chiun informed him, grinning now.

"You could have helped," Aurelia said.

"You needed no help," the old Korean answered.

Next thing Cuvier knew, the wizened little man
had picked him up with one hand, gripping the
denim fabric of his shirt, and toted him back to the
bed. He tossed Jean onto the mattress as if he were
slinging a sack of dried beans.

"Sleep now," the scrawny apparition said. "No
more chitchat. No more hanky-panky."

Cuvier felt obligated to respond somehow. He
found his voice—it had been hiding somewhere in
the neighborhood of his left kidney.

"Hey, Chinaman!"

The little Asian faced the bed again, no longer
smiling, and leaned over Cuvier, a slim hand reaching toward the junction of the Cajun's neck and
shoulder.

"Too much noise," he said. "Too little brains."

The Asian barely touched him, but at once the
pain below his waist evaporated, swallowed in the
sudden, wrenching agony that gripped his upper
body. Cuvier was frozen, powerless to move or even

scream, until the lights went out again and blessed darkness carried him away.

THE GROUND ON WHICH New Orleans stands has been so wet, historically, that corpses are entombed above the earth instead of buried in it. Wealthy individuals and families lean toward elaborate vaults and monuments, while those without the surplus cash on hand wind up in simple tombs resembling the foundations of so many narrow toolsheds swept away by tropical storms. The graveyard Remo chose that night was more elaborate than most, and offered countless hiding places.

The goon squad trailing him had the combined IQ of a normal human being. It took them a while to figure out where Remo had got to. "Criminy," he complained, making it easier for the goons by lingering at the curb outside the cemetery gate. Finally one of them spotted him and started bawling at the others, pointing out their quarry. Even then, Remo stalled until the first of them had churned free of the crowd and come toward him. Only then did he continue into the boneyard, merging with the night.

It was no challenge to avoid them. Remo could have led them in and crept around behind them, disappeared while they were hunting him among the tombs and monuments, but that wasn't his plan. The way he saw it, Fate had handed him four chances to improve upon the information he had gained from

Étienne DuBois, and he would be a fool to throw that opportunity away.

The goons who stalked him now were leg breakers and killers, undeserving of sympathy. He heard the four gorillas fanning out. They called to one another in the darkness, sounding nervous, making noise enough to wake the dead around them as they combed the cemetery for their mark. Remo decided it would be a smart move to secure at least one POW first, in case it got too hairy later on, and so, while they were stalking him, he did a little hunting of his own.

As luck would have it, Remo came upon the human fireplug first. Like many small men with tough attitudes, this one had tried to compensate with iron. His weapon was a .357 Magnum Desert Eagle semi-automatic, stainless steel with jet-black plastic grips. He held the massive pistol well in front of him—his first mistake—and swung it in an arc before him, as if it had been a flashlight rather than a gun.

Remo came up behind him and pulled the punch that should have crushed his adversary's skull. The gunner's consciousness winked out as if someone had flicked a light switch, and before he crumpled, Remo plucked the Desert Eagle from his fist and twisted the barrel like a wrung-out washrag.

A quick frisk of his dozing captive turned up knuckle dusters, a blackjack, a switchblade knife—

it was a wonder that the little bastard didn't rattle when he walked. He squashed every weapon.

"Sleep tight," he told the fireplug, and went off to find his friends.

The next one was a relatively tall man pushing six feet, with the shoulders of a high-school jock and waistline of a slacker who had lost the taste for exercise. The goon had reached a point where his physique could still go either way, but it was nothing he would have to be concerned about from this night on.

Remo sped up to intercept him, marking where the others were by their insistent jabbering. His chosen target didn't answer them, but as he closed the gap between them, Remo heard the shooter whistling softly to himself, and understood that these tough guys were frightened of the graveyard, more like children than the soldiers they aspired to be.

He passed the shooter, moving swiftly, covered by the night, and ducked behind a minimausoleum that stood directly in his target's path. Someone had placed a small bouquet of flowers on the threshold of the tomb, and Remo stepped around them, noting that the blooms had wilted and were on their way to dropping petals in another day or so.

A moment later the tough guy's pistol nosed around the corner of the mausoleum. It was a snub-nosed .38, blue steel, and Remo waited for the arm to follow, using both hands as he grabbed the shooter's wrist and elbow, whipping him around the corner, to his knees.

The wrist bones and the elbow snapped together, but he had a grip on the shooter's throat by then, bottling up the scream.

"You want to live?"

The kneeling gunner tried to nod, eyes bulging with surprise and pain.

"So take a nap."

The death grip shifted slightly, fingers finding the carotid arteries on either side and cutting off the flow of blood to one befuddled brain. The shooter wilted. Remo made scrap of the his snubby and another switchblade.

It was a moment's work to dump his latest prize beside the human fireplug, and he went back to the hunt. His third mark was of average height and heavyset, a waddler who compensated for his flab by packing a Colt .45. His wingtip shoes made little squishing noises as he moved among the tombs.

With half the crew already snoozing, Remo had an urge to wrap up the preliminaries and proceed to his interrogation. Waiting in the shadows of another tomb, he jabbed a punch at number three and dropped him in his tracks. As the shooter fell, a reflex action of his muscles triggered off a loud round from the Colt and brought his final sidekick on the run. Remo hadn't planned it that way, but it was okay. The next goon would come to him.

Three goons were plenty, Remo calculated, and he met the fourth man with a palm thrust that took him underneath the chin and broke his neck. The guy was dead before he hit the ground, and Remo crushed two more shooting irons into steel lumps.

Remo gripped a shooter's belt in either hand and hoisted them, moved back in the direction of the tomb where he had stashed the other two. He swung the flaccid bodies as he walked, for all the world resembling a man out for a stroll with two light shopping bags—except that each of these weighed just about two hundred pounds.

He dropped the living gunman near his fellows, propped the dead one up against a nearby tomb, where he would be immediately visible to his companions when they came around. One small adjustment to his posture, and the scene was set.

Reviving his three captives took only fifteen seconds of pinching, probing, slapping. They were slumped together, muttering and shaking heads that throbbed with pain when Remo stepped in front of them and spoke.

"I guess you're wondering," he said for openers, "exactly why I called you all here this evening."

"What's that?" the fireplug asked, addressing no one in particular.

"I'm glad the three of you could join me," Remo said, still smiling. "I'll be your inquisitor this evening. Anyone who wants to live can simply answer all my questions honestly, first time around. There will be penalties for bullshit, bluffing or attempting to walk out before the game is finished. Do we understand the rules?''

''Where's Gabby?'' asked the goon who had been carrying the .45.

''Oh, right.'' Remo pretended that the fourth punk had already slipped his mind. ''We played a practice round while you three sleepyheads were snoozing. I'm afraid he lost.''

That said, he stepped aside to let them see their friend. At first, the groggy shooters didn't understand what they were seeing, and it took a moment for the details of the scene to register: the late, lamented Gabby sitting with his back against a marble tomb, his head inverted so that he was kissing stone.

''Poor sap thought he was Linda Blair,'' said Remo. ''That's the breaks. Hooray for Hollywood.''

The other three were staring at him now. The thug in the middle cradled his shattered arm, in too much pain to make a move, while the others were wondering if two-on-one was good enough to let them walk away from this alive.

''You've got two choices,'' Remo told them. ''We can talk or we can fight. So far tonight, you haven't done that well with muscle.''

The silence stretched between them, dragging on, until the fireplug spoke at last.

''Okay,'' he said, ''what is it you wanna know?''

11

Late Thursday morning, Armand Fortier was noti-
fied by Eulus Carroll, one of his least favorite prison
guards, that he was favored with a visitor. The Cajun
mobster was perplexed, because he hadn't summoned anyone to call on him, and no one he could
think of had the balls to come and see him uninvited.
Oh, the Feds had come a few times in the early
weeks of his imprisonment, mostly to taunt him,
hoping they could make some kind of deal now that
they had him caged, but they had long since given
up.

"Who is it?" he asked Carroll.

"How the hell should I know, shithead?"

Eulus Carroll was six foot eight and weighed at
least three hundred pounds, most of it muscle. He
was as black as coal, head shaved and took no shit
from anybody in the joint. The story was that he had
killed two inmates with his bare hands when they
made the grave mistake of coming after him with
shanks, and while Armand could never verify the
tale he had a sneaking hunch that it was true. Carroll

hated convicts, which at first blush seemed peculiar for a man who chose to spend his life with prisoners, but story number two involved a budding pro football career, sidelined when Eulus had been run down in a crosswalk by a car thief and escapee from the Fulton County jail. The doctors told him he would never play again for money, and as soon as he could walk—or so the story went—he had signed on as a corrections officer to get some payback happening.

And payback was a bitch.

"You know the drill," Carroll said, and shook the chains in Armand's face for emphasis.

"Yeah, yeah."

Embarrassed by the routine even now, the Cajun raised his arms above his head while Carroll wrapped the belly chain around his waist and locked it at the back. Next came the shackles. Carroll crouched behind him, and while it was tempting for Armand to kick old Eulus in his big black face, it also would have been the next best thing to suicide. The cuffs were last, secured to the belly chain so that Armand could neither scratch his balls nor wipe his nose.

"Let's go."

They had to clear three different checkpoints—double sets of heavy sliding doors controlled by guards secure in bulletproof glass boxes. It was all about security, the Cajun realized, but he believed that part of it was also psychological, reminding

every convict in the place that he was under someone else's thumb.

Visitations were strictly controlled in Atlanta,
with the main visitors' room patrolled by multiple
guards whenever convicts were present, rigid barri-
ers blocking any contact between inmates and their
visitors. Aside from that, there were four smaller
rooms, as well, where screws weren't supposed to
peek or eavesdrop, and these were used for inmate
conferences with lawyers and occasionally psychiatrists employed by the defense team on particularly
sticky cases.

Fortier was all the more confused when Eulus
Carroll led him to the block of private rooms and
opened number three. With nothing in the way of
explanation, Carroll opened up the door, shoved
Fortier across the threshold, closed and locked the
door behind him. Glancing back, the Cajun saw his
keeper's face framed briefly in the door's small window, double panes of glass with wire mesh in between, before it disappeared.

His visitor was standing in the corner farthest
from the door, hands in his trouser pockets, watching Armand with a crooked little smile. If Fortier
had ever seen his face before, it didn't stick.

"You've gained some weight," the stranger said.
"Must be that starchy prison food."

"Who the fuck are you?" demanded Fortier.

"You want to have a seat?" the stranger asked as if he hadn't heard. "Relax a little while we talk?"

"My mama told me not to talk to strangers," Fortier replied. He made no move toward either of the straight-backed wooden chairs.

"That's fair enough," the visitor replied. "I'll talk, you listen. It'll do you good."

Armand said nothing, but the stranger didn't seem to mind.

"You've got a motion for a retrial coming up in June, before the Seventh Circuit. Some new evidence, your mouthpiece says. Right now, you look to have a fifty-fifty chance of winning that round."

"I feel lucky," Armand told him, never able to resist a timely gloat.

"That wouldn't be because you're weeding out the prosecution witnesses who sent you up, now, would it?"

"You must be an idjit, come in here and ask me that."

"You're right," the stranger said. "There's no point asking questions when we both know what the answers are."

The Cajun felt like telling him that what he knew and what the state could prove were very different things, but he decided not to push his luck. The room was more than likely wired, with tape recorders rolling. This wasn't a privileged conversation, and he didn't want to push his luck.

"You've killed nine people that I know of in the past two months," the stranger said.

"I been right here," said Fortier. "I'm sure the warden will be pleased to verify that fact."

"That's nine plus half a dozen Gypsies who were killed last night."

Armand allowed himself a puzzled frown at that one. For the first time since the stranger started talking, Fortier had drawn a blank. He knew nothing of dead Gypsies, nor was he especially concerned.

"Oh, wait," the stranger said. "You didn't know about the Gypsies, did you? My guess is that Leon was working on his own."

The name set Armand's scalp to prickling, but he couldn't scratch it, even if he had been willing to display surprise—which he was not.

"Who's Leon?" he inquired, hoping he sounded calmer than he felt.

The stranger grinned, a predatory flash of strong white teeth. "You haven't started going senile, have you, Armand? Hey, I know it happens, but you're young yet. Got your whole life still in front of you, if you call this living."

Fortier ignored the taunt and shook his head, in case they had a camera running, in addition to the audio. "This Leon don't mean shit to me," he said. "Don't know him. Don't know anything about no Gypsies."

"I believe you," said the stranger. "Well, the last

part, anyway. See, how I figure it, Leon found out
one of the Gypsies had a line on him, so he decided
what the hell? He didn't know which one it was, so
why not take 'em all? Of course, he missed a few.
The one he wanted, in particular. Tough luck that
sheriff's squad car passing on routine patrol.''

Another troop of phantom ants swarmed over Armand's scalp and down his back. He ground his
teeth, felt tremors starting in his knees and willed
them to be gone.

"You got this guy, how come you come and
bother me?"

"Did I say that?" The stranger frowned. "I don't
think so. No, see, your wild man got away."

"Ain't none of mine," the Cajun said. Relief
coursed through his veins, reviving him as fresh air
does a drowning man.

"Or should I say your loup-garou?"

It hit him like a slap across the face, but Armand
didn't flinch. At least, he didn't think he had.
"You're a crazy fool," he said, and forced a bark
of nervous laughter. "Believing old wives' tales like
that. You got some garlic in your pocket?"

"That's for vampires," said the stranger. "Trust
me."

"Shee-it. I wouldn't know."

"About the loup-garou? That's strange, you
know, because I had a talk with several of your men
last night, and they were very helpful."

"Bullshit." It was coming at him much too quickly now. Armand could think of nothing else to say.

"You know Étienne DuBois? Friends call him Ham? I grant you, he's a little on the porky side, but hey, that gives you one more thing in common."

"I don't know no Étienne What's-his-face," Armand replied.

"That's weird, because he sure as hell knows you. In case you're wondering, he gave me Leon's name. Your other four gorillas helped fill in the blanks."

"Bullshit." With less conviction this time. "Ham, gorillas, loup-garou. Sound like you talkin' about some kinda zoo."

"Hey, that's not bad." The stranger grinned. "Too bad for you, these apes could talk. Did you see *Congo,* by the way? They weren't quite that advanced but they came up with the answers I needed."

The Cajun's mind was reeling; he had no small difficulty keeping the reaction from his face. He knew the pig DuBois, of course. As for the others, if he found out any of his men had spoken to this stranger, any stranger, he would see them dead before the week was out.

"I don't know what you want with me," he said at last. It sounded lame, but he could think of nothing else to say without tipping his hand, in some way admitting guilty knowledge of the crimes this stranger was discussing.

"That's okay," the stranger said. "Mostly, the reason why I'm here is to remind you that there's different kinds of justice, see? Sometimes the system works all right, but other times it gets clogged like a drain, and little bits of crud start floating to the top. See what I'm saying?"

"Can't say that I do."

"Okay, let's put it this way. I'm the plumber. When the drain backs up, I have to ream it out. I don't involve the courts, see what I'm saying?"

"That supposed to be a threat?"

The stranger smiled, stepped forward, reached down with his right hand for a corner of the wooden table. With his thumb and forefinger, he pinched the inch-thick oak and gave a twist, as if it were nothing, and a jagged piece of wood snapped right off in his hand. It left a scalloped wound perhaps two inches wide, as if the father of all termites had been gnawing on the table.

"Call it food for thought," the stranger said, as he advanced and slipped the piece of wood into Fortier's hand. That said, he brushed past the Cajun godfather and rapped his knuckles on the metal door.

"We're done in here," he told the guard outside.

Armand Fortier was trembling in his chains when Eulus Carroll came to fetch him back, and he couldn't have said if it was fear or rage. Perhaps some combination of the two.

"Let's go, shithead," the black man ordered.

"Not so fast," said Fortier. "I need to use the telephone."

A PHONE CALL from the joint could only be bad news. First thing, the convicts always had to call collect, since none of them had calling cards inside, and that meant money out of pocket if you took the call. Worse yet, as soon as Bettencourt found out it was Atlanta calling, then he knew it had to be Armand, and Armand never simply called to pass the time of day, much less to share glad tidings. He called to give instructions or to bitch and moan, more often all of the above, the orders springing typically from some complaint that had occurred to him while he was sitting on his ass and killing time.

Still, turning down the call wasn't an option. Bettencourt's houseman was under orders to accept the charges, and he found Merle in the playroom, working on a solitary game of nine ball.

"Boss's on the phone," he said, and wandered off to God knew where.

Merle felt like yelling after him that he was the boss, but it would have been a waste of breath, aside from downright dangerous. Instead, he made a bee-line for the nearest telephone and lifted the receiver.

"Hey, Armand."

"Hey, Merle."

"Is this line like, you know, safe?"

"How should I know?" Armand snapped at him. "I'm callin' from the damn joint."

"Oh, yeah. What's up?"

"What's up is I just had a visitor," the Cajun godfather replied.

"Who is that?"

"I didn't catch his name, all right?"

That seemed a little odd to Merle, a total stranger showing up to visit at the federal pen and he forgets to give his name, but Bettencourt suspected that wasn't the problem Fortier had called up to discuss.

"So, what'd he want?"

"Came by to tell me he been talkin' to some boys down your way," Fortier replied. "My boys."

You could at least have said our boys, Merle thought, but kept it to himself. And said, "Talkin' about what?"

"This thing with Leon," Fortier replied.

"Aw, *merde.*"

"You see now why I'm callin'?"

"Yeah, I think so. This guy give you Leon's name?"

"Come out with it like it was nothin'," Armand said. "Made like he knew all about that other business, too."

Merle had to puzzle over that one for a moment. Other business? Finally, it came to him that Fortier was making reference to the purge of prosecution witnesses for which Leon had been retained. The knowledge made his flesh crawl uncomfortably. The way he felt right now, his mama would have said someone had walked across his grave. But how the hell could they do that, when he was still alive?

"He say what boys was talkin'?" Bettencourt inquired.

"One name he give me," Armand said. "The pig man."

Pig man. Pig man? Wait, he had it! "Yeah, okay. Who else?"

"I said one name! You got spuds in your ears?" When Merle made no reply, the Cajun godfather continued. "Another thing. Some shit about Leon and Gypsies."

"Gypsies?"

"That's what I said! You got a fuckin' parrot on your shoulder?"

Bettencourt was reaching up to check before he caught himself. "Uh-uh," he said.

"So check this out," said Fortier. "Leon and Gypsies. All I know. And take care of that other thing."

"Okay."

"You keep a lookout for this bastard, Merle, you hear me?"

"Right."

The line went dead without so much as a goodbye, and Bettencourt returned the telephone receiver to its cradle. Jesus Christ, as if he didn't have enough problems to deal with as it was. Now one of the prosecution witnesses was still out there, and old Armand was nagging him to get the job done. He had started thinking lately that it wouldn't be so bad if Armand lost his damn appeal and had to spend a few more hundred years inside. Like anyone would miss him but his bimbos.

Bettencourt could run the show himself. God knew he had been handling the grunt work long enough, while Armand got the cream and accolades. So much for justice. Now this shit about the Gypsies, and he couldn't even find out what it was supposed to mean, because Armand was worried that the pay phone in the joint might sprout an extra pair of ears.

Leon and Gypsies. What the hell? Of course, the more he thought about it, turned it over in his mind, the more they seemed to go together. Gypsies had that spooky reputation, and old Leon, well, they didn't come much spookier than that.

Merle knew exactly what he had to do, and while he didn't like it one damn bit, there was no viable alternative.

He grabbed the telephone again, but it was dead. Now, what the—? Instantly it came to him. His houseman, who had taken Armand's call, had left the damn extension off the hook. Merle cradled the receiver, biting off an urge to slam it down with crushing force, and reached the playroom's door in three long strides.

"Arno? Arno, you idjit, where you at?"

"What, boss?" Arno emerging from the kitchen with a turkey leg in hand, grease smeared around his lips.

"Would you be kind enough to go hang up the telephone?"

"Okay."

Sweet Jesus. Now Merle had to make the call he had been dreading ever since the Feds sent Armand to Atlanta. There was no way to avoid it any longer.

He was bound to fix himself a meeting with a goddamn loup-garou.

THE ROUND-TRIP TO Atlanta took four hours, not including time spent at the prison, picking up and dropping off his rental car and dawdling through the traffic-crowded streets. All things considered, it was well into midafternoon when Remo disembarked at New Orleans International Airport, west of town, and bid a sad farewell to the incessant squalling of the two brats who had occupied the seats behind him. The whole way back, he had been mulling over Fortier's reaction to the bits of information he had dropped. The Cajun boss was hanging in there, had let nothing slip from his side, but the grim expression on his face when Remo mentioned "Leon," although quickly covered by a sneer, had shown that he was stung. The mobster's brain was working overtime when Remo left him, that was obvious, and he would not allow the game to start unraveling if there was anything that he could do to bring it back on course.

Remo was counting on it.

The sooner Fortier demanded swift results of his staff, the quicker Remo would be treated to a one-on-one with his pet loup-garou.

And what would happen then?

Before he left New Orleans, Remo had inquired about the Gypsies and was told that five were dead, two others barely hanging on with life support, six others treated and released for injuries that ranged from broken bones to multiple dog bites. Survivors who were capable of talking told police a pack of wolves had burst into their camp and run amok. Of course, the only wolves known to reside within Louisiana's borders lived in zoos, and so police assumed the Gypsies were mistaken, possibly hysterical. There had been problems in the past with feral dogs—some wild-born, others cast-off pets who joined a roving pack in order to survive. They came in from the bayous now and then, attracted by the city lights and smell of food, reacting viciously if humans tried to run them off.

It was a logical description of events, one that the media could swallow and regurgitate with sidebars

about leash laws and the tragedy of heartless bastards who dumped their unwanted pets without a
second thought. King Ladislaw, one of the evening's
battle-scarred survivors, had spent time enough with
the police in several states to know that there was
no point in disputing the official version of events.
As soon as he was reasonably satisfied as to his
daughter's short-term safety, he had packed up the
remainder of his tribe and hit the road. Aurelia had
her ways of keeping in touch.

When she had spoken with her father, he had told
a vital bit of trivia. The attackers had witnessed her
leaving. The Romany had, as well, and they assumed she was fleeing, leaving them to their fate.
Until the attackers ran off after her. Then the Gypsies had understood that the loups-garous were after
her specifically. She had done a brave thing leading
them away from the camp, alone and unprotected.
And they all agreed it would be the best thing for
her to stay away for the time being.

That was when she and Remo decided it would
be best if she stuck with them.

Remo was getting his own little merry band of
followers. Chiun spent most of his time lost in his
own little world of meditation or Spanish-language
TV. He was being uncharacteristically aloof, and he
wasn't interested in telling Remo why. This was
standard behavior for Chiun, who loved to create his
little mysteries and impart wisdom by letting Remo

learn things for himself. Right now Chiun claimed that he was allowing Remo to immerse himself fully in the role of Reigning Master of Sinanju. As far as Remo could tell, that meant he did all the work while Chiun "meditated" in front of the Mexican soap operas. With Chiun only physically present and with his two new companions, Remo felt like the guy in some bad TV show who wakes up to find himself living with the wrong family.

But between Cuvier and Aurelia, he sure had a full bait bucket.

"The best way I can help my people," Aurelia told Remo, "is to stay with you and see these monsters finally destroyed."

Since Remo was trying to accomplish exactly that, it was hard to turn her down. Come to think of it, it would have been hard to turn her down on anything.

But he knew he couldn't guarantee her safety, because he still didn't know for sure what they were up against. Was there one loup-garou, Leon, and a pack of trained dogs? Or were there several loups-garous?

Was he—or were they—really the product of the mad genius of Judith White? Or was there something different, something less explicable?

Remo frankly didn't have a clue what he was up against, except that Armand Fortier and company were at the root of it, their bloodstained Cajun fingers pulling strings behind the scenes.

With that in mind, he had decided on a visit to Atlanta, no real plan in mind except to meet the Cajun godfather in person, try to shake him up and crank his paranoia up an octave with the news that members of his home team in New Orleans had begun to crack.

Aside from Ham DuBois, in fact, it wasn't strictly true. The three gorillas in the cemetery would have talked, he was convinced, but they were simple button men, the kind of bottom feeders who digested rumors from the street and spit them back in garbled form. They would admit to serving Armand Fortier and "knew" he had a loup-garou on call for "special jobs," but anything beyond that point was garbled nonsense. Remo exhausted their meager store of intelligence and left them there, fresh customers for the New Orleans boneyard.

Which left Remo with his most important unanswered question—how to get to the loup-garou, the one he now knew was named Leon. But nobody really seemed to know how to get to Leon.

Fortier and friends would have no difficulty tracking down the stiffs in the graveyard, but short of scheduling a séance, there was no way to discover what, if anything, they had divulged before they died. With any luck at all, the prospect of informers in the ranks would amplify the innate paranoia that was part of every gangster's personality, alert to treachery from "friends" and relatives around the clock.

The first rule of organized crime had always been, would always be to do unto others before they could do it to you. Armand had come up through the ranks the hard way, killing or subverting those who blocked his path to power, and he knew damn well that others had been waiting in the wings, hoping for him to fall. His prison term had cleared the way for Bettencourt, but now that Fortier was trying for a comeback, with his bid for a new trial, he had to know that some of his old buddies would be just as glad to have him stay exactly where he was.

And maybe, if the Cajun godfather got anxious, if he started pushing hard enough, something would snap. If he began to whistle for his loup-garou…

That's what Remo was hoping for. That someone, anyone would draw out the werewolf. And the sooner the better. Every hour in New Orleans gave the enemy another chance to tag Jean Cuvier, another chance to kill Aurelia Boldiszar. He knew the woman and his witness were secure with Chiun, for now.

It was a dicey business, he decided, when you had a werewolf by the tail.

THE CROWDED STREETS PUT Leon off, disturbed him, conjuring sensations that were almost claustrophobic, but the summons had permitted no denial. If he had refused, as he was first inclined to do, there would be trouble. Exposure, on some level. He and the pack would have to flee their home and find another place to hide, outside the bayou country.

He hated to think of that happening. So he had come into the city, trusting Bettencourt's assurance that the free-for-all of Mardi Gras would mask him better than a physical disguise. No sweat, the go-between had promised him. Boss said just be himself.

And so he was.

Against all odds, he found a parking space two blocks from his appointed rendezvous and wedged the van into it, ramming bumpers fore and aft. If anybody noticed in his absence, they were free to jot down his license number. The plates were stolen and would be discarded once he got back home.

He locked the van and stepped into the maelstrom of activity that swirled around him, checking out the costumes, men on stilts, half-naked women, fireworks going off at random in the crowd, an all-pervasive smell of alcohol, gunpowder, sweat and lust that made him giddy, brought a hot rush of saliva to his mouth. It was the biggest, most frenetic freak show he had ever seen, but as he started for the sidewalk, part of Leon's brain still felt as if a spotlight followed him, some cosmic finger pointing to alert the dipshit normals that he wasn't one of them—that he was real.

As if in answer to his fears, a short man in a diaper stepped into his path, a beer bottle in one hand, giant pacifier in the other.

"Hey, man!" the intoxicated creature said to Leon. "That's some crazy costume. Where'd you find it?"

"It's homemade," the werewolf told him, stepping to one side.

The tipsy "infant" moved to block him. "Awesome," he said. "You got a card? How much did it cost?"

"It's not for sale," said Leon, finally brushing past the stranger, merging with the crowd. His skin was crawling, but another part of him was starting to relax.

Some crazy costume. If they only knew the half of it.

Leon had reviewed an ancient street map, creased and mildewed, prior to starting on his journey. He had memorized street names and landmarks, the historic buildings that were spotted on a map and unlikely to change their names. Thus readied for the challenge, he had no great difficulty finding where he meant to go, but there was still a nagging sense of others staring at him.

But nothing happened, and he made his way into the heart of the French Quarter. He could smell the

Mississippi River, not so far away. Its smell was reminiscent of the bayou country, but without the stagnant odor of decay that was so common in the swamp. Now all he had to do was find the intersection and a certain restaurant.

The limousine was parked outside a smallish Cajun restaurant, the engine idling. One of Fortier's leg breakers stood beside the car, the only person visible to Leon who had opted for a business suit in lieu of more exotic garb. The Cajun did a double take as Leon stopped beside the car, and then a window powered down, in back. Someone inside the car spoke to the goon in French, the blacked-out window closed again and Fortier's gorilla held the door for Leon as he climbed into the car.

He settled on a jump seat, facing three more men in stylish suits. One of the younger pair leaned forward, reaching for him, but the Cajun in the middle hauled him back and shook his head.

"Don't be insultin' Leon, now," the oldest of the three men said. "He didn't come here to shoot me, did you, Leon?"

Leon shook his head. It was a stupid question, but he knew it would be rude to say so.

"I'm Merle Bettencourt," the boss man said. "I don't believe we've met before."

The Cajun knew damn well they hadn't met. Leon had only met his boss one time, and that had been enough for both of them. Merle glanced at Leon's shaggy hands, as if considering if they should shake, deciding he would pass.

"I guess you wonderin' why I call this meeting, hey?"

Leon had no response beyond a shrug. The man would tell him what he wanted when he got around to it. These "normal" men weren't always direct in dealings with one another, much less with a creature they regarded as a freak of nature.

"What it is," Merle Bettencourt went on, "is about that last man on the list you were supposed to handle for us."

It sounded like a question, but he didn't think it was, so Leon sat and waited.

"We need to get that job took care of right away, soon as you can," said Bettencourt. "And there's another thing come up just recently. Some guy been askin' around about you, like maybe he was lookin' for you."

Leon knew that, too, but he wouldn't reveal his knowledge to this stranger. He would deal with it in his own way and time.

"You hear me, Leon?" From the pinched expression on his face, Merle Bettencourt couldn't decide if he was puzzled or pissed off by Leon's silence.

"Yeah," the loup-garou replied. There was no reason he could think of to elaborate.

"Okay, then." Bettencourt relaxed a bit, but he

was frowning. "Just one other little thing. About these Gypsies, now. What the hell is that about?"

Leon considered his reply, took more time than most men would have required, since conversation was a lost art in his world. He knew exactly what he meant to say, but picking words to spell it out required some study.

"Friend of mine told me they askin' questions about my business," Leon said at last. "Which by, I mean your business, too."

One of the Cajun mobster's eyebrows crinkled in surprise. "That so?"

"What I was told."

"Who say that?" Bettencourt inquired.

"This Gypsy. I been knowin' him some time."

"You trust him?"

Leon shrugged at that. "He scared of me. Come told me what he seen."

"And you took care of that?" asked Bettencourt.

"I think so. Shook them up, at least."

"I'm wonderin' if maybe they mixed up with this old boy I told you about," the Cajun mobster said. "They mention him at all?"

"They didn't tell me nothin'," Leon said, as if it should be obvious. "Just scream and bleed is all."

"Uh-huh."

The mobster glanced at his gorillas, left and right, but both of them were staring at the wolf man, fingers on their gun hands twitchy with the urge to draw and fire. Leon imagined he could rip their throats out if they tried.

"Best watch out while you handlin' that job we talk about," said Bettencourt. "See maybe if you can't take out this other guy. Clean up the whole damn thing."

"I'll keep an eye out," Leon said.

"Do that," said Bettencourt. After a brief silence, he said, "I guess that's all."

Leon didn't see the signal, but the limo's door was opened by the outside man, as if on cue. Leon was half out of the car when Bettencourt called after him, "And finish up that job right quick, you hear?"

Outside, the freaks were still in charge. Leon felt more at home with them than he had with the "normals" in the limousine, and he didn't look back to see if they were watching him as he began the walk back to his van.

12

"Another expert?" Remo kept his voice down, leaning in toward Cuvier so that Aurelia couldn't hear him from the bathroom, where she had retired to freshen up. "I'm getting tired of these side trips to nowhere."

"Jamie knows all about them loups-garous," the witness answered, sounding peevish. "You just wait and see."

"And you just thought of it?"

"He slipped my mind," said Cuvier, defensively, "with all the shit been goin' on."

"Uh-huh."

Remo glanced back at Chiun and found the Master of Sinanju Emeritus sitting three feet from the television, watching one of Reverend Rockwell's infomercials, piety and politics mixed up into a gumbo that was hard to swallow. Remo wondered what Chiun was gleaning from it, and decided it was better not to ask.

"Where are you going this time?" Chiun inquired when he was halfway to the door.

Remo could feel the angry color in his cheeks as he replied, "I have to see a man about a wolf."

It took him half an hour, winding through the crowded streets on foot, to find the address he was looking for. A block off Charles and up a narrow flight of stairs that smelled like mold or urine. He knocked and waited, knocked again and was about to leave when he heard footsteps on the other side. A little trapdoor opened to reveal one bloodshot eye.

"What you want?"

"Jamie Lafite?"

"What you want?" the owner of the eye repeated.

"I was sent here by a friend of yours, Jean Cuvier. He figured you could help me find a certain loup-garou."

The small hatch on the peephole slammed shut in a heartbeat, and he heard the tenant fumbling with some half-dozen locks and chains. The door creaked open seconds later, showing half a pallid face and one arm beckoning for Remo to come in. No sooner had he crossed the threshold onto threadbare, mousy-colored carpet than the door was closed again behind him, chains and latches rattling into place.

"You can't just talk about loup-garou like that, where anyone can hear you!"

Christ, he thought, another Cajun. This one seemed to be in his late thirties, but it was impossible to tell with any certainty. He had the waxy pale complexion of a movie vampire, evidence that he was rarely caught outside in daylight, and his long hair was parted in the middle, hanging down on both sides of his face in dusty-looking dreadlocks. He was anemic looking, skinny even by the standards of the modern diet generation.

"Jamie Lafite?"

"That's right. Who sent you here?"

"Jean Cuvier."

The pale man blinked. "Thought he was dead."

"Not yet."

The small apartment looked like something from *The Texas Chainsaw Massacre.* It had been weeks, or maybe months, since anyone had dusted, and the furniture had all the charm of cast-off items from a going-out-of-business sale at a Salvation Army thrift shop. All except the coffee table, which appeared to be a coffin, decorated with a pair of mismatched candlesticks. The centerpiece, a plastic human skull, was painted gray to make it seem more natural.

"Nice place."

"I did it all myself."

"It shows."

"How you know Jean?" Lafite inquired.

"I'm looking out for him right now," said Remo. "He's in danger."

"Tell me something I don't know."

Remo considered giving him the address for *House Beautiful* and then decided not to push his luck. "I need to find the people who are after him. The werewolf and his buddies. Got his address?"

"Loup-garou ain't people," said Lafite. "You need to get that notion out of your head right now. But they like us, in some ways. All different, see? Some got more power than others. All the more you know about what you huntin', that one special loup-garou, the better chance you got of killing them."

"I don't know all that much," said Remo, "but I'm told he lives around New Orleans somewhere, and his first name may be Leon."

"Leon!" the pale man exclaimed when he regained a vestige of composure. "Leon Grosvenor, that has to be."

"You know him?"

"I know of him," the scrawny Cajun said. "Ain't nobody really knows a loup-garou, except maybe them he's killed. For Jean's sake, I can tell you this much on the house. Some people say Leon was born with powers of the loup-garou. That make him stronger, see? Not like the ones what have to sing the songs and beg for help. Ol' Leon had it goin' in."

"That's it?"

"They lots of stories go around," Lafite went on. "Some of them contradict the other. One say Leon killed and ate his mama, but another say folks took one look at them and left them on the bayou, sink or swim. Don't make no difference after thirty, forty years, whatever. Thing you gotta remember is that Leon's had a lifetime to find out what he can do.''

Remo considered that. A lifetime? Leon had always been this way? That didn't fit into the puzzle he was building in his head. "Leon only started working for the local bosses recently," he observed.

Lafite got more nervous and his eyes twisted from side to side. "Leon came into his own. Not sure how or why. He offered up his services and did a free job. And he did it real good. That's when he went on the payroll.''

"Yeah. So when did this happen?''

Lafite's face made a grimace that was the equivalent of a shrug. "No more than nine months ago. All of a sudden he a star player. This is what I heard.''

"So where would I look for Leon?" asked Remo.

"You don't want do that, friend.''

"Humor me.''

"Most of the stories say he live out past Westwego somewhere, in the bayou country. Way back there, you don't find nothin' man, I guarantee.''

WHEN LEON GROSVENOR came back to New Orleans, hours after meeting with Merle Bettencourt, he brought other members of his pack along. The Dodge Ram van was crowded, ripe with feral smells: excitement, tension, lust. As he negotiated teeming streets, he kept an eye out for potential obstacles and danger. Once, a mounted traffic cop bent down to peer at Leon through the driver's window of the van, examined him from less than fifteen feet, then smiled and flashed a cheery thumbs-up gesture.

Leon was amazed.

Such fools these normals were.

There was no magic in the fact that he had managed to locate his quarry. Bettencourt's informers on the street had been engaged in canvassing hotels, and one of them had bribed a night-shift bellhop at Desire House to describe any "peculiar" guests. It was the ultimate in long shots during Mardi Gras, when damn near everyone was more or less peculiar, but the bellhop had recalled this group specifically: two white men, an old Chinaman and one extremely pretty girl. The female, dressed in Gypsy clothes, had shown up at Desire House on the same night Leon staged his raid against the Romany encampment outside town.

And so, he knew.

Who would the Gypsy woman run to in New Orleans, when she fled her tribe, but to the man who had come seeking after information about loups-garous? The very man, according to Merle Bettencourt's intelligence, who had prevented Leon from completing his clean sweep of targets on the present contract.

The question, then, was whether he could reach his prey in the hotel without creating so much chaos that police were summoned to the scene while he was still at work. Leon had no fear for himself, but men with guns might kill the other members of his pack, and he had no desire to jeopardize them needlessly.

No problem, he had finally decided. They could do it.

Turning down an alley half a block west of Desire House, Leon snarled and mashed his foot down on the brake pedal. Ten feet in front of him, a six-foot mummy was engaged in sex with what appeared to be a human skeleton. It took a closer look, illuminated by the van's headlights, for Leon to discover that the "skeleton" had small, firm breasts beneath her skintight costume, part of which had been unzipped and disarranged to let the sweating mummy ply his stout Egyptian tool.

The glare of headlights did not seem to faze the frantic fornicators, so Leon leaned on his horn. Two faces—one a skull, the other swathed in gauze— swiveled to face him, and the mummy flashed a bandaged middle finger toward the van, went back to thrusting with an urgency that said he wasn't getting much in all those years he spent beneath the pyramids.

That did it.

Beside Leon, the bitch was growling, anxious to be on about their business. Leon took his right foot off the brake and moved it back to the accelerator, gentle pressure on the pedal moving the van forward, inch by inch.

It took a moment for the undead lovers to discover what was happening, the visceral excitement of discovery turned into panic as the van bore down on them. The mummy disengaged, backed off a yard or so, his fleshy member bobbing in the Dodge Ram's high beams as he turned and ran. The living skeleton, for her part, scrambled for the cover of a nearby garbage bin, pale cheeks mooning Leon as she tumbled out of sight amid the trash.

He chased the mummy to an intersection, where the north-south alley met another running east-west at the rear of the hotels and shops on Tchoupitoulas Street. Leon turned right, or east, and wondered how long it would take the bandaged sprinter to decide that he was safe. If he forgot to check his fly before he hit the next main street, the mummy would be in for more exposure than he had originally planned, but who could say? He might just find another willing ghoul to help him with his problem.

Anything was possible at Mardi Gras.

The service entrance to Desire House had a little plaque beside the door for the convenience of deliverymen who lost their way. Leon drove past it, hissing at the bitch to stop her grumbling, and parked the Dodge Ram three doors farther east. The van was wearing stolen plates, but he preferred to take no chances with an eyewitness description, just in case.

The bellhop had informed Merle Bettencourt's gorilla that the foursome Leon sought had occupied a third-floor suite that fronted Tchoupitoulas Street. He had the number—304—and took it as an omen that the digits added up to seven, which was always lucky. He ignored the small voice in his head that asked, Lucky for whom?

The true risk started when he parked the van. From that point on, he and the pack would be exposed, their every move a gamble. There was no one in the alley to oppose them at the moment, but there would be staff members and guests in the hotel, and precious time would pass as he led the pack upstairs, the ruckus starting when he crashed the door to 304 and tore into the people he had come to kill.

Four targets now, instead of one. The witness, he would recognize from photographs. The Gypsy woman and the Chinaman would both be obvious on sight. The only man remaining would be Leon's nemesis, the hunter who was seeking information on the loup-garou.

This night, that one would learn more about the wolf man's power than he ever cared to know.

He left the van unlocked, the youngest male detailed to guard it, brooding in resentment when he realized that he would miss out on the kill. It mollified the youngster slightly that there would be no real time for feeding, but they rarely got the chance to kill four humans at a time, and it was still a treat to savor, if you got the chance.

The bitch was on his heels as Leon stepped out of the vehicle, the other four beside him in a moment. They were silent shadows as they moved along the alley, Leon taking point. From somewhere to their left, the muffled sounds of revelry from Tchoupitoulas Street reminded him that there was still a party going on.

So much the better, then. His pack would join in the festivities and add a little flavor of their own.

The taste of blood.

CHIUN'S MOOD HAD GONE from bad to worse since his arrival in New Orleans, but the Master of Sinanju knew he concealed it well, presenting a facade of perfect calm to the pathetic specimens around him.

It was bad enough that he was traveling with strangers, forced to stay in a hotel where noisy drunkards lurched about the halls and made commotion in the street around the clock. The desk clerk had insulted him by staring when they registered. The scrawny dwarf who led them to their so-called suite was more respectful, glancing only twice at Chiun, but he had prattled on incessantly about the "big, big party" that was going on outside.

The hotel was an older building, ill maintained, and while Chiun saw evidence of cleaning in their rooms, the maids were clearly not enthusiastic in their work.

But the television was the worst insult of all.

It was an ancient Motorola, ten years past its prime, with washed-out color and sporadic bursts of static that appeared to coincide with the flush of toilets in adjacent rooms. He could have tolerated poor reception, though, if there had been a reasonable choice of channels. As it was, despite the size and splendor of New Orleans, he could pick up only six. One broadcast constantly in French. French!

When it came down to it, New Orleans was far too French.

The holy man was on the television again, his face distorted as he waved a Bible at the camera, calling on his Christian brothers to get out and vote for God's anointed candidate. He spoke of Christian love, but with the sound turned low, his face became a twisted mask of hatred, spewing silent bile from narrow, bloodless lips.

Chiun wondered who would vote for such a man to lead them, and the answer came to him at once: Americans.

New Orleans, Chiun decided, was far too American.

Despite the revels that continued incessantly in the streets, Chiun heard the approaching pack long before they reach the room. He knew that they were not human.

"Get to cover!" he barked. Cuvier and the woman, wrapped in their own thoughts, looked at him bewildered.

"They come!" Chiun said sharply.

The pair of imbeciles scrambled for cover. Chiun heard the rush of flesh and positioned himself in the middle of the room when the door burst inward, dead bolt shattered, pieces of the locking mechanism hurled across the room to scar wallpaper.

A gray wolf lunged into the room, immediately followed by another and another. To Chiun's left, the Gypsy woman screamed again and took off running for the nearest bedroom, with a snarling canine in pursuit. The white man yelped, his wind pipe closing on him, hastily retreating to the balcony, where he would soon be trapped.

A manlike shadow loomed behind the wolf pack, filling up the doorway, but Chiun had no time to examine the intruder. A stocky canine rushed at him, leaping furiously toward his face.

REMO SMELLED TROUBLE, literally, when he walked into the lobby of Desire House. It was too subtle to have been noticed by the few jabbering guests or the night clerk nodding at his post, but Remo caught a whiff of it instantly. It was the smell of animals. Canine. A lot of them.

He took the stairs in lightning leaps and picked up the first sounds of combat when he tore through the landing for the second floor. A woman's scream, a crash of furniture, mixed up with snarling and the snapping of fangs.

Remo reached the third floor a second later. He was at the west end of the hall, perhaps one hundred feet from number 304. In the dim lighting he saw the door to his suite of rooms was open, spilling light into the corridor. The crashing continued but the snarling had turned to animal yelps and whines, and then a hulking man-shape cleared the threshold, followed rapidly by one, two, three sleek canine forms.

Remo never slowed, tearing after the fleeing attackers, but glanced through the open door of 304. The smallish parlor was totaled, furniture upended, stuffing ripped out of the sofa's lacerated cushions, coffee table halved as if by an ax-wielding lunatic. A large dog, charcoal gray, lay stretched out near the center of the room, unmoving, obviously dead.

Jean Cuvier was gaping at him from the balcony, crouched and peering through a small gap in the curtains like a Peeping Tom. Aurelia Boldiszar stood in the doorway to her sleeping room, with Chiun beside her. At their feet, another lifeless canine, this one with more brown than gray to his untidy coat.

The attackers had speed. Animal speed, goaded by blind panic. The man-thing in the lead was faster even than the others.

But not faster than Remo Williams.

The man-thing looked over his shoulder and barked an order. One of the beasts skidded to a halt at the bottom of the stairs and stood his ground, baring his teeth and growling menacingly. He started the growl, anyway, and then realized the human wasn't showing fear. Wasn't even slowing and was coming at him with the speed of an avalanche.

Then the avalanche hit him. The creature barely had time to think about snapping at the human before the human brought a fist down hard on his canine skull, reducing it to jelly.

Remo was back in the lobby. The wolf man got lucky. A couple was coming in at that moment, the doors open wide. If the wolf man and the pack had slowed enough to open a door or even to crash through the glass, Remo would have been upon them.

As it was, he was just inches behind them as they slithered between the entering couple and into the thick of Mardi Gras. Remo made a bounding leap and caught the last of the beasts by the tail. And pulled hard. Pulled fast. Between the beast's forward momentum and the strength of the yank, something had to give.

Remo quickly came upon the yowling, wounded beast in a rapidly clearing space in the street. The thing turned to face him.

"Looking for this?" Remo held up the bloody tail. "I think I'll use it to make a hat."

The beast's growl became a leopard screech, and it came at him in a bound that was fast. Very fast. Remo knew in that instant that he was facing no ordinary dog.

That confirmed his suspicions. And it pissed him off.

The dog was airborne and homing in on his throat with fangs like saw blades, but the teeth never connected with living flesh. Remo grabbed and flung the creature, which found itself flying way beyond its planned trajectory.

Up over the soaring crowd and onto the balcony of a hotel room that faced the street. It took Remo less than one second to shot put the beastie, but for a moment he thought it had been too much. The pack was gone.

He continued moving fast, slithering through the masses like some impossibly quick serpent, and his senses fanned out. He struggled to identify the countless sounds around him. Hundreds of human beings with noisy heartbeats and thunderous breathing, not to mention the miasma of intoxicated chatter.

But through it all he heard one unique sound.

Panting.

He concentrated in vain to pin down its precise location.

Time to use the old noggin.

Not his. Everybody else's.

Remo took a step up, and the step carried him six feet off the ground, where he began running along the heads of the revelers. Without thinking about it, his feet found the correct pressure level of each head of hair they landed on and used it to support him momentarily before he moved to the next.

Nothing to it. As easy as walking on water.

From his elevated vantage point it was easy to find the scattered bodies his adversaries left in their wake. The beasts and their werewolf leader were intent on getting away fast and muscling anyone and everyone out of their path. Remo stepped back onto solid earth—in his own wake he left several drunks scratching their heads and wondering what had just brushed over it.

Remo suddenly had the advantage, using the path through the crowd that the werewolf's pack was clearing, which slowed them. In a flash he came alongside the last dog in the pack and gave him an openhanded shove just between the shoulder blades. The beast was crushed into the pavement like a bug under a shoe, his spine a shambles.

The pack was veering into an alley. Remo snatched the next dog by the scruff of the neck and lifted it to shoulder level.

The dog flailed his powerful canine legs and craned this way and that, snapping his powerful jowls. It was all wasted energy. He couldn't reach far enough to sink his great canine fangs into his captor. He was helpless.

Remo didn't even notice his prisoner's struggles. He was too pissed off.

Because the alley was empty. The wolf man was nowhere to be seen.

Then he heard the squeal of tires and he sped off in search of it, into the street and then another alley. He was behind the Desire House.

There were human bodies scattered at the far end of the alley where a vehicle had gone through the crowd. Some of those people looked like they wouldn't be getting up again.

Remo had a new path to follow and sprinted along the trail of victims around another building. Another narrow street.

There had been revelers in the street, but the werewolf's vehicle hadn't even slowed. There had been nowhere for the revelers to run. Remo saw an astronaut and a green alien and a belly dancer, their costumes making a mockery of their crushed and lifeless bodies.

Remo found the werewolf's vehicle a block later, but the werewolf was gone.

There were people dead underneath the van. People were screaming and shouting while only twenty feet away the drunk partyers were oblivious to the horror. A wounded woman wearing a coconut bikini top and a grass skirt was sobbing over a pair of man's legs that were attached to a pelvis that was pinned and flattened under the front tire of the van.

Remo smelled the animal odors from the vehicle. He reached out his senses fervently again, and for a moment, through the steady clamor of voices, he thought he heard the canine panting. Then it was gone.

The hula girl started screaming. She was screaming at Remo Williams. "He's one of them! That's one of the dogs!"

Remo had virtually forgotten his prisoner, who was hanging limply in one hand, paws groping weakly at the air.

Remo moved fast into the nearest alley, too fast to be followed.

How many dead? Innocent, stupid party drunks. Just a bunch of people out having a good time, and now how many were dead?

How many of them wouldn't be dead if Remo Williams, Reigning Master of Sinanju, had put a stop to Judith White once and for all? It wasn't as though he hadn't had the opportunities.

The blood of the dead partyers was on his hands.

"And you," he said menacingly, swinging the dog underhanded and sending him flopping down the alley, scoring a perfect strike on a collection of overstuffed garbage cans. The beast scrambled to his feet with amazing speed, but his speed wasn't nearly amazing enough.

Remo was on the beast and struck with both hands at his forelegs. The legs didn't just break. They broke off. The dog yowled and frantically tried to make his front stumps work.

"I know what you are," Remo said. "Come on. Show me."

"Ohmigod! What are you doing to that poor dog?" A rotund woman in a great purple paisley muumuu and purple face paint moved to intervene. "Stop it this instant!"

Remo ignored her. His hand snicked at the beast and came back with a bloody ear. "Show me!"

The huge purple woman tromped down the alley with an illuminated wand of some sort. "Stop it! Stop torturing that poor animal!"

Remo was in a fury and when he turned on the massive purple blob, she stopped cold. Nothing she had seen in all her years of Mardi Gras prepared her for the eyes that radiated death.

"Oh, yeah? A poor animal?" He took the whining beast off the ground with one hand and slammed him against the brick wall. The blood from the severed front legs flew in twin arcs. "Show us!" Remo raged at the creature.

"Stop! Stop!" the woman sobbed.

"Show us both, you freak!"

The blazing red eyes of the dying beast looked into the black dead eyes of the Destroyer.

"Who…you…callin'…freak, freak?" the dog said.

13

The bitch howled until the stolen station wagon overflowed with her mournful cry.

"Shut up!" Leon Grosvenor growled.

She howled again, a desolate canine figure collapsed against the door in the passenger seat.

"I said, shut up!" he groused, clawing the air at her.

The bitch responded with a vicious snarl and she chomped at his hand, which he quickly withdrew to the steering wheel.

Leon Grosvenor, the alpha male, had just been subdued by his own bitch.

The other male in the car witnessed the alpha's submission.

The bitch raised her head at the roof of the Toyota and wailed like a lonely graveyard wind.

The male, with a disdainful glare at Leon in the rearview mirror, raised his voice to join her.

The bitch had forgotten how to cry real tears. There had been a time when she could truly weep, but that was before, when she was a normal.

The time of pain had changed everything.

Once she had been human. Then came the time of pain. She still didn't understand what caused it, but the time of pain was hell on Earth. It was agony beyond endurance, and yet she endured. Day after day. Week after week. She never knew how long the pain went on.

The leader was always there during that period, nursing his pack through the agonies of the change. The bitch hated him in the early days, when the pain had just started and she was still mostly normal.

Soon she forgot her reasons for despising him and she learned to love the leader. He brought her fresh meat and water. He stroked her hair as she writhed against her torment. She felt her bond growing with the alpha male.

Her human side and her wolf side both admired his compassion as he cared for his pack during that marathon of suffering that went on night after night, as the moon went from full to new to full again.

Some of them didn't survive. She saw the leader take their clenched and contorted bodies away.

But those who survived the time of pain were remade, no longer normal. Now they were these very special beasts, and together they made up a very special pack. The alpha male was accepted as the pack leader without question in those early days. He protected them and fed them and commanded them.

But he protected them no longer. Instead he took them away from the safety of their isolated bayou home and, for reasons none of them could comprehend, he transported them into the open where they were exposed. The feeding was good, but they could feed in the swamp.

They had been discomfited by the danger, but none dared oppose the alpha male.

But now he had brought them death.

The bitch understood death. And she knew that tonight, one of the dead beasts from her pack had been an individual she had known well when she was human.

Back when they had both been human, before the time of pain, before the change, before she had become the alpha male's bitch, she had been a...a wife. That was the word.

There had been a human who had been her—man? No, the word was "husband."

She and her husband had come to the bayou, back when they were human. They had come with all the others to sleep in small cloth houses and see the trees and the animals.

The husband had a name when he was a human. He had been Jasper.

The bitch didn't understand why she cared so much about Jasper. She was the alpha male's bitch now. That was simply how it was, after the time of pain. Jasper had become just another member of the pack.

Now Jasper was dead. The inexplicable pain she felt now was almost as bad as the pain of the change. It was also the most human feeling she had known in all those long months since she had stopped being normal.

"YOU MEAN it wasn't even a *dog?*" Remo asked incredulously.

"It was a wolf," Chiun explained in his singsong voice. "Anyone can tell a wolf from a dog."

"I've seen German shepherds that look a lot like that."

Chiun shook his head. "But this is a wolf. As much as it was anything."

When Remo switched to Korean he got stares from Aurelia Boldiszar, who was standing off to one side of the room silently, her arms folded beneath her breasts. Cuvier was on the threadbare couch trying not to go fetal. "The thing talked to me, Chiun," Remo said.

The old Korean showed surprise. Just for a moment, he froze. It was such a brief reaction that the Romany beauty and the Cajun ugly missed it entirely. "Spoke?"

"I forced it to."

Chiun looked at him questioningly.

"I knew the minute I saw them that they weren't natural dogs. Or wolves or whatever."

"As did I," Chiun said, looking seriously at one of the beasts sprawled dead in the hotel room. "And yet I was not inclined to converse with it."

"I wasn't after some polite chitchat. I was trying to prove something."

"What?" Chiun looked at him.

Remo switched to English without realizing it. "You know goddamn well what. That it was human."

"You kill old loup-garou," Cuvier interjected, "he change back to what he was before."

Remo shook his head morosely. "Don't count on it."

"How could one of these things talk?" Chiun continued in Korean.

"Well, it didn't do it very well, but it was good enough for me to understand," Remo insisted. "They used to be human, Little Father. Anyway, none of them was Leon Grosvenor."

Cuvier stood up fast when he heard the very non-Korean name amid the otherwise unintelligible conversation. "Leon? You didn't tell me Armand got Leon Grosvenor after me."

"You know the guy?" Remo asked.

"I hear some story," said the Cajun, sounding even more depressed. "Reckon I'm dead." He turned to Aurelia Boldiszar.

"That was no man," Aurelia said. "I saw it, felt it. We were in the presence of a devil."

"Well, he ran like one," Remo said.

Chiun made a small, exasperated clucking sound and shook his head.

"What about them other wolves?" Cuvier demanded.

"I took out a few before they slipped off. I don't know how many got away with him."

Another cluck from Chiun.

"Go shove it, Chiun, you couldn't have done any better," Remo griped.

To Cuvier he said, "Get packed."

"What?" Jean Cuvier had gone from frightened to confused, with no real change in his expression.

"Get your things. We're clearing out before the cops get here."

"Cops! *Merde!*" he blurted, and rushed to pack his suitcase.

Aurelia Boldiszar had come to Remo with nothing but the clothes she wore. She was as ready to bail out, right then, as she would ever be. While the Cajun completed his hasty packing she stood over one of the dead creatures, staring at the lolling tongue and the half-open eyes.

"These weren't ordinary wolves," she said. "They're not werewolves. Still, they may share the werewolf's spirit and commune with him in other ways. They are familiars."

"Like a witch's cat, you mean?"

"Perhaps."

"So you think this is witchcraft, whatever made the werewolf?" Remo asked. "You're saying these are spirit wolves? I told you, they're science experiments. Laboratory freaks."

"You are not listening," she said. "The loup-garou is closer to an animal than normal men. It doesn't matter what created them—he still may commune with others of his kind, draw strength from them."

"Collaborate?"

"Perhaps."

"So, he's the alpha male? Top dog?"

"The others followed him," Aurelia said. "That's all I know."

Cuvier rejoined them then, his heavy suitcase dragging down one shoulder. "Where we going?" he asked.

Remo had formed the answer in his mind already, without knowing it. "Your friend Lafite told me where we can find this thing," he said. He could have added, "more or less," but kept it to himself.

"Where is that?" The Cajun sounded gravely ill at ease.

"Where do you think? We're going on a camping trip," he said.

Remo stripped the blankets off the bed Cuvier had used and quickly wrapped the wolf corpses.

Aurelia asked, "What will you do with those?"

"Present for a friend."

ONLY WHEN THEY WERE safely back on the hermit's land, deep in the swamp with the rest of the wolves, did the leader howl with his pack. His grief was at last allowed to come out, and the sound of it echoed among the cypress trees for miles around.

For almost a year his pack had lived and run and thrived together. None of them had ever been lost, no matter what the dangers. But tonight the tables turned. So many of his brothers cut down, dead, in a matter of just minutes.

What had gone wrong?

The old Asian should have been the first to die, an easy target, but he stood his ground as if the sight of hungry wolves in his hotel room was nothing new. When the little old man struck, it came with speed that Leon's eyes could barely follow, wielding lethal force the wolf man's brain still couldn't comprehend. Within a fraction of a second Leon saw his proud young brother stretched out dead on the floor.

Another of the pack pursued the Gypsy woman as she tried to run away, when the Chinaman had struck again!

Leon couldn't have honestly described the way the old man moved from one point to another, traveling some twenty feet to intercept the second wolf before it reached the woman. Another flurry of the

old man's fists—or was it feet?—and Leon saw a
second brother crumple lifeless on the hotel carpet.

It was then that Leon knew fear.

Before Leon could react to the old man, his warning instinct shrilled and he knew help was coming
for the old Asian—someone else who carried death
in bloodstained hands. Leon's nerve broke.

He retreated, knowing that the bitch would blame
him—possibly the others, too—and that they would
be right.

He led his brothers and the bitch in a coward's
retreat—and they were struck down like cowards by
a foe even more lethal than the Chinaman. Leon had
caught a glimpse of the horror and still couldn't believe what he had seen. The younger man with the
dead eyes had ripped the tail right off one of his
brothers, then had launched the wolf into the side of
the building. With one hand. And had done it with
enough force to shatter the beast.

He and his brothers bullied their way through the
crowd, but the mass of normals slowed them down.
The one with the dead eyes caught up in seconds.
Another wolf dead from a single blow to the spine.
Another wolf snatched up by the scruff of the neck
like a housecat!

That was when a lucky break in the crowd allowed Leon to streak back to the van. He was already blinded by his own tears, which blurred the
shapes of the people that got in the way of his ve-

hicle. He simply drove through them and remembered feeling the thump of bodies bouncing off the van. Screams followed in his wake, but all Leon could think of was that his brothers were dead.

Another crowd. He didn't even try to slow. Just let the van slam into the mass of costumed humans and come to a stop—then he and his companions emerged and fled through the city of horrors.

He had taken fully half the pack with him on this trip, and now there were just two wolves remaining—the bitch and the guard wolf he had left with the van during the hotel incursion.

It took the pathetic trio twenty minutes more to find another vehicle, because most Mardi Gras participants were roaming aimlessly on foot. At last they came upon a normal in a Toyota Tercel station wagon, just emerging from an all-night liquor store. He had a paper bag in one hand, a twelve-pack in the other, and he never knew what hit him, dying on his feet before he had a chance to be afraid.

They were too frightened to feed. They scrambled into the car and raced back to the bayou to mourn.

Those were his brothers—dead!

More than that—those wolves were his *children*. He had created them.

THE WOMAN WHO CAMPED on the Hermit's land, who called herself Thena, had asked Leon to come visit her laboratory on wheels.

Leon liked Thena. She didn't flinch from him. She had something of the animal in her, too. He had begun thinking that maybe, somehow, he and the woman...

Was such a thing totally out of the question?

He, Leon, the loup-garou, the killer and hunter, was shocked when he entered the laboratory. Thena had been busy collecting animals of all shapes and sizes from the bayou, and parts of them littered the interior of the laboratory. Many parts were stored in glass laboratory freezers. Other parts were chewed to the bone and tossed in plastic bins or simply scattered on the floor and the counter.

That was when the woman, Thena, made him the offer he couldn't refuse. With one simple sip of a solution, she could make him into a true hunter—a genuine, more-than-human loup-garou.

Leon accepted the offer without hesitation.

Thena laughed delightedly, showing her strong white teeth, and then she made him something to drink.

She took a small glass laboratory bottle from one of the little refrigerators—the one with the label 942 Solution—and poured the contents into a paper cup.

"Just drink," she said.

So Leon drank.

"What's the matter?" she asked as he sat heavily down on one of the folding chairs.

"It hurts," he said.

She looked confused. "Bad?"

"Not too bad."

But it lasted a long time. Hours. And he felt sore for weeks afterward. His face and his arms. His very bones hurt. He didn't know it that night, but his bones were changing. Lengthening.

But that night he became a true loup-garou. He and the woman hunted together, and she was delighted with his new strength and speed.

"My wonderful wolf man!" she exclaimed happily when he emerged from the water with a struggling gator draped over one shoulder.

Together they feasted on the gator, still weakly struggling as they tore it apart with their talons and teeth. Thena, he found, might look entirely normal, but she could kill and devour prey like a tigress.

On the way home, she told him to kill the hermit. Then the bayou would be all theirs.

"It already is," Leon argued. "He'll let us do as we please."

"I can't allow him to know what has occurred," Thena said with a heartless shrug.

Leon Grosvenor wanted very much to please her. But kill the old hermit, the only father he had ever known? "Never," he declared.

"You will do as I command!" Thena snapped, suddenly furious.

"Not that," Leon responded. They argued, but Leon stood his ground.

Thena became very quiet the rest of the way home.

THEY PARTED COMPANY that night with short words, and Leon waited in the woods a few hundred paces from the RV laboratory, then realized she might smell him. He moved into the nearest body of water, a stagnant pool of murk, and sank almost completely.

Near dawn he heard the woman emerge from the laboratory and scamper off into the bayou.

When Leon entered the laboratory, he found her notes. "Canis lupus 942 standard dilution too potent. Subject improved to dangerous extremes. Physical traits outstanding but diminished obedience and enhanced self-control characteristics make subordination of subject inadequate."

There was much more that Leon couldn't understand. Latin phrases, something about genetics, but the phrase "termination of subject" caught his eye.

What angered him the most was that she had never liked him. She had just used him. For a damn experiment. And now she was planning to kill him. Leon had thought that he had finally found companionship—someone like him. But every word she said was a lie.

Then Leon got a brilliant idea.

He would *make* himself some companions.

HE LEFT THE LABORATORY with a specially insulated pouch filled with glass bottles from the little refrigerator. Dry ice packs fitted inside to keep the bottles cold.

Heading for the hermit's cabin, he smelled the blood a half mile away. He found Thena squatting on the sagging porch with a chunk of red, bloody meat in her mouth.

"Join me," she called from the porch.

Leon stood in the trees, great sorrow over the loss of the hermit competing with a savage desire to join the feast. The blood scent called him like a siren song.

Then he saw Thena freeze, her eyes locking on the insulated pack. She knew at once, of course, what Leon had done.

"Give that to me." Her voice was cold and commanding.

"Never."

"Give it to me now!"

Compelled by his need to obey this strange woman, and burning with desire to sink his teeth into the fresh, warm kill, Leon did the hardest thing he had ever done.

He left.

Because to stay, he knew, would somehow mean his death.

The woman came after him.

Leon ran, and he was faster than she was. He

laughed at her from the distance. "I am stronger than you are!" he taunted.

He left her behind in the night, running miles into the bayou. Cautiously he returned in the daylight to find Thena and her mobile laboratory were gone.

He had scared her off.

The hermit was no longer so attractive a meal. He was cold and growing sour, but Leon filled his belly anyway and put the remains in the water where the gators would dispose of it. Then Leon went looking for campers.

He knew of a university field camp where the grad students spent their weekends taking samples of the water and plants and bugs. They made measurements of the depth of the bayou, set up no-kill traps, set up nets with lights to trap night insects. It all looked pointless to Leon.

Somehow, he liked the idea of using these brainy types for what he had in mind.

He found their camp deserted in midmorning. A collapsible five-gallon water jug was in the shade. Leon emptied it.

The bottles in the insulated pack were a little different from what he remembered, but the label still said 942. He poured every last drop of the stuff into the water jug.

The students returned, dirty and hot from a morning of toiling in the swamp. There were more of them than he had expected. Mostly men in their midtwenties. Two older men were addressed by the others as "Professor." One beautiful young woman stayed close by the side of a strong, bright-eyed young man.

One by one they began to help themselves to the water. It took fifteen minutes before the first one fell to the ground, screaming in agony. Soon they were all stricken, on the earth writhing and moaning, racked with monstrous pain.

Leon ran through the bayou this way and that, whimpering and whining in panic. By the time he returned to the camp the old men were already dead, their bodies locked in tight, contorted balls. The others were helpless in their agony—or unconscious from the pain.

It had not been like this for him! There was some pain. He still hurt, in fact. But nothing like this!

Only then did he bother to consider the labels on the bottles he had emptied into the water jug. They said 942, just like the bottle he had drunk from in Thena's laboratory. But his bottle had said "solution." What did that mean? Why would the word "solution" be on a bottle?

Then he remembered what the word "solution" might mean in that context. What he had consumed was a diluted solution of the 942. And what he had put in the campers water jug was plain, pure 942. Full strength.

What would undiluted 942 do to them? Would it kill them all, like the old men?

Over the next few weeks, a couple more of them did die. The rest of them were in such constant agony that they certainly wished they were dead.

Leon carried them to the hermit's shack, two painwracked bodies at a time. Soon the tiny structure was filled with moaning human worms too intoxicated with misery to even get to their feet.

Those who died were fed to the gators.

The screaming really started when their bones began to push through their skin. That was about the second week. There would be blood and thrashing and finally merciful unconsciousness. The wound would close in a matter of hours, but soon another bone would penetrate to the outside world.

The screaming never stopped. Leon thought he was going as insane as the students. He fed them with all the fresh meat he could find. He bathed them with buckets of swamp water to wash away the blood and their own waste.

It was only in the third week that he began to see clearly what was happening. The students were changing, just as he had changed, but they were changing faster and they were changing completely.

They were becoming true wolves.

The bitch was the first to be done with it, six weeks after the metamorphosis commenced. She was a real wolf now. She went to her still-prostrate lover, gave him a sniff and then walked unsteadily to Leon.

She licked his foot.

The next day, she went into the bayou with him and they hunted together for less than an hour. She was exhausted and invigorated when she came back with her hare, and she devoured it in front of the others.

Over the next several days, they all began to find their strength. The hunting parties became larger. And then one day the entire group of transformed creatures left the stench-filled hermit's shack all together.

They were a wolf pack.

And Leon was the alpha wolf.

And the bitch was his bitch.

Life was good.

He had been happy then, and he foresaw a long lifetime of hunting and running with his pack.

But less than a year later, much of his pack was dead, and the others no longer looked at him with the adoration and obeisance he was accustomed to.

Revenge would be sweet, but more importantly revenge was absolutely necessary if he intended to regain the trust of the pack.

The Chinaman would have to die. So, too, the woman who had managed to elude them at Desire House, the malicious Gypsy witch. And especially the younger man who ran faster than a wolf and killed with a touch.

He and the Chinaman were of a kind, but what that kind was Leon Grosvenor did not know. One thing for sure. Those two weren't normals.

REMO STOPPED at the first gas station outside town. It was a huge, brightly lit complex with something like eighteen gas pumps. Several of them were being used by rowdy partyers who shouted and whooped as they gassed up.

He found the pay phone at the far side of the parking lot and leaned on the one button. Somehow this connected him to Folcroft Sanitarium and the offices of CURE.

"Lucky Dollar Store and Incense Emporium," said a voice in heavily accented English.

Remo looked at the phone. Looked at the keypad. Had he accidentally held down the wrong button?

"Hello?" the voice said. "Hello?"

"Is Harold home?" Remo asked.

"Remo, it's about time," Harold W. Smith said suddenly.

"What's with the hired help who answered the phone?" Remo demanded.

"That's a new automated system for weeding out undesirable calls," Smith explained quickly. "Believe it or not, there are people out there who have nothing better to do than see what happens if they hold down their 1 button. The system will let you through as soon as you speak and it recognizes your voiceprint. Now give me your report.''

''Fine, thanks,'' Remo complained. ''The report is I just spent my evening chasing wolves around N'awlins.''

''Yes, we've been getting the reports of several wolf attacks in the French Quarter,'' Smith said. ''Also about the attack on the Romany camp. I spoke with Master Chiun about that earlier. I wish you would have phoned more quickly, Remo. Master Chiun is not, er, precise when it comes to details.''

''Yeah, well, I was busy.'' Remo quickly ran down the events that had occurred since arriving in New Orleans. He ended by describing his questioning of the last wolf.

''You questioned it?'' Smith asked dubiously.

''I tortured it, if you must know,'' Remo said.

''And?'' Smith asked noncommittally.

''It talked.''

''It *talked?*''

''Yeah.''

''The wolf *talked?*''

''Read my effing lips. It effing talked, Smitty. The thing used to be human. Dr. White's *really* outdone herself this time.''

''Remo,'' Dr. Smith said quietly, ''I agree that Judith White achieved some shocking physiological changes in her subjects. But to make a man into a wolf—it seems unlikely.''

"Figure it out for yourself," Remo said. "I've got one of the chatterboxes in the trunk of the rental. Test him out. You're gonna find all kinds of DNA or genetic material or whatever little buggies people normally have that wolves don't.''

"Is it—?''

"Dead as a doornail, and it'll be getting ripe by morning. Have somebody come pick it up.'' Remo gave Smith the location in Westwego he expected to be leaving the car and described his plans for moving into the bayou—and forcing Leon Grosvenor into the open.

"All right.'' Smith sighed heavily. "It'll take some doing, but I'll have it picked up and sent to a private lab for testing. When will you be able to report in again?''

"First phone booth I find in the bayou,'' Remo said.

"How will you get the test results?'' Smith asked. "They could be revealing as to the nature of these creatures.''

"I know their nature, and it ain't natural,'' Remo said. "My objective is to make them dead. Except Leon. Him I want to ask questions and then make dead.''

"You still think he'll give you a lead on Judith White?'' Smith asked.

Remo felt grim and he said, "No. But it can't hurt to ask. Can't hurt me, anyway. Now, Leon, it's gonna hurt."

"You sure about this, Reverend?"

"Course I'm sure," the portly televangelist told Jeremiah Smeal. "It's perfect, son. I know exactly what I'm doin'. Just you wait and see."

The Reverend Rockwell could sympathize with Smeal's misgivings, staring at the empty auditorium and hearing all that whoop-to-do outside. As far as he could figure out, no one had ever tried to stage a mass revival in New Orleans during Mardi Gras, much less right smack-dab in the middle of the French Quarter, but that was what appealed to Rockwell. He would be the first, which meant he would be noticed. That meant free publicity!

The campaign TV spots were eating up his money faster than he had expected, and he didn't like those rumors that the IRS was gearing up to scrutinize his books at JBN. Rockwell had a team of born-again accountants handling the money side of things, with strict instructions not to leave a paper trail, but there was always something for a bloodhound to latch on to if you let him sniff around for very long.

Rockwell's temporary answer to the twofold problem, ready cash and federal scrutiny, was Mission Mardi Gras, two nights of hellfire and damnation—with an option for a third night, if the crowds were large enough—that would replenish empty coffers and supply him with a whole new audience. The program would be run in its entirety on JBN, of course, but local TV news had also been alerted to stand by for something big from Reverend Rockwell.

The auditorium was one block south of Charles, near Audubon Park. It wasn't huge compared to some of the New Orleans theaters and concert halls, but Rockwell had chosen it both for its proximity to the French Quarter and for the nightly rental rate, which he found very reasonable.

And with any luck at all, there would be news cameras on hand to catch the show.

As if in answer to his thoughts, Smeal said, "You think they'll come?"

Rockwell didn't have to ask who they were. News people with minicams. The sacred talking heads.

"They'll come," the televangelist replied. "God told me so."

That wasn't strictly true, of course. The scheme had come to him while he was on the toilet, battling the chronic constipation that had plagued him ever since he tossed his halo in the ring to run for governor. Rockwell had been straining like a modern Jacob wrestling with the angel and refusing to give up before he got his blessing, when it hit him. First, the flood gates opened down below, and then a light went on upstairs: a Mardi Gras revival! Free airtime!

He would present the greatest story ever told to fans and new recruits alike, while just outside the door old Satan staged his biggest party of the year.

He scanned the silent auditorium, imagining a crowd that spilled into the aisles, all swaying, chanting, lifting hands to Jesus, opening their wallets, purses, cracking piggy banks.

"I want this whole place SRO tomorrow night," the reverend told his flunky.

"SRO?"

"Standing room only," Rockwell explained, and offered up a silent prayer for patience in the face of rank stupidity. "I don't care if you have to drag them off the street in costume," he continued. "Better yet, I want a few of them in costume. Maybe half a dozen."

"Right," Smeal said. "What for?"

"To show the power of the word," Rockwell said, remembering that patience was a virtue of the saints. "Poor sinners out there drinkin', fornicatin' in the streets, dressed up like demons out of hell itself, but even they find Jesus in New Orleans. Even they receive his message. Even they are saved."

He fell into the singsong pattern of his TV sermons automatically, from force of habit. "Even they can testify to Christ's redeeming glory. Everyone out there in television land will feel the power of His message."

"Amen!" enthused Jeremiah Smeal.

The Reverend Rock was on a roll.

"YOU SURE about this, Elmo?" Maynard Grymsdyke sounded dubious.

"Hell, yes, I'm sure," Breen said. "The polls tell
me we're twenty points ahead of that ol' son of a
bitch in New Orleans, nearly twenty-five statewide.
Besides, it's Mardi Gras."

"I still think—"

Elmo frowned and raised an open hand to silence
Grymsdyke. "Just this once," he said, "don't
think."

"But Elmo—"

"Son, I been in Louisiana politics for almost forty
years," Breen said. "One thing I know beyond a
shadow of a doubt is how to get things done. I don't
know how they play the game where you come
from, but here in Louisiana, money greases the machine. This weekend, I'll be spending time with
three of our top five supporters in the state."

It would have been all five, but two of them were
sadly "unavailable"—one shacked up with his latest teenage girlfriend, while the other had a sit-down
with a group of silent partners in Miami. Breen
would catch them in another week or two.

"I understand, sir. But a hunting trip? I mean, it's
not—"

"Politically correct?" Breen finished for him.
"Jesus, Maynard, why don't you wake up and smell

the coffee for a change? You think the folks who matter give a damn about all that shit down here?''

"So, you'll be out of touch all weekend," Maynard said, deciding it was useless to protest further.

"*We'll* be out of touch," the would-be governor corrected him. "You're going with us, Maynard."

Grymsdyke shook his head fervently. "The campaign! I've got a thousand things..."

Breen smiled. "None of that, now. It'll do you good to meet the boys, get out and breathe some fresh air for a change, instead of all this air pollution shit. I got an extra 12-gauge you can use. Who knows, you may get lucky. Make a man out of you yet."

Grymsdyke flushed, insulted and uncomfortable with the plan, but he knew better than to argue.

"I swing by for you in the limo," Breen said. "Make it half-past four, so we aren't late to meet the others."

"Half-past 4:00 a.m." Grymsdyke's enthusiasm knew no bounds. "And where is it we're going, once again?"

"Out to the bayou country, Maynard. Down below Westwego. It's a different world, believe me. You'll see things you never seen before, I guarantee."

14

The bayou country of Louisiana bears no great resemblance to Florida's Everglades. The Glades are mostly open to the sky, the water rarely more than five or six feet deep. Louisiana's bayous, by comparison, are dark and dreary places, sheltered by the looming cypress trees and mangroves that were old before the first conquistadors arrived with swords and muskets to "convert" the natives and turn them into slaves. Some of the swamp country has yielded, through the intervening centuries, retreating from the swarm of men and their machines, but much remains intact, still waiting for the men to drop their guard.

Remo thought the whole place smelled, well, swampy.

Their vessel followed Highway 90 to Westwego, on the fringe of bayou country. Most of the Louisiana coastline was consumed by swampland, dark and dangerous, with scattered settlements of fishermen and bankrupt shrimpers.

"I thought you said this tub was new," Remo complained.

Jean Cuvier peered back at Remo from beneath the long bill of a faded baseball cap. He seemed at home behind the wheel of the small rented cabin cruiser.

"I don't recollect saying she was new," the Cajun said. "New boat in these parts, I don't reckon you can find at any price. This baby gets us where we need to go, I guarantee."

That was another thing. It had seemed curious to Remo that the Cajun's "old friend" in Westwego didn't bat an eye when Cuvier showed up in such strange company, after a year in hiding from the mob, and asked to rent a boat. It smelled like a setup, and while Cuvier was wise enough to lie about their destination, Remo guessed that it wouldn't take much detective work for his good buddy at the rental dock to find out where they went and pass the word along. The swamp was full of eyes. Remo and Cuvier still had to get a fix on Leon Grosvenor's lair before they even knew where they were going, much less how long it would take.

"You're taking quite a chance," said Remo, "checking in with your old pals like this. What makes you think they won't sell you out to Bettencourt, or try to pick up the bounty themselves?"

"Truth is, this is my only chance," said Cuvier. "If you don't get Leon before he gets to me, I'm good as dead. These other folks ain't family now. They know all about my beef with Armand, but I reckon they hear Leon's in it, too. That will keep them off, I'm pretty sure."

"And if you're wrong?"

"Dead's dead," the Cajun said. "I just as soon get shot as be ate by old loup-garou."

"And if these folks are scared of Leon," Remo pressed, "what makes you think they'll tell us where to find him?"

"That's called 'head's I win and tails you lose,'" Cuvier said. "They figure Leon's looking for us and they sent us out there, they be doing him a favor. Make it easier for him to kill us, like. Now, if we get lucky and ol' Leon bite the bullet, they still come out clean. No loup-garou around to hassle them no more."

"Good thinking, I guess," Remo said doubtfully.

"You sell these bayou people short," said Cuvier, "you make a big mistake, I guarantee."

Their next stop was a mile or so inside the bayou proper. They had been traveling southwestward from the rental dock. Remo wondered if Cuvier had any idea where they were and where they were going.

Their pit stop didn't seem to be a settlement. No houses were visible, nothing, in fact, except a kind of general store that stood up on stilts above the water. A wooden dock protruded from the front porch of the store, and Remo tied off the cabin cruiser as Cuvier prepared to go ashore.

"Want company?" he asked.

"I best do this myself," the Cajun said.

It was another gamble, putting Cuvier within reach of the locals. Remo was still uncertain whether they would try to kill him or if Cuvier was working some weird angle of his own. But his reading of the Cajun told him Cuvier was doing everything within his power to survive.

Three men were lounging on the shaded front porch of the store. Remo thought they looked like extras from *Deliverance* or *Southern Comfort,* or maybe *Soggy Bottom USA.* Each was in faded denim overalls, two were barefoot, one without a shirt to hide his scrawny chest and shoulders. Thankfully there didn't seem to be a banjo in the house.

He leaned against the cabin cruiser's rail and eavesdropped as the three men greeted Cuvier without apparent animosity. One of the locals cocked his head toward Chiun, sitting the forward deck, and made a reference to "the Chinaman old enough to be the first emperor of China." They had no way of knowing Chiun could hear every word they said perfectly.

"No killing," Remo pleaded under his breath as the porch-sitters chortled at their tremendous wit. Chiun could also hear Remo, but the old Master of Sinanju ignored all of them.

A damn good thing, thought Remo, after their near miss with trouble in Westwego. Cuvier's old friend had smiled at Chiun and cranked the volume up a notch, apparently believing it would help the old man understand what he was saying. More specifically, the redneck said that he had never rented to Vietnamese before, although he heard they did some righteous shrimping on the Gulf, and he didn't believe in holding folks responsible for what had happened in the war.

Chiun had been examining the combination rental shop and bait shack with the keen eye of a demolition engineer—preparing to dismantle it by hand, one sagging timber at a time—when Remo managed to dissuade him.

Remo was surprised at Chiun's tolerance, but it was just a matter of time until some lippy local yokels encountered the casual wrath of the Master of Sinanju.

"Do you think they'll help?"

He had sensed Aurelia arrive at his elbow, and it wasn't a bad sensation at all. She was close enough to touch, if either one of them was so inclined.

"He seems to think so. I'm reserving judgment."

"I think you will find what you are looking for," Aurelia said.

"And what about yourself?" he asked.

"I must be done with this before I can rejoin my people," she replied.

"That's it?"

Aurelia frowned at him and said, "What else?"

He was distracted from the question by the sound of Cuvier returning, boot heels clomping on the wooden pier. The cabin cruiser shuddered as the Cajun landed aboard.

"So, what's the word?" asked Remo.

"Word is," Cuvier replied, "we got ourselves a loup-garou."

MERLE BETTENCOURT was feeling more uneasy by the minute as the day wore on. He kept expecting one of those collect calls from Atlanta, and he didn't have a clue what he would tell Armand about the previous night's screwup on Tchoupitoulas Street.

Armand ought to take the blame himself. He insisted they have old Leon and his bowwows handle it, as much because Leon already had the contract, cash up front, as from Armand's desire to see his enemies destroyed by something from Friday Night Fright Theater.

Instead of good news in the paper this morning, Bettencourt was looking at a report of several wolves that had been killed on Tchoupitoulas Street and several dead and wounded Mardi Gras revelers.

The night clerk at Desire House told reporters and police that he had three guests missing in the wake of what appeared to be some weird, destructive prank. The police were interested in the absent

strangers—two white men and "one old Chinaman," the night clerk said—in an effort to clear up
the matter of the wolves. No mention of Jean Cuvier
by name. The white men had been registered as
Remo Gillman and Alex Holland, the Chinaman as
Kim Ho Sun.

Damn comedians.

Merle's fury, generated by the first reports from
Tchoupitoulas Street, had settled down enough that
he could think straight and focus on his problem
rather than his rage.

Leon had to go. That much was obvious, and Bettencourt no longer cared what Armand thought
about his so-called loup-garou. The hairy bastard
was a menace, flubbing vital contracts, leaving dead
wolves as his calling card. Merle didn't intend to let
the cops take Leon, wouldn't see the wolf man turn
and rat him out, as others had betrayed Armand.

Before he took off on a wolf hunt, though, there
was another problem to deal with. In the past two
hours there had been three phone calls to his office,
each describing a peculiar foursome headed for the
bayou country southwest of New Orleans. Two
white men, some kind of Oriental and a woman
dressed in Gypsy clothes. Merle didn't know what
that was all about, but he recalled Leon's recent hassle with the Gypsies near Westwego and assumed
the woman was now mixed up with Cuvier and his
bodyguards somehow.

The foursome had acquired a boat, and they were well into the back country by now. His spotters had them moving roughly south-southwest. Even though they traveled on the water, it would be no great challenge for a team of swamp-bred Cajuns to track them. Nip their little half-assed expedition in the bud.

Merle had already picked the shooters he would use, the same boys he should have sent the previous night to Tchoupitoulas Street. A six-man team was overkill, no doubt about it, but he wanted no more screwups, nothing to make Armand think he couldn't handle it. If this petition for a new trial made the grade, and Armand walked because the feds were suddenly bereft of witnesses, Merle knew he would be set for life.

Leon was history. He simply didn't know it yet.

That shaggy freak had seen his last full moon.

THE HUNTING PARTY was assembled on a private dock on the outskirts of Westwego. Four limousines had come and gone, depositing their passengers and cargo: backpacks and camping gear from L.L. Bean, long guns in hand-tooled leather cases from Abercrombie & Fitch. Four of the six men standing on the dock wore tailored camouflage, including long-billed caps, and heavy boots designed for rugged wear. Each of the four wore Ray-Ban sunglasses, carried long survival knives and shiny semiautomatic pistols, either on the hip or slung under one arm. They smoked cigars and laughed politely at one another's jokes.

The last two members of the team stood out. One was the guide, a wiry swamp rat with a patch over the empty socket where his left eye used to be and a two-day growth of beard. Decked out in rumpled Army-surplus fatigue pants, he stood apart and waited for the others to complete their socializing. Every now and then he spit a stream of brown tobacco juice into the water, wiping his lips with his sleeve.

Then there was Maynard Grymsdyke, in denim shirt and jeans, a jacket he would have to shed once daylight started heating up the swamp and a pair of brand-new hiking boots that hurt his feet. It seemed impossible that he could already have blisters, but his heels were killing him, and he had only walked a few steps, first from his apartment to the limo, then to the dock.

It was damn chilly in the predawn darkness. The cold mist rolling off the bayou dampened Maynard's spirits—as if he needed any help in that department. He was sleepy, cold and generally miserable, revolted by the prospect of the next two days with this miserable company.

The tallest of Breen's guests was Marshall Dillon. "No relation," he was quick to tell each new acquaintance before miming a fast draw for some nonexistent movie camera. Dillon was the founder, president and CEO of Petro-Gas Conglomerates, which dominated oil and natural gas leases from Port Arthur, Texas, to Biloxi, Mississippi. At fifty-six, Dillon had indulged himself along life's highway, and his six-foot-four frame wasn't quite tall enough to stretch three hundred pounds and make it look like muscle. When the oilman laughed he had a tendency to spray saliva, but he was so filthy rich that no one seemed to mind…at least, until his back was turned and he was out of earshot.

Hubert Murphy was a huge name in the Southern banking world, but reputation didn't reflect size. A veritable dwarf to Dillon's giant, Murphy might have been five-three in cowboy boots, and everything about him seemed a trifle underweight, except the small paunch that he had developed from good living and a lack of daily exercise. Murphy wore steel-rimmed bifocals that made his eyes appear to shrink or bulge each time he moved his head. His politics, well known to Maynard Grymsdyke, placed him somewhere to the right of Heinrich Himmler when it came to taxes and social welfare.

The last of Breen's supporters to accept his weekend invitation was a portly man of average size named Victor Charles. He made his home in Baton Rouge, where he could keep an eye on the state government from day to day, and his most striking feature was a total lack of striking features. Grymsdyke guessed that Victor Charles was closer to the fifty mark than forty, but he could as easily have pegged the guess at thirty-five or sixty. Charles had that kind of face, ageless and bland, the next best thing to nondescript, but there was nothing commonplace about his bank accounts. His first few million had been made in cotton, then he branched out into big-time shrimping in the Gulf. A year or two back his politics became more extreme, to the ongoing concern of his allies. When shrimp prices plummeted forty percent due to a surge in overseas imports of cheap farm-raised shrimp, Charles went on a rampage. Almost single-handedly he funded a slew of illegal-dumping lawsuits against several Asian governments, which made him a hero to scores of bankrupt bayou shrimpers. Truth was, he cared a lot less about their livelihood than about getting even with the foreigners who kept interfering with his country.

Grymsdyke wouldn't have chosen these three as companions for a two-day bayou killing spree, but he was wise enough to know that Breen's safari had no more to do with hunting than it did with acid rain or women's rights. Elmo was bent on strengthening his bonds with three men who could help him buy the statehouse in November, making sure they understood that he was on their side. Before the hunting trip was over, Grymsdyke had no doubt that new deals would be struck, with cash exchanged for promises that Breen could only keep if he was governor. It was the way things worked in politics, on both sides of the Mason-Dixon line, and Grymsdyke had no personal objections to the game.

Their shifty-looking guide, answering to Jethro, no last name, expelled another stream of murky fluid from between pursed lips and checked the eastern sky, where gray dawn had begun to show itself.

"We best be going," he said, and moved off toward the cabin cruiser they had rented.

Sweet Sixteen was stenciled on the stern, but Maynard Grymsdyke would have bet that twenty years or more had passed since this tub had its sixteenth birthday party. It was still afloat, and that was something, but he was relieved that they wouldn't be putting out to sea, where sudden squalls blew up from nowhere and the depths were full of sharks. If *Sweet Sixteen* went down, he'd find himself in quiet, brackish water filled with alligators, water moccasins and leeches.

What a break.

"You ready, Maynard?" Elmo asked him, putting on a crooked smile he never showed the TV cameras.

"Yes, sir," said Grymsdyke. Adding to himself, As ready as I'll ever be.

LUKE SEVERIN HAD BRIEFED his team while they were checking out their hardware, stripping auto-

matic weapons down and reassembling them with
practiced ease, loading the magazines, a couple of
them sharpening long knives for close-up work.
They heard him without seeming to, absorbed the
sparse details and gave them back almost verbatim
when he quizzed them.

The boss had filled him in on how important this
job was, both parts of it. First up, they were supposed to find four people—one of them a rat who
had rolled over for the Feds and sent Armand to
prison. They were somewhere in bayou country
southwest of Westwego. Once those four had been
taken care of, Severin's crew was ordered to proceed
and take out Leon Grosvenor.

It was the second part that troubled Luke the
most. If anyone had asked, he would have said that
he was no more superstitious than his fellow Cajuns,
less so than his daddy or his granddaddy before him.
Lounging in a comfy booth at Cooter's, in the Quarter, sipping bourbon on the rocks, Luke might have
said that he didn't believe in loups-garous. It was
another story, though, when you were out in the
bayou, shaded from the sun by looming trees and
veils of Spanish moss, the smell of death and rot
filling your nostrils.

In the bayou country, Luke may well have said
that anything was possible. But he would never have
admitted he was scared.

They had sufficient firepower to do the job, God

knew. Two M-16s, three Uzis and a 12-gauge shot-gun with extended magazine that held nine rounds. In addition to the long guns, each man had at least one pistol. Florus carried twin .45s in double shoulder holsters. Little Remy set the record for their hunting party, with a Glock slung underneath one arm, a sleek Beretta on his right hip and a Colt .380 Mustang tucked into his boot.

No silver bullets, but Luke didn't think they would need any. Put enough rounds into some guy—any guy—and he'd go down, werewolf or not.

"Don't like this much," Jesper said, moving up beside him at the cabin cruiser's starboard rail. They had been chugging over stagnant water for the best part of an hour, scenery scarcely altered by the passage of their boat or time. For all Luke knew, they had been traveling in endless circles.

"What's to like?" he asked Jesper. "We do a job, go on home, get paid."

"I reckon you know exactly what I'm talkin' about," Jesper replied.

"Leon?"

Jesper brought up one hand to cross himself, an awkward gesture that revealed a lack of practice during recent years. "Damn foolish sendin' us to kill ol' Leon. How we supposed to kill a loup-garou?"

"First thing," Luke said, "you best forget them fairy stories. Keep your powder dry and hit what you be aiming at."

Jesper wasn't convinced. "My grandpa try to kill a loup-garou one time, before I was born. Got right up close and let him have both barrels. Damn thing mauled him anyhow, got clean away. Grandpa weren't good for much of nothing after that."

Luke was almighty tempted to suggest that Jesper's grandfather had belted too much moonshine, maybe sneaked up on a panther in the swamp and missed his shot before the damn thing turned on him, but he wasn't about to start an argument with Jesper when he needed every man behind him, giving 110 percent.

"Do like I told you," Luke instructed. "When we got him, take good aim and just keep shootin' till he don't get up no more. That's all you gotta do."

"I surely hope you right."

I hope so, too, Luke thought.

A NERVOUS CAJUN BROUGHT the word to Leon shortly after noon. The bitch was first to smell him coming, and she was in no mood to take prisoners, but Leon warned her off and listened to the man. The Cajun got his regular twenty dollars and left unmolested—he was the closest thing Leon had to a telephone and Leon needed him.

Four people were coming for him, looking for him on his own home ground. One of them was the witness he had failed to kill in two attempts. The sawed-off Chinaman was with him, and the Gypsy woman. Plus another man, the one who had pursued him like a demon through the streets of the Quarter and killed more of his dogs.

It seemed impossible to Leon that the outsiders would find his lair. That meant he would be forced to scour the swamp himself and run them down, but that was fine.

He needed to do something, and damn quick, before the surviving members of his pack began to think he was completely ineffectual. Their trust had already been shaken, and one of the older males was casting little sidelong glances back and forth, between the bitch and Leon, trying to decide if it was time to make a challenge to be leader of the pack.

Just try it, Leon thought. He wasn't done yet, no matter how it looked.

But he was getting there. Another failure like the one on Tchoupitoulas Street, and he would have no pack to lead. It wouldn't even matter if they trusted him at that point, since they'd all be dead.

He missed his brothers who had died on the abortive mission to Desire House. He would find the ones responsible and punish them, share their destruction with the pack.

But not share too much. He wanted the pack to see him bring down the hunters. A show of force such as that would put to rest any ambitions the other males had to take him down and assume the leadership of the pack.

He was top dog around here, and he was going to prove it.

He was looking forward to taking out the white hunter, but especially the little Oriental.

It had been years since Leon ate Chinese.

15

Darkness didn't descend upon the bayou country by degrees, but rather closed in like massive velvet curtains drawn across the sky. If you were sailing open water, stars were sometimes visible between the treetops. But on what passed for dry land in the swamp, the canopy blocked any but the most persistent moonbeams, cloaking all in blackness more akin to midnight at the bottom of a coal mine than to any forest glade. A campfire drove back some of the shadows, but at the same time attracted swarms of insects.

Remo was sitting back from the circle of the fire, leaving Jean Cuvier to curse and swat mosquitoes as they settled on his skin. When the Cajun noticed that none of the insects were pestering Remo he tried sitting back from the fire, too. It didn't make a difference.

"They just don't like how I taste, I guess," Remo said.

Chiun had opted to remain aboard the cabin cruiser, tethered to a mangrove root some fifty yards downstream. His explanation—that a night of sleeping on the sodden ground was "detrimental to these ancient bones"—fooled Remo not at all. He knew about the Casio handheld TV the Korean carried, and decided from the angry tone of Chiun's voice, audible across the water, that reception in the swamp was nothing to write home about.

He heard Aurelia coming up behind him, and was pleased to note that she avoided making excess noise. An average man wouldn't have heard her footsteps on the spongy ground and would have been surprised.

"Watch out for snakes," he said before she had a chance to speak.

"I've never been afraid of animals," she told him. "Want some company?"

"Suits me."

She stood beside him, touching-close, and he could smell her in the darkness. Not perfume—she hadn't worn any since they had met—but an enticing, healthy woman smell. He wondered if a loup-garou could track her by that scent alone, or if he needed footprints for a guide.

"You're not afraid, either," she said.

"Not yet."

"Do you believe we'll find him?"

"One way or another," Remo said. "He may find us. It all comes out the same."

"You're pretty confident." Her own voice seemed to harbor doubt.

"We beat him once," he said. "He lost some of his little pets last time."

"I have been wondering," Aurelia said, "how much of that was luck, and how much skill."

He didn't answer her. The silence stretched between them for a while, before the Gypsy spoke again.

"This is a little strange," she said, "don't you agree?"

"Which part? The werewolf, or his working for the Cajun mafia?"

"Our hunting him like this," she said. "I mean, we really don't know where we're going, do we? All he has to do is lie back like a spider, waiting for us. Make a move when it's to his advantage, and he has us where he wants us."

"That's assuming he's still here, or ever was," said Remo.

"Oh, he's here, all right." There was a tremor in Aurelia's voice. "I feel him. Not on top of us, just yet, but getting near."

"You could have stayed back in New Orleans," he reminded her, "or gone to find your people."

"And what good would that do? If he wants me, there's no place for me to hide. It's cost my family too much already."

Remo said nothing.

"You blame yourself for that?"

He looked at her. In the blackness of the night his pupils dilated to an extraordinary degree, allowing him to see with catlike clarity where the Romany woman could only see his shadow. She thought the darkness hid her expression, and so allowed her interest, and her simmering passion for him to show on her face.

"You think," she continued, "that by coming to me, you led the loup-garou to me. Which makes you responsible for the deaths."

Remo shook his head. "I could have stopped this long before that, and I didn't. That's why I'm responsible for your dead."

She was surprised. "You could have stopped the wolf man before this?"

"I could have stopped the woman who made him into what he is. She was a scientist. She tampered with genetics. She somehow put animal DNA in the blender and came up with a secret potion to turn people into whatever she wanted them to be."

The Romany woman considered this for a moment. "You mock me," she asked gently, "when you try to tell me that this thing of magic and spirit is instead just a freak of science."

"Hey, I was being the victim here, not you. Remember, poor, guilty Remo?"

She was waiting for an answer.

"I'm not mocking you, Aurelia. What I told you

is true. I failed to stop this woman twice before. She is what made Leon Grosvenor into an honest-to-God werewolf. But that is not to say I don't believe what you say. That you can feel his evil. That you can feel his presence approaching us. I've seen all kinds of creepy junk hanging out with the wacky old Korean.''

In the distance, in a voice too soft for Aurelia to hear, Chiun said, "I heard that!"

Remo heard something else far away, too. Aurelia started to speak, and he shushed her with a finger pressed against her lips.

The sound that reached his ears stood out from the noises he had grown accustomed to since nightfall in the swamp. Aside from the unearthly call of birds, the whir of bats in flight, the splashing sounds of turtles, leaping fish or gliding alligators, there was…something else.

When Remo spoke again, it was a whisper. "Are you any good at climbing trees?"

She answered him in kind. "I do all right. What is it?"

"We've got company," he said. From the sound of things, the camp was practically surrounded.

"Leon?" There was something close to panic in Aurelia's voice, although she tried to hide it.

"We'll see," he said, and jerked a thumb in the direction of the nearest sturdy tree. "Just get upstairs, and don't come down until I call you or the sun comes up and you can see to get away, which-ever happens first.''

Aurelia abruptly experienced levitation. It took her a moment to realize that it was Remo lifting her by the waist as if she were weightless, and she found herself eye-to-eye with a branch that had been above her head.

''Where are you going?'' she whispered as she scrambled onto the cypress branch.

''I'm putting out the welcome mat,'' Remo said.

THE PACK HAD a trail now, picked up at the water's edge, almost by accident, and followed over marshy ground. Leon could thank the bitch for taking them directly to the camp.

He used hand signs to send the bitch and her brothers on their separate ways, encircling the camp-site. They had the critical advantage of surprise.

Leon hadn't gone hunting in this sector of the swamp for months, and he reflected that the normals had to have taken bad advice if they were searching for him here. It was a fluke that he had found them when they were so far off track, a touch of destiny perhaps, a signal that his run of miserable luck had changed.

Leon didn't care if they had guns, grenades and body armor. They were his, and they couldn't escape him. They had made one fatal error too many, coming to his own backyard in search of trouble, and he meant to help them find it one last time.

The crackling fire was closer now. His first sight of the men was a lone shadow figure, squatting near the fire, hands stretched out toward the flames for warmth.

The others should be in their places now, he thought, and started moving in a more direct line toward the fire.

Pausing in the midnight shadows of the tree line, less than twenty paces from the fire that had been kindled in a forest clearing, Leon threw his head back, breathing in the scent of his intended prey, mouth watering.

The wild, bone-chilling howl erupted from his throat, almost without a conscious thought. It warped and warbled through the tall dark trees and brought the startled humans lurching to their feet.

Too late.

Leon was snarling like a wild thing as he broke from cover, running in a crouch, and charged the fire.

CHIUN HAD EMERGED from the boat of his own accord, sensing the presence in the woods almost in the same instant as Remo. A moment later Remo heard the first gunshot echo from the cabin cruiser downstream and he glanced back just in time to see a rag-doll figure vaulting backward through the air, head over heels, to strike the nearest mangrove like a sack of dirty laundry and slide down the trunk to vanish underwater with a muffled splash.

Remo knew without taking in the too-large size of the recently deceased that it wasn't the old Korean. One of their uninvited guests had made his way aboard the boat and learned the hard way that Chiun could take care of himself.

The gunshot from the boat may not have been a scheduled signal, but it had the same effect. Streams of automatic fire swept the bayou camp, converging from no less than five distinct points of origin, the bullets drilling cookware, sleeping bags, exploding into showers of embers when they hit the fire itself. He recognized the sounds of SMGs and automatic rifles but they were all just bullets, and bullets were swords were arrows were rocks. All just something sent in your direction in a big hurry with the intent of hurting you. You dealt with them—if you were Sinanju—in the same way. You got out of the way.

But there was no sign of Cuvier, and Remo couldn't tell if he was down, somewhere beyond the fire, or trapped inside one of the bullet-riddled sleeping bags. In either case, it was too late to help him now.

THE WEIRD, UNEARTHLY howling shattered Maynard Grymsdyke's fragile grasp on slumber. He had turned in early, physically exhausted by the first day of their so-called hunting trip, afraid to even think how he would feel the following day, when they actually had to leave the *Sweet Sixteen* behind and travel overland. The punishing humidity and heat, blood-hungry insects, Grymsdyke's lifelong fear of snakes and spiders, all combined to make him dread the sunrise.

And all for what?

Breen and his cronies could have held their meeting in an air-conditioned office, ironed the details out within an hour or two at most, but here they were, intent on some pathetic macho bonding ritual that made them look like primal idiots.

And I'm the biggest idiot of all, Maynard thought. I'm the one who knew it was a frigging waste of time and tagged along with Elmo anyway, to kiss his ass and keep my job.

Grymsdyke dozed off to visions of himself confronting Elmo Breen in righteous indignation, saying all the things that he would never have the nerve to say in waking life. When he was wakened by the howling, Maynard needed several heartbeats to remember where he was and how he got there, why he felt both frightened and empowered by his dream.

As for the howling, now, it called up one emotion only.

Terror.

A massive shape burst from the tree line, moving toward the campfire and its ring of startled millionaires. Manlike in form, the howling creature was fantastic in detail, a nightmare come to life that hurdled Maynard's sleeping bag as if he weren't there. He told himself that much of what he thought he'd seen had been a mere trick of the lighting, flames and shadows playing head games, but his bowels weren't buying it.

Over by the campfire, men were scrambling to their feet and screaming, shouting curses, while the man-thing fell upon them, baying harshly with what had to be a set of leather lungs. As Grymsdyke struggled from his sleeping bag and made it to all fours, he realized that the intruder who had leaped across his prostrate body hadn't come alone. Off to his left, beyond the fire, he had a fleeting glimpse of Marshall Dillon grappling with what seemed to be some kind of savage mongrel dog. The snarling beast had locked its jaws on Dillon's arm and seemed intent on dragging him to earth, no matter how the oil-and-gas man wept and pleaded for his life.

A shotgun blast ripped through the wild, chaotic sounds of combat, drawing Grymsdyke's full attention to the right. There, Elmo Breen had somehow reached his weapon and was standing with the customized Benelli Montefeltro Super 90 braced against his hip, smoke curling from the muzzle. There was madness in the politician's eyes, and Maynard knew his boss was not so much frightened as he was thrilled.

Away behind the would-be governor, he caught a glimpse of Jethro in retreat, high-stepping toward the water and the relative security that he would find aboard the cabin cruiser. Maynard didn't know if he would make it, didn't really care, but Jethro's flight was all it took to cut through the hysterical paralysis that held him captive, freeing him to run.

He didn't know where he was going, much less whether he had any chance at all of getting there, but Grymsdyke knew he had to do something before the howling man-thing and his pack of killer canines finished off the other, more demanding targets and went looking for an easy kill.

There was an instant, watching Hubert Murphy lifted high above the man-thing's head and dashed to earth, when Maynard felt that something snapped inside him, and before he knew it, he was running with the campfire at his back, no destination fixed in mind. He wasn't headed toward the *Sweet Sixteen,* but there was still a chance to find it, work back through the reeds and grass along the shore, if he could only find the water first.

Maynard hit the bayou running, went down like an anchor, sucking water as the scummy surface closed above his head.

16

The first shot startled Leon, even though he knew the normals might have guns, but it wasn't enough to slow him.

He lived to kill, seize normal flesh and rip it into pieces with his taloned fingers, taste the fresh blood of his enemies. A part of Leon's mind told him that something had gone wrong—he saw no Chinaman in camp, no Gypsy woman, and there seemed to be too many men—but it was too late to consider his decision now. The battle had been joined, and there was nothing for it but to charge ahead and finish off the job—or die in the attempt.

A tall man, six foot four or five, was closest to the charging loup-garou. He held a hand-tooled gun case, yanking at the zipper, which was giving him some difficulty, keeping him from joining in the gunfire that tore through the camp. Leon leaped through the campfire's licking flames and came to grips with his first target, swept the leather case and useless gun aside. The fingers of his left hand gripped the old man's throat and bottled up a scream, his right hand clamping tightly on the normal's genitals. It felt like nothing to him when he jerked the gasping scarecrow off his feet and hoisted him to arm's length overhead. With yet another howl, he slammed the man to earth and straddled him, face lunging toward his throat.

The next shot scored, but not on Leon. As he raised his bloodstained face, one of his brothers catapulted through the air and struck the ground unmoving, less than thirty feet away. Off to his left, another male had grabbed one of the normals by an arm and shook him wickedly, with strength enough to separate the shoulder joint. The man was squealing like a sow even before he lost his footing and went down. The gray male instantly released his grip and tore a mouthful from the screaming mortal's face.

Leon craned his neck and found the bitch. She stood astride a dead man's chest, her muzzle buried in the scarlet fountain of his throat. He saw the normal with the firearm, and another breaking for the trees behind him, running for his life without a thought for those he left behind.

The normal with the shotgun hadn't seen him yet, or else was choosing not to credit what he saw. Instead of bringing Leon under fire, he raised the semiautomatic shotgun to his shoulder, sighting another male and squeezing off a blast.

More of his pack were dying!

The roar that burst from Leon's throat was primal fury amplified. He crossed the ground between the gunman and himself in loping strides, long arms outstretched as if his hairy hands could stop a buckshot charge from opening his chest.

It didn't matter now that he had clearly led his pack against a group of total strangers, led two more of them to violent deaths. The only thing that mattered was revenge, while there was time for him to strike a killing blow.

He saw the shotgun's muzzle pivoting to meet him, looking like a cannon at close range. He didn't know if there was time to reach his enemy before the gun went off, but he could try.

The blast was like thunder, and he heard the angry swarm of hornets hurtling past him, some of them on target, biting deep into his flesh. He howled and launched into a headlong dive, directly toward the gunman.

THE SHOOTER WAS awfully confused right about now.

What he was firing was an automatic rifle and that meant it automatically sent bullets flying at the target in very rapid succession. The man on the receiving end of all those bullets usually hid, ran away, something like that. Also, the guy on the sending end of those bullets usually didn't miss a close target. The shooter had fired automatic rifles lots and lots of times and knew those facts to be true.

So what was happening now was just plain wrong. The shooter's victim wasn't hiding or running from the automatic-weapons fire. He was, well, dancing around the bullets if what the gunner saw was right. There would be maybe a little shift this way and a little jig that way and the guy never ever got tagged by a single one of the damn bullets!

And the guy was coming right for him.

And the guy didn't have any gun of his own to shoot back with. Not a knife. Not even a cypress branch to use as a club.

The shooter was still trying to make sense of it all when Remo Williams stopped in front of him.

"It's empty."

Remo nodded at the shooter's trigger finger, still working the gun uselessly.

Oh, the gunner realized, he's right. No more bullets.

Then Remo grabbed the sizzling hot gun barrel. The gunner held on, thinking the guy was going to try to take it out of his hands. Instead, Remo propelled the gun at the gunner.

It slammed into him. Hard. All the internal parts between the bottom of his rib cage and the top of his pelvic bone turned into just so much mush. The gunner felt it happen.

Those, the gunner thought, were really important internal parts.

But that was the last thing he ever thought about, flopping down, gore flowing from his mouth.

One down—two counting the intruder who had tangled with Chiun aboard the boat—and Remo counted four more automatics still unloading on the camp.

The second shooter, fifty feet beyond the first, had an Uzi submachine gun. He had emptied one magazine, and Remo sprinted at him as he was reloading. He slashed hard and fast with his fingernails as the gunner half turned.

Then the gunner's vision momentarily went haywire. He was spinning through the air in an impossible way, and when he fell to the ground he saw, a few feet away, his own headless body falling to the ground in the darkness.

The gunner knew he had been decapitated and his only thought—before his thoughts ceased altogether—was that his attacker had to have had a really big knife.

Three guns still raked the camp with automatic fire, as if the men behind them were on automatic pilot, bent on firing endlessly until they got an order to desist.

Remo's third quarry had a Ruger Mini-14 rifle with a folding stock, a bandolier of spare clips slung across his chest. Instead of hosing down the camp at random, he was squeezing off short, measured bursts, aiming at first one sleeping bag and then another, keeping up his pinpoint fire despite the fact that all the bags were plainly riddled, tufts of cotton stuffing floating in the air around the campfire like exotic insects. From the smile etched on his face, Remo decided that the rifleman enjoyed his work.

Again Remo didn't bother approaching from the sniper's blind side. He just came in too fast for the sniper to do anything about it. The shooter started to turn his gun at the newcomer. When Remo jabbed rigid fingers under the shooter's rib cage, the move was too quick for the shooter's eye to follow. But the concussive, channeled force brought death as swift and sure as any point-blank gunshot to the head.

The next-to-last assailant had another stubby submachine gun. Moving up behind the tall man like a silent shadow, Remo clapped his hands over his assailant's ears with stunning force. The shooter's body shivered through a brief convulsion, then slumped forward.

One more to go.

By this time, Remo's last target had to know that there was something wrong. The other guns that had been pouring fire into the camp were silent now, the absence of their multiple staccato thunder plainly obvious. The final shooter had ceased firing, as well, attempting to discover what had happened to his friends.

Metallic clicking sounds told Remo that the gunner was reloading, just in case he had to make a fight of it. After that, it was the simple sound of breathing that betrayed his quarry.

At last, when he could stand no more silence, the shooter began calling out to his companions.

"Remy? Florus? Where you at, goddamn it! Harry? Claude?"

The gunner started running, crashing through the ferns and undergrowth like a stampeding water buffalo. Conveniently, he was coming straight at him. Remo gave him a nice quick punch without even needing to move from where he stood. The gunner's head caved in, and he fell right over.

LOUISIANA'S WOULD-BE governor had gone stark raving crazy, and the hell of it was that he knew it. Elmo Breen was on the razor's edge of laughing at his own insanity, prevented only by the fact that he was trying to remain alive.

It was the first time in his fifty-something years on Earth that Breen had suffered from hallucinations, drunk or sober. And it could only be a wild hallucination, after all. A wolf man, for Christ's sake! According to the hallucination, the wolf man had hoisted Marshall Dillon overhead and dropped

him like a sack of laundry, as dead as hell when he
hit the ground.

As for the wild dogs or coyotes or whatever the
hell they were, one of them had Hubert Murphy by
the arm, attack-dog style, and yet another was attacking Victor Charles.

Breen saw three-fifths of his campaign support
fund being ripped to bloody shreds before his eyes,
and there was only one thing for a Southern boy to
do in such distressing circumstances, even when he
knew the whole damn thing was an illusion conjured
up by a disordered mind or tainted booze.

He grabbed his thousand-dollar shotgun and proceeded to give battle as his great-great-granddaddy
had done at Shiloh.

Breen turned his weapon on the nearest of the
wolf-dogs, aiming for a rib shot, so the buckshot
pellets wouldn't spread and injure Victor when he
fired.

The big Benelli shotgun kicked against his shoulder, but he held it steady, dead on target, grinning
triumphantly as his first round tore into its shaggy,
snarling target with the force of an express train. It
was almost comical, the way the mutt went down,
rolled over once, then lay still.

He swiveled toward the wolf-dog that was maul-
ing Hubert Murphy. The dog rushed in and took a
bite from Hubert's face, retreating with a hefty portion of his fat cheek clutched between its teeth.

Breen knocked it sprawling with another shotgun blast.

His ears were ringing with the gunfire, but it didn't keep the howling out. Breen swung back to face the hulking man-thing lunging in his direction, wild-eyed, lips drawn back from huge yellow teeth, nostrils flaring in a face that looked like something off a Halloween mask. No time to aim the 12-gauge this time, and he jerked the trigger. Breen got lucky, saw his charging nemesis lurch sideways, thrown off stride, as pellets tore into its arm and side. Still it wasn't a killing shot, and when he tried to fire again, the shotgun's hammer snapped against an empty chamber.

Shit! Shit! Shit!

Breen dropped the 12-gauge, reaching for the stainless-steel Colt Double Eagle on his hip. The special tie-down holster he had purchased for this outing had a flap secured with Velcro, slowing his draw enough that he had barely reached the .45 before his freakish adversary hit him with a flying tackle, slammed the breath out of his lungs and drove him back against a nearby tree.

It was impossible for Breen to catalog the bolts of pain exploding through his body. A kaleidoscope of colored lights spun on the inside of his eyelids when his skull collided with the tree trunk. Lower down, it felt as if his spine had snapped, but that couldn't be right, or else he wouldn't feel the brittle agony that emanated from a hard knee's point of impact with his testicles. If that weren't enough, he sensed he was drowning, tried to draw a breath and found the burning muscles of his diaphragm unwilling to cooperate.

The shaggy man-thing took a backward step, then lunged again, one heavy shoulder slamming into Elmo's chest. Breen felt a couple of his ribs go, snapped like chopsticks, and a pain beyond pain as the jagged ends lanced deep into a lung. Whatever hope he had of drawing breath was canceled in a heartbeat, and the would-be governor saw darkness opening around him like a ghastly flower blooming.

Through the darkness came his frightful enemy, hands that resembled something from an ape-man costume reaching toward his face. Before they found him, Breen had time to wonder how a figment of his own imagination had acquired such rotten breath.

CHIUN WAS STANDING by the fire, his hands in his kimono sleeves. "Have you finished?" he asked, merely curious.

"Yes."

"You could thank me for lending you assistance," Chiun suggested.

"Huh? What? You took out one guy and then let me take care of the rest of them."

"It is your job to do so. You, not I, are the Reigning Master of Sinanju," Chiun explained reasonably. "It is you who are charged with carrying out the edicts of the Emperor. However, since I was in close proximity to that one at the boat, I thought I would lend you my assistance."

"Yeah, well, thanks a whole lot."

Chiun beamed. "You are welcome."

"All done?"

Aurelia Boldiszar jumped down from her hidden perch, rejoining them. If she had seen Remo disposing of their enemies, it didn't seem to bother her unduly, though her face was solemn as she scanned the camp. "Did they hurt Jean? Where'd he go?"

"I smell him that way," Chiun said with a slight tilt of his head.

The Cajun's voice reached out from the surrounding darkness. "Is it safe to come out?"

"Yeah, come on," Remo said.

"I had to tap a kidney," said the sheepish-looking Cajun as he stepped into the firelight. "Barely found myself a place, before all hell broke loose."

There was a dark stain on his blue jeans, and Cuvier attempted to conceal it with one hand.

Remo retrieved the lifeless gunners and lined up their bodies near the fire, then asked the Cajun, "Friends of yours?"

"No way," said Cuvier. "I recognize some of them, though. "That's Florus Pinchot on the far end. Next to him, Claude Something, I don't know his last name. That one—'' he pointed to the next-to-last body in line ''—he Remy Arridano. Them be Armand's boys.''

"No werewolf," Remo said. "Surprised?"

"Shee-it, man," Cuvier replied, "I got surprises comin' ever time I wake up still alive."

THE BAYOU WATER TASTED foul, and Maynard Grymsdyke came up spouting like a porpoise, gasping for fresh air. He thrashed his arms to stay afloat, the closest he had come in years to swimming, but his feet couldn't make contact with the bottom. Once again, his head slipped underwater, and he fought back to the surface with a desperate strength he didn't know that he possessed.

That strength wouldn't last long, in any case. His wild dash from the camp into the water had covered not more than fifty yards, but Grymsdyke felt as if he had been sprinting all-out for a mile. His heart was pounding, hammering against his ribs, and even with his head above the brackish water Maynard found it difficult to catch his breath.

Somehow Grymsdyke turned himself around and faced back toward the bank. Tall grass and reeds combined with darkness to obscure his vision of the camp, but Grymsdyke stared into the night regardless, more than half expecting some demented nightmare to come crashing through the undergrowth where he had lately passed. He tried to listen, too, but his own splashing in the water made the effort futile.

Christ, what was that in the camp?

The wolf-dogs were no mystery to Grymsdyke. They were something he would have expected to inhabit bayou country, one more reason why sane men should stay in town. The first creature, however, had been something else.

No matter how he tried, Grymsdyke couldn't persuade himself that he had conjured up the man-thing out of nightmares. He most desperately wanted it to be a man—even a man who roamed the swamp with vicious feral dogs, attacking other men—but he had glimpsed its face, and one glimpse was enough.

Whatever it had been, despite the fact that it was wearing denim overalls and big, mud-clotted boots, Grymsdyke knew it wasn't human. Not with those long arms and burly shoulders covered by the same dark, matted hair that sprouted from the creature's head and face. And that mouth. That distended, tooth-filled maw...

Grim silence descended on the swamp—or rather, the expected night sounds returned, after their rude disruption by the sounds of mortal combat. There were no more gunshots from the campsite, and the angry snarling sounds had also ceased. Maynard was terrified to think what that had to mean.

Grymsdyke lost track of time before he drifted very far. For all he knew, he could have floated thus for hours, or it could have been brief moments. He was slipping in and out of consciousness until he woke with water burning in his throat and sinuses. Blinking scum out of his eyes, he saw a log, nearly submerged, floating directly toward him, shining where an errant beam of moonlight found rough bark. Grymsdyke beheld salvation, thrashing toward the log, intent on climbing aboard and allowing it to carry him wherever it might go.

He was within arm's reach before he realized this log was moving steadily against the current, driven by some power of its own. Too late, he saw the alligator's glinting eyes, tried to reverse directions, swallowing foul water as he tried to call for help.

Only the reptile heard him, opening its trapdoor of a mouth to swallow Maynard Grymsdyke's helpless scream.

17

Merle Bettencourt was eating shrimp cocktail and chasing it with chilled chablis when Ansel Rousseau showed up at his elbow with a cell phone in his hand. A green light on the telephone was blinking, signaling an open line.

"What?" Bettencourt demanded.

"Some guy say he gotta talk to you," said Ansel. "Say it's about some huntin' party on the bayou."

Bettencourt set down his wineglass, careful not to tip it, startled and unnerved to find his fingers trembling. "What's his name?"

"Won't say." Ansel shrugged. "Guy tells me you be pissed if I don't pass him on. Want I should hang him up?"

The Cajun mobster thought about it, wished the question were as simple as it sounded. Only six men were supposed to know about his little bayou hunting party—those involved as trigger men—and any one of them who felt a need to call him would have given up his name. It made no sense, but he could say the same of so much else that had been happening the past few days.

"Gimme," he said, and took the telephone from Ansel, waiting for the other man to leave and close the door behind him. Then, into the cell phone's mouthpiece, he said, "Yeah, who's this?"

"You wouldn't recognize my name," a very average voice replied. "I'm calling for Jean Cuvier."

"Don't rightly recollect that name," Bettencourt replied eventually.

"That's funny," the stranger said. "He sure recognized the boys you sent to waste him. Most of them, at least. You want them back, I'll tell you where to send the garbage truck."

That's all I need, thought Bettencourt. Admit to knowledge of attempted murder on an open line and get myself shipped to Atlanta for conspiracy. No, thank you very much.

"I don't know where you got this number," Bettencourt replied, as cool as he could manage in the circumstances, "but there must be some mistake. Sounds like you need to talk to the police."

That was a nice touch, Bettencourt decided, smiling to himself. He was about to disconnect, but then he heard the stranger speaking almost casually, as if he didn't care if Merle was listening or not.

"If that's the way you want it, fine," he said. "Thing is, Jean wondered if you could get together, maybe work this whole thing out before somebody else gets hurt. But since you never heard of him—''

The Cajun's mind was racing, one thought stumbling on another, but he knew it would be madness to admit a link to Cuvier or the hunters in the swamp.

''Can't say I have,'' he said, ''but I could ask around with my people, for the hell of it.''

''No, never mind,'' the stranger said. ''I should have gone to the police first thing, as you suggested. They can check out the bodies, see who they worked for, whether they had—''

''But let's suppose one of my people recognized this name…what was it?''

''Cuvier.'' The stranger paused and spelled it for him. ''First name Jean.''

''Where would a person get in touch?'' asked Bettencourt, heart stuttering against his ribs.

''Go south of Charles,'' the stranger said. ''You've got an auditorium near Audubon Park, some kind of church revival going on. Across the street, you'll find a little Cajun restaurant, Justine's. The man you don't know will be there at half-past five o'clock.''

The line went dead, and Bettencourt switched off the cell phone. He had other calls to make, but not on that instrument. He would reach out for Leon, get the hairy son of a bitch cracking on the job he should have finished long ago. And just in case the loup-garou was losing it, Merle would have backup waiting to complete the contract, maybe take out the wolf man while they were at it, to prevent him squealing later, if he got his leg caught in a trap.

Merle wouldn't lead the team himself, of course; that would be risky. But he would be in the neighborhood, by pure coincidence, to watch the play go down. It would be more fun than the prize fights scheduled out of Vegas that night, running live on HBO.

He set the cell phone beside his plate and called for Ansel, waiting for the fat man to appear.

"Yeah, boss?"

"Give me a telephone, a real one this time, and be quick about it, hear?"

LEON WAS SICK of driving to New Orleans. Normally, he made the trek no more than three, four times a year, but this would be his second time within as many days. In his condition—wounded, hurting, weak from loss of blood, still grieving for the brothers he had lost—Leon was in a mood to scorn the summons from Merle Bettencourt, except for one small item.

Vengeance.

Leon hungered for it, had convinced himself that he couldn't survive without inflicting catastrophic payback on his nameless enemies. Without revenge, he was persuaded now, his bloody, aching wounds would never heal. The thought had seemed ridiculous at first, even to Leon, but he had been raised with magic, this and that kind, to imagine that he knew it all.

His wounds weren't as bad as they had first appeared to be, but they still pained him, and he was feeling somewhat light-headed from loss of blood. He had a shotgun pellet in his shoulder, burrowed deep into the flesh, no damage to the bones, apparently, since he could use his arm. Another piece of lead had grazed his biceps, left an ugly, oozing furrow, with flesh and fur peeled back and dangling until he had ripped it free. He didn't know how many pellets from the shotgun blast were buried in his side, but guessed there had to be two or three at least. Again, they had struck nothing vital.

There was no pack with him this time. They were shunning him. Leon had tried to leave the bitch behind, as well, but she was having none of that. The two of them would finish it together, but he didn't know what to expect from her once they had settled with their enemies. He was unfit to lead—that much was obvious—and Leon didn't know if she would stay with him when he was expelled from the pack.

No. He knew. She would stay with the pack. She would gravitate to the new alpha male.

Leon pushed that away and turned to business. He wondered how Merle Bettencourt had traced the enemy so quickly, and it bothered Leon that the Cajun mobster was directing him again. The first tip, sending Leon to Desire House, had been disastrous, and he had never seen his hated adversaries in the swamp, could not have sworn that they were even there. Now, Bettencourt said they were back in the French Quarter, hanging out around some Cajun restaurant.

Leon decided he would have to kill the mobster if his tip proved wrong this time. Three strikes, you're out, he told himself. It would be difficult, of course, but not impossible. A man—or loup-garou— who didn't care if he survived was the most formidable enemy on Earth.

The part about the restaurant made Leon smell an ambush. How could Bettencourt know where his enemies were having supper? And, more to the point, if he did know, why would he summon Leon for the job when he could easily have sent some guns along? It was a fact that Leon owed one body on his contract, but with all that had been going on, it seemed to him that Bettencourt would have preferred to trust his own.

Unless, of course, he planned to kill two birds with the same stone.

He had dispensed with the disguise, since there was still a final night of Mardi Gras ahead, permitting him to travel more or less at will, without the mummy wrappings. It was dark out, sidewalks crowded with a host of drunken revelers whose costumes made the wolf man's normal look seem positively tame. Raw wounds or no, Leon knew he would fit in with the herd and pass unnoticed through their ranks—at least until he found his prey and started raising hell.

He cruised past Justine's, saw no familiar faces from Desire House or the Cajun syndicate, but he was still ahead of schedule. Anyway, Merle Bettencourt could have a hundred gunners on the street disguised for Mardi Gras, and Leon wouldn't pick them out until they pulled their guns and started blasting.

Never mind.

He hadn't come this far, the need for vengeance churning in his gut, to simply turn around and go back home. He needed blood, and wouldn't rest until he tasted someone's, be it Cajun, Yankee, Chinaman or Gypsy witch.

Directly opposite Justine's, an auditorium's marquee displayed a sign for Mission Mardi Gras in foot-high letters. Underneath that cryptic legend hung the name of Reverend Marvin Rockwell. A line of folks waited outside the auditorium to get in, their Sunday-best clothes marking them as a distinct and visible minority in the riotous throng.

Leon dismissed them from his mind. He had no interest in religion, and damn little in the world of men, which had excluded him from birth and thereby canceled any debts he might have owed to a "polite" society. To Leon, all the festive crowd meant was potential cover when he made his move.

He found a place to drop the station wagon two blocks from his destination, parked the stolen car and waited for the bitch to make her exit, locked it up and pocketed the keys. Leon couldn't predict if he would ever pass this way again, but just in case, he didn't want to find a bunch of alcoholic elves or gargoyles sprawled out in his vehicle when he was running for his life.

"Let's go," he told the bitch, and felt her walking close beside him as he moved into the crowd.

"I DON'T NEED any preachin', thank you all the same," Jean Cuvier protested.

"I didn't say you had to sign up," Remo replied. "It's handy, and you'll blend in with the crowd instead of standing out like a sore thumb. I think it's safe to say your old friend Bettencourt won't have a hit team working the revival."

"They aren't after me," Aurelia said. "Why should I go?"

"Because the wolf man is," Remo reminded her. "That's how you wound up here, if I recall correctly. If things get nasty, I don't need any excess baggage."

"Thank you very much." Her tone was stiff.

"Don't mention it. You'll stay with Chiun and do exactly what he says, exactly when he says it. Understand? Survival means cooperation. Don't start making up new rules to suit yourself. A deviation from the plan could get you killed.''

"Ain't been to Sunday school since I was six or seven," Cuvier complained. "Feels downright odd, you wanna know the truth."

"I mean to save your life," said Remo. "You can think about your soul some other time."

It was still entirely possible, he realized, that Bettencourt would keep his men away from the restaurant. Remo hadn't been assigned to trash the Cajun Mafia per se, but Remo wasn't shy about using his own initiative if it wasn't too much of a bother.

Chiun was miffed, of course. He wished to accompany Remo to meet the enemy. He wanted to see the wolf man in the flesh. Mostly he didn't wish to take the servile position of bodyguard.

He made one last snipe about the issue. "You want me to go mingle with the carpenter's rabble while you hog the glory," he accused Remo.

"Aren't you supposed to be meditating?" Remo asked. "You can go do that if you'd rather. But I'm Reigning Master, and I'm the one who's supposed to be doing all the work. You made that clear enough. So I'm gonna go to the restaurant. You can protect the civilians or go find a nice spot for your butt mat."

Chiun huffed and argued no further, which was

as good as acquiescence, but Remo could tell the old Master was already planning some payback.

Aurelia stared at Remo for a moment, as if memorizing details of a face she wouldn't see again.

"Follow me," Chiun ordered. When Cuvier hesitated, Chiun took him by the elbow in his gentle fingers. The Cajun yelped.

A moment later, they were gone, merged with the gaudy foot traffic beyond the alley's mouth.

YOU HAD TO GET UP pretty early in the morning to surprise Merle Bettencourt. He hadn't risen from the lousy shrimp boats, climbing through the family ranks as runner, strong-arm, pimp and captain, to command the syndicate in Armand's absence, without picking up some tricks along the way.

If you received an invitation to a sit-down, for example, and your gut told you it was a trap, you didn't automatically decline. Instead, you took precautions—showed up early, scouted out the territory, checked for indicators that you ought to stay at home, or maybe show up with your own gorillas and reverse the gimmick, turn the whole damn thing around.

He could have sent a spotter to perform that function, but instead had chosen to take care of it himself. You want a job done right, his daddy used to tell him, don't give it to someone else. His old man had been sober that day, for a change, and Merle

had listened to him. Every now and then, the
scrawny bastard got one right.

His rooftop perch gave Bettencourt a clear view
of Justine's, across the street and south of where he
stood, together with the auditorium directly opposite. The street was crawling with a motley crowd
of party-goers sporting costumes that ranged from
simple dominoes to weird full-body suits that turned
them into movie monsters, cowboys, clowns or men
from Mars. It was like Halloween down there, except it was adults, not kids, and they were after
booze or sex, not penny candy.

The binoculars brought everything up close and
personal, gave him a ringside seat to a colossal freak
show. Bettencourt had no idea what kind of masks
his men were wearing and he didn't care, as long as
they were armed and ready, their team leader standing by his walkie-talkie for the signal to attack. He
knew their general positions, staking out Justine's
without being too obvious about it. They were all
professionals, and he would trust them to perform
as such.

Unless they blew it, in which case he meant to
have their balls for cuff links, boiled and bronzed.

The problem with his plan—a huge one, Bettencourt admitted to himself—was that it only worked
if Cuvier showed up as Cuvier, revealed his face to
let Merle get a fix on him and tell the gunners where
to strike. As far as Bettencourt could guess, the odds

were sixty-forty, anyway, in favor of some kind of setup, meaning Cuvier was nowhere near Justine's, but there were federal marshals, local cops—whatever—staking out the restaurant to bust whomever Bettencourt sent in to make the tag. Another possibility was that the rat would show, but in disguise like everybody else, in which case he could pass within arm's length of Bettencourt and not be recognized. All things considered, it was a pathetic long shot, but the last, best hope he had of nailing Cuvier and opening the road for Armand Fortier's appeal.

He had been concentrating on the sidewalk near the restaurant for half an hour, maybe longer, when he took a break and swept his glasses slowly to the right, across the crowded street. He scanned the made-up faces, traffic creeping down the center stripe while geeks of all descriptions spilled over the sidewalk, milling in the street. It crossed his mind to look for Leon, but he spotted two werewolves no more than twenty feet apart and quickly gave it up.

Another long shot.

If the hairy freak decided to show up, would he have any better luck at picking Cuvier out of the crowd? Would Leon sniff him out, like some bizarre and ghastly bird dog from *The Twilight Zone?* What powers did the bastard really have, beyond the strength of his broad shoulders and thick arms?

Merle Bettencourt was so caught up in thinking of his troubles that he almost missed his target, standing right there on the street before him, no disguise. The rat was just emerging from an alleyway, perhaps a block south of the auditorium where Jesus people had been trooping in to hear the word. Cuvier was followed by a woman dressed in clothing that resembled Gypsy garb.

Screw it.

Bettencourt followed the mismatched pair with his glasses, making sure that there was no mistake. You would've thought that Cuvier had sense enough to grow a beard or mustache, anyway, some effort to disguise himself while he was wandering around the very heart of Armand's territory, but there was no accounting for stupidity. If Cuvier had been half-smart, he never would have testified against his boss man in the first place.

Bettencourt kept watching, waiting, for the pair to veer right, across the street, head for Justine's, but they kept walking north until they reached the Holy Roller crowd and got in line. The line was moving swiftly now, and Cuvier and his lady friend were at the front door of the auditorium before Merle got the walkie-talkie unhooked from his belt and brought it to his lips.

"Brunelle, you there?"

"Here, boss," the leader of his hit team answered.

"They're across the street," Bettencourt said, "going in the auditorium right now. He's with a

Gypsy woman and I think—I think maybe I saw the Chinaman. Maybe not.''

"We're on it."

Merle stowed the two-way radio and watched Cuvier and the Gypsy a moment more, until they disappeared inside the auditorium. He could have sworn he saw the little old Chinaman, just for a second. But he didn't see him again.

Merle put down the glasses and retrieved the latex mask rolled up in his pocket. Bill Clinton, looking swollen and red-nosed with cartoon hair. Merle slipped it on and double-timed in the direction of the service stairs.

There would be no harm watching while his soldiers did their thing, if only from a distance. He could verify the kill himself and be on hand to help if anything went wrong.

But it had better not go wrong, Merle told himself. It damn well better not.

LEON WAS TALLER than three-quarters of the other people in the crowd, excluding those who had arrived on stilts, and so he had spied his targets even as Merle Bettencourt was spotting them from farther up the street. The wolf man recognized all three of them, the stoolie from his photos and the Gypsy woman and the little Asian man, who moved through the crowd with such fluidity and speed that even the wolf man's sharp eyes had trouble keeping up with him. Leon felt his blood begin to simmer, hackles rising, as his lips curled back from yellow teeth.

The bitch couldn't have spotted them, as short as she was, but she picked up on his tension, the excitement thrumming in his veins, and gave a little whimper that became a snarl. A tall transvestite dolled up like Reba McEntire retreated from the growling wolf and wobbled on his comical stiletto heels.

"Ooo, keep that beast away fom me," the person of transgendered persuasion cautioned in a hoarse falsetto.

Leon's right hand lashed out, dark fingers snagging in the neckline of the he-she's party dress, and ripped the garment to its owner's waist. Pink rubber falsies hit the sidewalk like two balls of Silly Putty, bounding off in opposite directions through the teeming crowd.

"Oh, my babies!" squealed the she-male, diving for his disembodied left tit in a move that cleared the way for Leon and the bitch to pass beyond arm's reach.

Leon was tracking all the while, saw his three targets get in line outside the auditorium whose marquee wore the brand of Mission Mardi Gras. He watched them disappear inside and cursed his luck, surmising that the ushers on the door wouldn't admit a loup-garou, much less his canine date, to hear the

Reverend Marvin Rockwell speak. Leon could lay them out in seconds flat, of course, but the effort would attract whatever passed for muscle at a Holy Roller outing, and his quarry could escape while he was dealing with the hired help.

There had to be a better way.

He saw the alley coming up, between a deli and the auditorium, and steered the bitch in that direction, shoving through the crowd. Another werewolf was about to take offense, until he got a look at Leon and his painted cheeks immediately crinkled with a smile.

"Hey, brother," the bogus wolf man said, "us lycanthropes should stick together. Put her there!"

He groped for Leon's hand, too shocked to scream as Leon crushed his fingers in a grip of steel and left him kneeling on the sidewalk, retching through his pain.

The alley wasn't quite deserted, but the figure sprawled across their line of march was already unconscious. Leon stepped across the scrawny legs and heard the tick-tack-tick of claws on pavement as the bitch kept pace. In other circumstances, she would almost certainly have paused to taste the wino, but her blood was up. She felt the call to vengeance and would let nothing distract her from that quest.

Leon hadn't devised a plan yet, but the auditorium would have a back door, and if it was locked…well, he would take one problem at a time.

In fact, the back door to the auditorium was standing open when he got there, with a sixty-something man leaning next to it, in shirt and tie, smoking a cigarette.

"My gracious, brother," said the old man, smiling at Leon's approach, "you look a—"

Leon snapped his neck and flung him into the garbage bin some twenty feet down the alleyway. The man was gone in seconds, and no one had been there to see where he went.

"Now," Leon told the bitch, "we going have some fun tonight!"

THERE IS A GOOD DEAL more to saving souls than many people realized. Most thought it boiled down to a rousing hellfire sermon followed by an altar call, and then the sheep came forward to surrender. That was part of it, all right, but Reverend Rockwell had learned his trade from masters of their craft, the planning and the details that went into it.

Making salvation pay.

There were a million different things to think about, from the selection of a meeting place to lighting, sound effects, emergency precautions, all the rules imposed by zoning boards and fire inspectors.

Once you had picked the place, there was a whole new list of details to arrange, from musical selections to the proper shills, if you were healing for the cameras. It wouldn't do to hire some yokel who would make it look too easy—or, conversely, one so drunk that he was unable to leap up from his wheelchair and begin to dance on cue.

Most critical of all, however, any preacher worth his salt planned for passing the collection plate—or bucket, as the case may be. The Reverend Rockwell preferred a shiny metal pail to the traditional collection plate for two good reasons. First, it held more cash, its very size encouraging his faithful audience to dig deep and give until the bucket didn't seem so empty anymore. And second, since the pail was made of metal and produced a ringing clang when coins were dropped inside, the first couple dozen contributors were encouraged to give folding money, thus sparing themselves the embarrassment of looking—or sounding—like cheapskates. That got the ball rolling each time, and those who saw a wad of greenbacks in the bucket when it came to them were more inclined to give in kind.

Psychology was a marvelous gift from God.

So far this evening, everything had gone like clockwork. Music for the first half hour, from a cheap piano and a choir donated—naturally—by the pastor of the Ninth Street Free Will Apostolic Church. They weren't half-bad, at that: more like three-quarters, with a couple of alleged sopranos in the ranks who couldn't hit high C if they were using antiaircraft guns.

Oh, well, Rockwell told himself, it wasn't quality

that counted so much in revival meetings as the quantity. More people meant more money, and more souls to trail the first few shills when Rockwell made his special altar call. Same thing at healing ceremonies, only more of them were apt to be in wheelchairs, pushing walkers, maybe hobbling down the aisle like Quasimodo. Reverend Rockwell would "heal" them all, with just a prayer and a light touch. Next night, same thing, his press gang making sure that no one hired the same street people two nights in a row.

Show business was a gas.

This night, the well-oiled, finely tuned machine was running like a Swiss watch. The choir had done its thing and shuffled off the stage, immediately followed by Rockwell's sidekick, Jerry Pratt. Jerry could milk an audience of cash the way an expert snake handler milked vipers. Only Rockwell himself was better at it, which explained why he took personal charge of the untraditional second collection, made concurrently with his dramatic altar call.

Reverend Rockwell was pleased with the crowd, noting that the auditorium was SRO, with only a handful of the spectators in costume, and all of those except a giant Tweety Bird had doffed their headgear in a gesture of respect. Rockwell made no effort to convince himself that he had won them over yet; in truth, he didn't even care. The whole point of his Mission Mardi Gras was getting on the tube, grab-

bing some airtime that that hell-bound sinner Elmo
Breen could not begin to emulate. A few months
down the road, when individuals were lined up at
the polls and they began to think about what really
mattered—family values, sacred principles, the right
to life—they would remember Reverend Rockwell
as Christ's own candidate.

This night, in keeping with the holiday, he had a
hellfire message for the crowd, straight out of the
Book of Revelation, strong enough to make the die-
hard drunkards in the audience take notice.

"The final days are coming!" he proclaimed, his
bull voice amplified by the acoustics and sound system of the auditorium. Without missing a beat, he
shifted to scripture, leaving the faithful to decide
which words were his and which were God's.

"'Before the throne,'" cried Reverend Rockwell,
"'there was a sea of glass like unto crystal, and in
the midst of the throne, and round about the throne,
were four beasts full of eyes before and behind.'"

There was a stirring in the audience, a couple of
the women gasping, while a tall man pointed toward
the stage. Rockwell wasn't used to that particular
reaction, but he made the most of it, leaning forward
with his full weight on the podium, shouting directly
at those brothers and sisters in the front row.

"'And the first beast was like a lion, and the second beast was like a calf,'" he bellowed, "'and the
third beast had a face like a man, and—'"

Christ, the whole front row was screaming now, some of them bolting from their seats and making for the nearest aisle. Distracted, Reverend Rockwell wheeled to his left, faced toward the wings and saw a most ungodly apparition rushing toward him, long legs eating up the stage.

He wouldn't have described the face as like a man's exactly, even though the thing was wearing overalls and boots. It struck him more as something from a nightmare, spawned by too much pepperoni on his late-night pizza, but Rockwell knew that he wasn't hallucinating. Not if everybody in the audience could see it, too.

Without a weapon close at hand, nowhere to run, Rockwell did the only thing that he could think of, lifting up his Bible in both hands and holding it in front of him to ward off the monster. No one was more surprised than Reverend Rockwell when one long, shaggy arm reached out and swept the book aside, immediately followed by a shoulder slamming square into his chest.

The words that poured from Reverend Rockwell's lips as he began to plummet off the stage and down into the pit bore no resemblance to a prayer.

18

Chiun was slightly amused. He was mostly annoyed. These were the worst kind of spectacles, greed cloaked as religion. For some reason, the followers of the carpenter from Galilee had an abundance of gaudy exhibitions such as this. What was most miraculous was that the worshipers came to them and enthusiastically permitted their pockets to be emptied.

But this was as good a place to meet the enemy as any other. Chiun would simply use the crowd to personal advantage when his foes arrived. Remo would probably find himself twiddling his thumbs in the restaurant and fighting the temptation to order some sort of fried cattle entrée.

The entertainers on the stage went through their paces. They were all familiar to Chiun from his channel surfing. He wondered if these actors thought there was some sort of supposed secret hypnotic quality that came from referring to the carpenter as ''Jay-sus-uh.''

The greed-preachers were experts when it came

to flogging simpleminded viewers into a state that was equal parts ecstasy and pain. When they attained that level, crimson-faced and weeping, brandishing their pudgy hands aloft like baseball fans rehearsing a coordinated wave, the salesman at the podium had little difficulty separating them from any cash they carried. Some of them collapsed, while others hopped about and babbled gibberish, like caricatures of small children pretending to speak a foreign language.

Chiun, despite the entertainment, was instantly aware of the first two Cajun gunmen slipping into the auditorium. He left his charges with strict orders to remain exactly where they were, awaiting his return.

Three more assassins were inside the auditorium as Chiun approached the first he had seen. They kept their weapons out of sight, but it was obvious that they were armed, with awkward bulges visible beneath the jackets they would not have worn this night if they had nothing to conceal.

Chiun had no idea if they had been forewarned to watch for a Korean, but he knew beyond the shadow of a doubt that nothing in their wasted lifetimes had prepared them to confront a Master of Sinanju. He was standing at the first one's elbow by the time his adversary knew that he was being hunted in the crowd. Too late, the big man with the rubber skull-mask tried to draw his weapon, dead before he reached it from a strike no human eye could follow.

It was child's play for Chiun to hold him upright, although the dead man's head wobbled as they moved together through the press of worshipers who were compelled to stand against the back wall of the auditorium for lack of seats. Ahead of him, a second gunman—this one with the plastic face and dangling hair of Fabio—glanced over, saw his comrade coming, and began to drift toward him, clearly having failed to spot his targets in the crowd.

When the second gunman came within arm's reach, Chiun reached around the corpse and delivered another lightning strike. Half of Fabio's unyielding countenance imploded. Chiun was now bracing two dead men and looking for a place where he could prop them up together without setting off a stampede and a chorus of screaming.

Then he saw movement on stage, far below. The hulking, hairy man-thing he had last seen at Desire House was charging at the startled minister. As Chiun dropped his pair of corpses, the manlike demon swept away the preacher. One of the wolf-dogs ran on stage with the creature.

The audience erupted into screaming chaos as Chiun homed in on his nearest living enemy with greater speed.

LEON HAD KNOWN they would be entering a crowded room, but the marquee for Mission Mardi

Gras meant nothing to him, and he had expected something in the nature of a barn dance, people milling everywhere, instead of wedged in seats and watching while a fat man paced around the stage, a microphone in one hand, black book in the other. Leon didn't know what the occasion was, nor did he give a muskrat's ass. The moment that he cleared the wings and heard the screaming start, he knew exactly what he had to do.

The fat man was first, turning to face Leon with his face contorted, shock and fear most evident among the jumbled senses flickering behind his eyes. Leon went for him in a rush, ignored the flare of pain from recent wounds as they collided, snarling triumph as the fat man tumbled backward, off the stage, to the unyielding concrete floor below.

Leon couldn't begin to guess how many people there were in the auditorium—it had to be hundreds, possibly a thousand—but he knew that every one of them was staring at him now, some of them pointing, screaming, many scrambling from their seats and making for the nearest exit in a rush. He needed time to find the three he had come looking for, but there would be no time, he realized, as panic seized the audience at large and individuals began to scramble over one another, elbowing their fellows to the side and trampling those who fell.

The bitch streaked past him, bounding off the

stage without a moment's hesitation. Leon didn't know where she was going, whether she had spotted their intended quarry. By the time he spun in that direction, tracking her, she had already disappeared into the crowd.

Goddamn it!

Someone came at Leon from the wings directly opposite, another fat man, this one with a badge pinned to his sweaty shirt. Some kind of rent-a-cop retained for the occasion, and he didn't even have a gun. The club he brandished overhead might have intimidated a normal, but Leon didn't give the stick a second thought.

He met the man halfway, his good arm reaching out, lips curled back in a snarl. The fat man blanched and tried to change his mind, but it was too late now. Before he could retreat, Leon had grabbed a handful of his shirt and jerked him forward, lunging at his triple chins with sharp, discolored teeth. The fat man's scream was drowned in gurgling crimson, and his night stick clattered on the stage, rolled toward the footlights, useless and forgotten.

Leon didn't pause to feed, but rather thrust the dead man from him after he had swallowed enough blood to quench his sudden thirst. If he was going to retrieve the moment, find his quarry in the milling, shrieking crowd, he had to get down there among them, on the main floor of the auditorium.

Each moment wasted gave his targets that much time to get away.

Without hesitating, Leon charged the footlights and leaped off into space.

MERLE BETTENCOURT KNEW something had gone wrong the moment he heard screaming from the auditorium. There was no sound of gunshots, so he had to figure that his men had not yet connected with their targets, and that meant something else had roused the audience to screaming panic in the time it took for him to cross six feet of sidewalk and approach the double doors out front.

It wasn't Jesus-screaming. It reminded Bettencourt of what you expect to hear inside a crowded theater if fire broke out.

Entering the smallish lobby of the auditorium, Bettencourt was greeted by a tide of frightened-looking people running in the opposite direction, toward the exit and the street beyond. He ducked behind a concrete pillar, braced himself, then plunged into the crowd, prepared to slug his way upstream if necessary, anything to find out what the hell was going on and what had happened to his crew.

He hadn't drawn his pistol yet, preferred to wait until he had a target or the stampede of humanity required more drastic handling than mere fists and elbows. As it was, Merle took a few knocks going in, but he was gaining ground. He guessed that there were other exits at the rear or to the sides, draining a portion of the crowd. That meant his targets could have wriggled through some other loophole, but he wasn't ready to give up on them just yet. He had to find his shooters first, and try to figure out exactly what was happening.

In fact, he literally stumbled on the first one, several yards inside the main room of the auditorium, where total chaos reigned. Merle caught himself before he went down on his face, and recognized the ape mask Terry Joslin had been wearing to disguise himself. Still, there was something odd…

It took Merle Bettencourt another moment to decipher what was troubling him. His soldier lay facedown, arms splayed as if to clutch the earth, but the ape mask he wore was facing upward, toward the ceiling. Reaching out to prod the rubber with a shaky index finger, Merle could feel his supper coming back as he discovered that the shooter's whole damn head was turned around like something from *The Exorcist.*

Merle drew his pistol then, stepped back from Terry Joslin's corpse and started looking for his other boys. Where were they, damn it? How could they have missed their targets, even in a zoo like this, when they had been so close behind them and the marks wore no disguises?

The crush was clearing out where Merle stood, and he spotted two more of his boys where they had fallen, not just side by side, but one atop the other, stacked. Benny Foch and Gilles Petiot, he recognized from their respective masks. A skull and a long-haired Fabio, for Christ's sake, stretched out dead together on the concrete floor.

That left three to do the job, if they were still alive. Merle didn't know if he could get to them in time, if they were even still inside the auditorium, but he couldn't cut and run, no matter how he longed to do exactly that. Rank had its privileges, but they were balanced by responsibilities.

He started toward the nearest aisle that led between the rows of seats, down toward the pit and stage, sidestepping as an old man charged directly at him, wild-eyed, running for his life. More panicked Christians followed, jostling Merle, unmindful of the automatic pistol in his hand. He slashed at one of them, a farmer type, opened his cheek and sent the damned hick reeling off into an empty row of seats, where he collapsed.

Merle was suddenly alert to a snarling sound that emanated from his left. He turned in that direction, toward the stage, and found himself confronted with a canine apparition from his wildest nightmares.

It was larger than a German shepherd, smaller than a Dane, with blood smeared on its muzzle and its matted, tangled coat. Bright eyes regarded Bettencourt as nothing more than food, lips curled back from a set of yellow fangs streaked crimson from a recent taste of flesh and blood. Behind the monster, he saw bodies scattered—two, three, four of them, all missing pieces of their throats and faces, crimson spilling from their wounds onto the sloping floor.

"You wanna piece of me?" the Cajun mobster challenged, but his voice cracked and he felt his bladder straining toward release.

The wolf-thing snarled again, in answer to his question, gliding forward with a click-click-click of claws on concrete, picking up its pace. Merle tried to raise his pistol, but it seemed to weigh a ton all of a sudden, and he knew he was too late as the demented hound from hell sprang toward his throat.

AURELIA BOLDISZAR was worried. There had been no warning this time that the loup-garou was coming, and she wondered if her powers might be failing her, perhaps disoriented by her feelings for the man called Remo. Or maybe she had been distracted by the fear of being shot by those who hunted her contemptible companion, the crude Jean Cuvier.

Whatever the excuse she chose, this time the wolf man had surprised her absolutely. She hadn't been listening attentively to Reverend Rockwell, but rather feeling out the crowd, wondering what had distracted their Korean baby-sitter and where he had gone off to after warning them to keep their seats. When the crowd started screaming, scrambling from their seats in panic, she turned once more to face the stage.

And saw a nightmare in the flesh.

It had been dark the first time, in the Gypsy camp, and she was fleeing for her life at the hotel on Tchoupitoulas Street when he had come for her the second time, but she saw every detail of the monster now. He was indeed a wolf in human form, the denim overalls and boots he wore looking ridiculous with hairy shoulders, chest and arms exposed. And then there was the face—the hideously distended muzzle and the snarling fangs.

By the time the monster rushed at Reverend Rockwell and swept him off the stage, Cuvier was on his feet and shoving toward the nearest aisle, elbowing frightened Christians left and right. She caught him by the shirttail, yelling at him, "Wait! Chiun told us to stay here!"

Rounding on her furiously, Cuvier spit back, "You stay here, then! Be damn dog food, all I care. I'm gettin' out while gettin's good!"

She followed him unwillingly, as much in fear of staying where she was as from a need to see that he was safe. She had distrusted Cuvier on sight, despised him since he made his clumsy move on her, back at Desire House, but if Remo wanted him alive, she was prepared to help the Cajun stay that way.

Aurelia only hoped it wouldn't cost her life.

She slipped in behind him as he started bulling

through the crowd. One thing about the Cajun, she decided: he made a fair human battering ram. It made no difference if the individuals who blocked his way were men, women or children—he shoved them to the side to save himself.

Twice in their stampede toward the street, Aurelia paused to help one of the people Cuvier had toppled in his rush. The first one was a little girl, no more than six or seven years of age; the other was a woman old enough to be his grandmother, who may have tipped the scales at ninety pounds if she had weighed in with her cane and orthopedic shoes. Aurelia mumbled vain apologies but kept moving in the Cajun's slipstream.

They were within sight of the lobby doors, and there was still no sign of Chiun, when suddenly Aurelia glimpsed a door off to her left. It stood in shadow, with no Exit sign above it, and incredibly, it seemed that no one in the crowd had spied it yet. Once more, she grabbed at Cuvier's loose shirttail.

"What now?" he snapped.

"This way!" she urged him, pointing toward the other door.

"We at the lobby," he reminded her. "It's this way to the street."

"And anyone who's looking for you knows it," she replied. "They'll be expecting you, but suit yourself. I'm going out this way."

With that, she turned her back and heard the Cajun cursing, screwing up the nerve to follow her. She glanced back once, to make sure he was coming, and it cost her, as she stumbled over someone's prostrate body, stretched out on the floor.

Aurelia caught herself, face inches from a leering vampire mask. It was an incomplete, almost pathetic costume, worn as it had been with a sport shirt, windbreaker, denim jeans. Not that it mattered to the man behind the mask what other people thought, since he was clearly dead or dying, his head cocked at an impossible angle, fresh blood leaking from one ear she could see.

Aurelia was recovering her balance, scrambling to her feet, when she saw the shiny automatic pistol tucked inside the dead man's belt. She grabbed it without thinking twice—he wouldn't need it now. She identified the make and made sure she had the safety off.

There was a great deal more to being Gypsy than just reading tea leaves, after all.

Jean Cuvier was past her, almost to the exit, as Aurelia scrambled to her feet. The bastard would have left her, she was sure of it, but he wouldn't get rid of her so easily. In fact, if he had any plans for ditching Remo and Chiun, she now had means to stop him and make sure he didn't slip away.

She was perhaps ten feet behind the Cajun when he reached the door and threw his weight against it.

Nothing. With a curse, he seized the knob and shook it, shouldering the metal door again.

"Try pulling," she suggested.

"Merde!" He pulled, without result. The door held fast.

"They can't do this!" he raged, and pointed at a message stenciled on the flat gray steel that barred their way: This Door Must Be Unlocked At All Times During Business Hours. "Jesus, man! They breakin' they own rules."

Aurelia thought about blasting the lock with her liberated pistol, as Cuvier started back to the lobby, then froze.

"Shee-it!" the Cajun blurted.

Before him stood a wolf-dog like the ones that had attacked her family's camp and the hotel suite. This one was smeared with blood, its muzzle gleaming crimson. Dark eyes shifted constantly between Aurelia and the Cajun, watching both of them at once, deciding which of them it should kill first.

Aurelia wondered if she ought to fire, risk missing, maybe hitting someone in the crowd still shoving, milling at the lobby exit. It was a long time since she had actually fired a gun, and if she didn't score a vital hit with her first shot—

The beast made the decision for her, yelping furiously as it sprang to tear the Cajun's throat. Aurelia raised her gun and fired once while the wolf was in midair, then saw its jaws clamp onto Cuvier's right arm, raised to protect his face. The two of them went down together, thrashing, with the animal on top.

Recovered from the first explosion of the pistol, fired by reflex more than anything, Aurelia Boldiszar lunged forward as the wolf-dog sank its fangs into Cuvier's arm and shook him as a terrier might shake a rat. The Cajun was screaming, his face flecked with blood, raw panic in his bulging eyes.

Aurelia dared not risk a head shot first, for fear of hitting Cuvier by accident. Instead, she moved to skin-touch range and fired two rapid shots into the creature's rib cage. The explosive impact blew her living target sideways, spraying blood from ugly blow holes, its fangs releasing the Cajun's arm.

Mortally wounded but still primed to fight, the savage canine turned on Aurelia, lunged for her on wobbly legs, jaws gaping. When the beast was three feet from her outstretched hand, she fired twice more into its gaping maw, slamming it backward like a tumbling sack of rags.

"Get up," Aurelia said to Cuvier when she could find her voice. "We're getting out of here."

REMO KNEW he had been suckered when a mob of screaming Christians started pouring through the front doors of the auditorium. Nothing in the preacher's repertoire would prompt such a reaction, even if he passed the plate three times instead of two. And then there were gunshots audible in the crowd noise.

No one had even sniffed around Justine's while he stood waiting on the sidewalk. Somehow, the enemy had zeroed in on Cuvier and Aurelia Boldiszar in the auditorium with Chiun, and now the racket from across the street told him that death had found them there.

Remo sped across the street, avoiding the sluggish traffic and finding a path through the panicking crowd.

Inside the auditorium it was a battlefield. Remo saw the first body as he cleared the threshold from the lobby, entering the main room of the auditorium. A gunman with an E.T. mask lay stretched out on the floor, the fingers of his right hand curled around a weapon he had never found the time to use. No blood was showing, but Remo didn't have to guess about the cause of death.

Off to his left, some thirty feet away, Chiun was finishing the last two members of the Cajun hit team. Remo might have reached the scene in time to help the Master of Sinanju, but no help was necessary. Chiun demolished his hulking adversaries with sublime economy of motion. Both of them were down and dead as Remo turned to scan the auditorium, ignoring scattered bodies and the walking wounded, searching for Aurelia and Jean Cuvier.

The howling told him where they were.

Remo slipped around a corner and down a narrow passageway that led him to an exit on the north side of the auditorium. Aurelia and his witness huddled back against the door, not using it for some reason, a bulky figure looming over them and snarling like a rabid dog.

This wasn't another of the Cajun shooters in a Halloween mask. The creature had a hairy back and shoulders, dark fur covering a power lifter's arms, long blackened talons at the tips of clutching fingers.

About time, Remo thought, and whistled like a man calling his dog. "Hey, Bigfoot! Someone forget to lock the cages at the zoo, or what?"

The loup-garou swiveled to face him, dark eyes blazing in a countenance as shaggy as the creature's arms and shoulders. The snout was distended just enough to be unnatural. The eyes were animal eyes. Dark, thin lips curled back from yellow fangs, as crooked and rotten as a long neglected picket fence.

"No orthodontists back in Transylvania, I guess."

The wolf man snarled at him, then spoke. "You wanna die before these two, it make no never mine to me."

"Use caution, my son. He is more than the others." It was Chiun who spoke, several feet behind him.

Remo nodded just barely in understanding. He sidestepped to see Aurelia, standing firm with both hands clutched around a semiautomatic pistol with the slide locked open. Empty. Cuvier was crouched behind her, fingers clawing at the concrete wall as if he longed to tunnel through it and escape.

"I hear you talking, Leon," Remo told the wolf man, pleased to see the savage eyes blink in surprise. "Is talking all you do? Or do you save the muscle for the ladies?"

The loup-garou sprang at Remo, arms outstretched to seize his throat. There was no planning to the move, and precious little skill, but there was animal speed and agility that shouldn't have been present in a brute that was six foot five or six and way better than two hundred pounds.

Remo had battled the mutated, half-animal creature created by Judith White, and he knew their capabilities.

Leon was better.

Leon was faster.

Leon came at him like a bolt of hairy lightning.

Remo watched him come and waited until the final instant, then stepped to the side and struck with his right hand, fingers rigid, hooking solidly into the wolf man's side.

Leon reacted with inhuman speed, twisting in midflight to dodge the blow. But he couldn't avoid it. Remo felt ribs snap on impact, heard the grunt of pain and saw his adversary stagger as he regained his feet. The loup-garou pivoted to face his enemy, returning to the fight with greater caution, snarling as he came.

Remo dropped and spun, lashing out at Leon's right knee with a kick and heard it snap. The wolf man clawed at the empty air where Remo had been, then yelped in pain and flung himself down, hoping to trap his adversary beneath him.

Remo was gone.

The wolf man pushed up off the floor, craning his head to find where his enemy had gotten to.

Remo was coming at him from behind, and he planted a palm on the wolf man's back. Leon Grosvenor was slammed to the floor with such force he felt as if a concrete wall had come down on him.

"Okay, dog-face boy," Remo said. "Time to talk."

The wolf man struggled weakly for a moment, dazed. "Fu—!"

Remo pushed harder. The wolf man's entire rib cage compressed, his lungs being squeezed into a smaller space as his ribs creaked like the timbers of an overloaded pirate ship of old.

"Speak, Fido," Remo commanded.

Leon wheezed and struggled. "It was Armand Fortier. Merle Bettencourt. Them's the ones that hired me."

Remo felt the stall. There was still a massive ripple of strength alive in the wolf man's body, and

Remo knew Leon was talking while he got his wits together. But talking was necessary.

"I don't give a fur coat for those two losers," he said. "It's you I'm interested in."

"Me?" Leon grunted.

"More precisely, your maker. How did you get this way?"

"I was born this way, you stupid son of a—"

There was a nerve in the neck. People had it. Leon probably had it, too. Remo felt around.

Leon howled.

"Yep. You got it," Remo said. Then he released the nerve. "Now, listen to me, you stupid piece of dog shit, and listen good. I want straight answers from you, and I want them fast. Because good answers is all you've got right now that makes you worth keeping alive."

"I'll talk," the wolf man moaned, long and low.

Remo pressed Leon Grosvenor a little harder into the floor, just as a reminder. Leon grunted. Remo wanted to keep pushing. He wanted to do things to Leon Grosvenor that would make a werewolf killing look tame. And for a moment the Reigning Master of Sinanju was surprised at the depths of his rage. "Who made you, dog?"

"A woman," Leon said. "She came to the bayou."

"And?"

"She asked me if I wanted to be a real loup-garou. She gave me something to drink."

"What did she look like?"

Leon described the woman.

Remo glanced at Chiun, who stood impassively watching. Chiun nodded and asked, "What about her arm, mongrel?"

Leon turned his head in surprise. "Her arm?" Then some sort of understanding opened on his face. "Her arm. It was smooth. It had skin like a baby's arm."

Remo breathed. There was the evidence. That was the kind of unusual detail that proved it. Judith White had lost her arm when she first encountered Remo. But by the time they had met the last time, she had managed to grow it back. The skin on the new arm was pink and new. "Even Smitty can't deny it was Dr. Judy."

Chiun nodded.

"How many others did she make?" Remo demanded.

"I made them. She ran away. I was too strong and she became afraid."

"How many?"

Remo knew the question wouldn't be answered when his hand detected the surge of impulses in the wolf man's muscles. Leon twisted violently to free himself—and Remo let him do it. One taloned claw slashed at him and Remo slapped it aside, shattering the bones. The other hand groped for him, weak and wounded, and Remo squeezed it into pulp.

The wolf man howled with rage and pain, and his eyes flashed to the left and right.

The wolf man's sanity had fled him.

He rose to his knees without warning, with the power of the insane, the speed of an unnatural creature and the adrenaline rush of a dying lunatic. His teeth gnashed at Remo's throat with dizzying speed.

Remo met the face full of fangs with his own fist, thrusting his hand into the wolf man's maw. The jaw full of fangs disintegrated. The back of his shaggy neck exploded.

Then Remo extracted the arm fast. But not fast enough to keep it from getting covered in blood and gore.

The loup-garou of Louisiana wavered. He was still alive and gagging on his own teeth and blood.

He struggled, amazingly, to get to his feet.

Remo sneered. "Forget about it. You can't even bite my legs off."

Angry breath wheezed out of the werewolf's bloody throat.

"You gonna huff and puff and blow my house in?" Remo demanded. "Not this house, Leon."

He struck hard and fast, his palm crushing the wolf man's skull with his palm, and Leon collapsed like a ton of bricks.

Incredibly, he was still alive, still moving weakly.

"No wonder Dr. Judy was scared of this guy," Remo said, "Whatever she gave him, it was kick ass."

Then the gurgle of death rattled out of the throat of the beast-man. The great, hairy brute went limp.

"Is he really dead?" It was Aurelia, without her pistol, stepping tentatively in Remo's direction.

Remo nodded. "He's dead. And too ugly even for a rug."

19

"Hey, Big Crawdaddy."

Armand Fortier awoke in a panic. He couldn't move. He couldn't breathe. There was someone in his cell!

"Be cool, Armand. I just need to talk to you for a little old minute."

Now he saw the shape of the man. It sure the hell wasn't the big black guard. It was—

The hand was removed from his mouth.

"Keep it down now, will you?"

"You're the one who came to visit me last week!" Armand accused.

"Oooo, eee. I guarantee that's me," said the Reigning Master of Sinanju.

"How did you get in here?"

"That doesn't matter. I just wanted to tell you that I came to wrap up some loose ends," Remo Williams explained.

"What loose ends?" Armand Fortier looked around wildly for some sort of an explanation. Sure enough, he was in his cell, in the middle of the night, just where he thought he was. The door to his cell was closed. The penitentiary was silent and lit only by the nighttime lights. Everything was as expected, except for the man in the cell with him.

"You see," the stranger was telling him, "I killed old Leon the loup-garou."

Fortier glared at him. "You killed Leon?"

"But one of Leon's pups took out old Merle before I got there."

"Merle's dead?"

"Also, about ten of your guys bought it tonight."

"No way—!"

Armand Fortier found himself paralyzed. The stranger was holding him by the neck.

"I asked you to be quiet, now, didn't I, Big Crawdaddy," Remo said. "Let me ask you this. I just snuck into a federal penitentiary in the middle of the night. Why would I lie to you about the other stuff?"

Fortier's eyes were wild.

"It's true. I guarantee."

Fortier tried to nod, but he couldn't.

"There are a few loose ends, though," Remo explained in a reasonable, quiet voice. "A few wolves running around in the bayou. I don't know if we'll ever find them all. And then there's you. You, I knew right where to find."

Fortier was confused.

"Got to tie up those loose ends," Remo Williams said.

Then he did. Literally.

20

The sour face of Dr. Harold W. Smith was more pinched than usual.

"You didn't have to knot him up like that."

"Yes, I did," Remo answered.

"He was still alive when they found him, you know," Smith added. "Paralyzed and mute, but conscious. They said his legs and arm bones had been broken in dozens of places."

"Had to do that," Remo said reasonably. "Had to make him all floppy in order to make the knots. You know, the little fox goes through the hole?"

Dr. Smith sighed. Chiun stood impassively at the corner of the desk. Mark Howard, in the other chair, added, "Fortier died while they were trying to untie him."

"Shame," Remo said, and found some interesting bird droppings on Smith's window to look at.

"They left him like that. I suppose the coroner will have a go at undoing him," Smith said.

"They should leave him in his present state,"

Chiun observed. "He would fit most conveniently in a garbage sack."

Remo smiled while Smith ignored the remark. "Louisiana state police are working on another case, involving several wealthy sportsmen who were found dead in the bayou country, shortly after your encounter with the so-called werewolf. One of them turned out to be a candidate for governor, an Elmo Breen. The others were presumably his friends, perhaps contributors to his campaign. One member of the party—Breen's campaign manager, in fact—is still missing. The party's hunting guide survived and told authorities that 'wild dogs' had attacked the camp. I would assume they'll try to pin the tragedy on Leon Grosvenor, whether he was involved or not."

"Feds see any wolves in the area?" Remo asked.

"No," Mark Howard answered. "Did you?"

"Not so much as moldy dog biscuit or a misplaced chew toy," Remo said. "We managed to convince some of the locals to take us to the hermit's shack this morning and the wolves had been gone for hours. They knew their pals weren't coming back, and they knew it wasn't safe to stick around."

"Any idea where they went?" Howard asked.

"They covered their tracks."

Smith said, "Excuse me?"

"They sought to confuse the trail, O Emperor,"

Chiun said in a pleasant singsong. "They used every trick to obfuscate and erase the evidence of their passing."

"Surely they didn't consciously try to obliterate their trail?" Smith said.

"They were people, Smitty," Remo said. "Just deal with it, would you? They talked. That means they could think."

"I suppose so," Smith said.

"We followed the path out of the bayou to a state highway," Remo reported.

"Remo lost the trail at a service station," Chiun announced casually.

"We both lost it," Remo said. "They hitched a ride. They must have stowed away on some truck. It was three, four hours before we reached the spot. Where they went from there? West. Maybe." He shrugged. "What about the others at the big God-fest?"

Smith looked down at his hidden computer screen. "Aside from Grosvenor and the several gunmen who arrived with Bettencourt, three persons are reported dead, with seventeen injured in various degrees."

"Reverend Rockhead?" Remo asked.

"Rockwell," Smith said. "He broke his left leg, hip and collarbone when he fell off the stage, but he's been quoted as insisting that it won't inhibit his campaign for governor. I understand he's also in negotiation for a TV movie of the week. Something about a modern exorcist who casts out demons.''

Remo had to smile at that. He had already seen the footage of Leon's attack on Reverend Rockwell. It had been aired on all the networks and repeatedly on CNN. The later broadcasts had been censored, but the early clips had captured Rockwell's exclamation as he vaulted off the stage, wailing for ''Jesus H. Christ.''

Then his amusement dissipated like vapor. ''We're not finished,'' he declared.

Smith sighed and sat up a little straighter, hands lifting from the glass top of his desk where he had been operating the hidden computer keys. ''We've found nothing more that will lead us to Judith White,'' he said.

''The FBI combed the land where her mobile laboratory was parked,'' Mark Howard said. ''They found a few very old traces that she had been there, but nothing useful. The evidence of her presence definitely predates the events at the water plant.''

''Definitely?'' Remo demanded.

''Definitely.''

''Leon Grosvenor, from what you've told us, seems like an experiment that almost got out of control,'' Smith said. ''If what he told you is correct, then she was afraid of what she had made. He was too strong. Stronger than she was. Maybe it had something to do with the purity of the genetic material.''

"The files on all CURE's old encounters with Judith White show she used complex genetic mixtures on her subjects,'' Mark Howard explained. "Tests from the animal corpse you obtained in Louisiana show it is genetically pure by her standards. Genetic signatures from just two species could be positively identified in the blood—*Homo sapiens* and *canis lupus baileyi*. Human and Mexican Gray Wolf, a subspecies of the North American Gray Wolf.'' He looked at Remo. "Maybe the bayou wolves were headed *way* west. *Canis lupus baileyi* lives in the Southwestern deserts.''

Dr. Smith added reluctantly, "The forensics report on Leon Grosvenor show that there were marked physiological changes, including signs of skeletal mutation, with bone-stress signatures indicative of extremely rapid growth.''

"So if Leon changed partially, then with a bigger dose of Dr. Judy's stuff—you change somebody almost entirely,'' Remo pressed.

Smith looked very uncomfortable with the concept. "Yes,'' he admitted. "It appears so.''

Remo stood abruptly. Chiun looked at him worriedly. Mark Howard and Harold Smith followed his agitated floor pacing.

"We gotta find that bitch,'' Remo declared.

"Why?''

It wasn't Smith or Howard. It was Chiun who asked the question.

"What do you mean, why?" Remo demanded. "Look what she's capable of!"

"Remo," said Mark Howard, "you are not responsible for what she does."

"How would you know?"

"You're going to get in trouble taking this too personally," Howard insisted.

"When I want your advice—"

"When I want to give you my advice I'll give it, goddamn it!" Howard said. "Would you just listen for a change!"

Remo stopped pacing. "Okay, Junior. I'll listen."

Howard looked flustered. "Well, I was done, actually."

THE DAY WAS BRIGHT and unseasonably warm outside. They left the windows down as they drove out of Folcroft.

Remo thought about Aurelia Boldiszar, back with her people now, picking up her life where it had been so rudely interrupted. She had suggested, at their parting, that she would be willing to remain with Remo for a while. The offer was appealing, but he said no. Aurelia seemed to take it well, and she had left him at the airport with a kiss Remo would not forget.

Chiun had been silent in the passenger seat for a

long while, staring straight ahead, before he finally said, ''Why?''

''Why what?'' Remo asked.

''Why we gotta find that bitch?''

''Huh? Oh,'' Remo said, realizing Chiun was using his own words. Remo opened his mouth to answer. But he didn't.

He was remembering the pronouncement of Aurelia Boldiszar. She was a freaking Gypsy. She was a crystal-ball gazer, for Christ's sake, but she had not been lying.

I see the swirling darkness and chaos of your life. I see your fathers and your daughters and your sons, battling one another....

She had seen it in her mind's eye. She believed it was a true vision of Remo's future. But was it?

What the hell could it mean?

And why was Remo Williams convinced it had something to do with Dr. Judith frigging White?

They drove in silence for a while. The sun was brilliant. The day was dark.

''My son?'' Chiun said finally.

''Yes, Little Father?'' Remo answered respectfully.

''Why?''

James Axler
Outlanders®

SEA OF PLAGUE

The loyalties that united the Cerberus warriors have become undone, as a bizarre messenger from the future provides a look into encroaching horror and death. Kane and his band have one option: fix two fatal fault lines in the time continuum—and rewrite history before it happens. But first they must restore power to the barons who dare to defy the greater evil: the mysterious new Imperator. Then they must wage war in the jungles of India, where the deadly, beautiful Scorpia Prime and her horrifying bio-weapon are about to drown the world in a sea of plague....

In the Outlands, the shocking truth is humanity's last hope.

**Readers won't want to miss this exciting
new title of the SuperBolan series!**

Don Pendleton's **Mack Bolan**

Line of Control

The powerful Kung Lok triad has set its sights on controlling the
U.S. narcotics market. Backed by Hong Kong's underworld, they
have the money, influence and bloodlust to get a foothold in the
West by destroying the competition—a Mexican cartel equally
determined to solidify its hold on the border pipeline. Mack
Bolan's mission: keep the destruction to a minimum...and keep
the bloodshed to the enemy.

Available in July 2003 at your favorite retail outlet.